STANDING ON THE EDGE OF ETERNITY

STANDING ON THE EDGE OF ETERNITY

T.J. Martini

with messages by Dan Frank

foreword by Bill Keller

-Founder - LivePrayer.com-

First Printing January 2005

Layout and Design: Jay Degn, Reno, Nevada
Editor: Melissa Van Vuuren, Bloomington, Indiana
Concept: Gary Lebeck, Reno, Nevada
Cover Design: Donald Zimmerman, Reno, Nevada

Photographs of T.J. Martini and Dan Frank: Spicer Photography, Reno, Nevada

Research information on religious institutes mentioned in this book were taken from Larson's Book of Cults written by Bob Larson and published by Tyndale House Publishers, Inc.

Printed in the United States of America
10 9 8 7 6 5 4 3 2 1

Vaughan Printing - Nashville, Tennessee

Library of Congress Cataloging-in-Publication Data

Martini, T. J., 1948-
Standing on the edge of eternity / by T.J. Martini ; with Biblical messages by Pastor Daniel Frank, foreword by Bill Keller.
p. cm.
ISBN 0-9705018-6-2 (alk. paper)
1. Death--Fiction. I. Title.
PS3613.A787S73 2004
813'.6--dc22

2004022628

Contents

Contents (cont.)

To my children:
Michael, Dennis, Jacquelynn, Ryan and Kara–Mia.
Forgive me for not teaching you when you were
younger about the awesome wonders and
love of our Heavenly Father and of our Savior,
Jesus Christ, and the sacrifice He made for us.

I pray that my writings will lead you all to know Him better,
and that, as you grow closer to Him, you will
give Him all that you have.

And as you go through your own trials here on earth,
never think for one minute that you have to go
through them alone.
You are loved more than you will ever know.
He is always with you.
God bless you all!

Acknowledgments

Throughout the course of putting this book together, I have come into contact with so many of God's finest children. I don't know what I did to deserve all of your help, guidance, friendship, and love, but whatever it was, I'm sure glad I did it! I am so very grateful to all of you.

To Pastor Dan Frank, I thank you for trusting me enough to share your incredibly powerful and extremely motivating messages with the world, and for wanting to do this project with me. This could be the beginning of something very special for both of us.

To Jay Degn, I thank you so very much once again for your incredible talent of laying out yet another book for me and designing each page as if it were your own. Your works are a true reflection of your loving, caring, and very faithful heart, and I am honored to call you my friend.

To my sisters in Christ Carol Dearing, Judy Frank, and Leah Witt, I thank you from the bottom of my heart for wanting to read my words, for giving me your thoughts and ideas, and for enduring the countless hours needed to prepare this book for the final edit.

To Dennis Keife, my second son and most challenging critic, over the years I have learned to lean on you and to trust your ideas, advice, and input, but mostly I have learned to trust your incredibly faithful and very Christian heart. Thank you for being truthful, encouraging, and even critical whenever it became necessary.

To my friend Bobby Foster from Engine Eleven in Reno, Nevada, thank you for taking the time to provide me with the vital information that helped me to better understand the dangers firefighters must face every day. No wonder the world calls you all heroes!

To Melissa Van Vuuren, I thank God for sending you my way at such a critical point in the final stages of this project. By using your amazing editing expertise, everything just seemed to fall into place. He knew exactly what I needed when He sent you. Thank you for making sure all the errors were corrected and for helping me sound so much better than I know I do! His timing is so perfect!

To my special friends Jeff and Martha Spicer from Spicer Photography in Reno, I thank you both so much for your phenomenal way of making every personal photograph a story, every story a treasure, and every treasure a memory to cherish forever.

To Bill Keller from Liveprayer.com, your daily devotionals have brought comfort, challenges, and answers to millions of people all over the world. You must know by now that our Heavenly Father is very proud of the incredible undertaking you continue to endure as you spread the good news of Jesus Christ. I am more grateful than you will know that even with your extremely busy schedule, you still found the time to be a part of this project. Your Foreword is the perfect beginning.

To Gary Lebeck—my husband, my partner, my friend—I thank you for your amazing knowledge and your extraordinary vision into things I could never imagine. This project went first from a dream to an idea and then from an idea to a reality because of your wisdom, talents, and fortitude. You are my right hand, my ears, my eyes, and my heart!

To Jesus Christ, my Savior, I know there is nothing I can do that would ever come close to what You did for me on the cross, but I pray that all my projects are a continuous fulfilling of Your purpose, plan, and will for me. I pray, too, that these books will help others to know both who You are and that You have an awesome plan and purpose for them as well. I am so grateful and humbled by Your love for me.

And to the reader, may the words inside this book be powerful enough to help you understand that you cannot fix your own life and must turn it over to Jesus Christ so that He can make you whole. I pray that one day you will know without a doubt that your eternity will be spent with the Author of Life... the Savior of the World. In God we trust!

TJ Martini

Foreword
by Bill Keller
Founder, LivePrayer.com

Death. This is obviously a subject that we aren't fond of talking about, though it is part of our human experience. You have probably heard the statement, "nothing in life is for sure except for death and taxes." Well, some have found ways of getting around taxes, and while modern science has done remarkable things, they have only added a few short years to the average lifespan. It is important to understand that God created man to live forever, not to die. Death became a byproduct, one of the consequences of the sin in the Garden of Eden. Now it is something we each must deal with during our lifetime.

Many people, even Christians, have a fear of death. That is normal. Death is an unknown to us. Of course, as those who know Christ as Savior, we have the assurance that when this life is over we will spend eternity in Heaven with Him. We know that, we believe that, but since we have never actually done it, there is that little bit of doubt, even fear. Again, don't feel bad. It is common.

However, the longer you walk with the Lord, the closer you get to Him, the more you realize that this whole life isn't just an accident or a coincidence. It is exactly like the Bible claims. We were created in the image of God, for the purpose of serving Him and glorifying Him with our lives. If that is true, then the rest has to be true as well, which means when we die we go to Heaven to be with our Creator for eternity.

Let me try to put this life in perspective for you. During our life we grow stage by stage. In our early years we learn the basic ways of functioning in this world, and get an education. In our early adulthood, we start working, get married, and have a family. In our elder years, we slow down, reflect on our life, and hopefully enjoy some of the fruits of our labor. Then death comes. Death wipes out everything that we did in this life: our education, our career, our human relationships, any position or power we ever possessed, and any financial resources we had accumulated.

When Bill Gates dies, his money stays in this world; it doesn't go with him. Rather than being someone special because of his financial wealth, he will be just another soul. All of the things of this world pass away. THE ONLY THING THAT WE TAKE FROM THIS LIFE IS OUR RELATIONSHIP WITH CHRIST. If you have no relationship with the Lord, then you leave this life with nothing. THE ONLY THING THAT WE TAKE WITH US FROM THIS LIFE INTO ETERNITY IS OUR RELATIONSHIP WITH THE LORD!

Understanding this, can you now see how important it is to know Him each day, to build that intimate, loving relationship with the Him? The things of this life will all pass away, but your relationship with the Lord carries on throughout eternity.

This book you have in your hands could be the most valuable thing you've ever owned. It may even save your life—your eternal life. The stories inside explain what happens to people when they die. Those who did not believe in God or understand that Jesus died on the cross for them will not be with Him when their earthly lives are over.

I pray that as you read about these five people's lives, you would understand how God reached out to all of them and continues to reach out to all of us. I invite you to know the lives of Dave Sanders, the fireman who was always willing to lend a hand; Morgan Taylor, the depressed teenage who turned to alcohol to fill the void in her life; Mary Burgoff, the young mother who rebuilt her life after losing two young children to an unpreventable accident; Andy Lynch, the Hollywood actor who grew up as a pastor's son and once planned to become a pastor himself; and Charlie McGee, the father and businessman who worked his entire adult life to build a successful business and provide for his family. As you read, you may find your own life or the lives of people you know mirrored in the lives of these five people.

Understand that while each of these people had both positive and negative aspects of their lives, only the ones who remained faithful and left all their struggles, losses, and heartache in the hands of God were granted eternal life in heaven. The ones who did not trust God with their lives—no matter how good their earthly lives may have seemed—were condemned to live out eternity in agonizing death and pain in hell. And this, my friends, is what it is all about—whether you will spend your eternal life in or out of the presence of the Lord.

I love you and I care about you enough to challenge you today to refocus your thoughts and priorities. Know how important your service to God is, since it has eternal significance. Your day–to–day life here on earth has no eternal significance, other than the things you do to impact the lives and souls of people. That is why witnessing and serving the Lord is so critical. Our jobs, our friends, and our recreation have such a big part of our life, but we need to try to refocus on the things we do each day that carry an eternal weight to them.

Death is something that we have to deal with and accept. But we have the knowledge and promise that when this life is over, we will be spending eternity with our God. That knowledge should motivate us each day to maintain our daily walk with the Lord and be about the things that will help others know Him, too.

If you want to know Jesus as your personal Savior and know for sure that when your life is over you will be forever with Him, take a moment, pray for God to open your heart and read the words on this link: www.liveprayer.com/bdy_salvatn.html.

In His love and service,
Your friend and brother in Christ,
Bill Keller

Introduction

This is the story of five individuals whose lives will simultaneously come to a tragic end on the first Sunday after Christmas. Although they all die in different ways and never know one another, all five of them must face the consequences of their earthly decisions as they enter into the only common ground they have among them: eternity! Do you know where you will be spending yours?

Death is a fact of life. We will either live a very long time, hardly any time at all, or somewhere in between. No one will escape. No one is invincible. But one thing is for certain: we are all eternal beings. God designed us that way. It doesn't matter what we think, what we've been taught, or what we believe. This is the truth!

When we die, our spirits will go on into the ever after and live forevermore. The decisions we make in this life will determine where we will spend our eternity. This should bring great comfort to those who know they have lived their lives according to God's plan and purpose for them, for it means they will spend their eternal lives in the presence of our Lord. However, the news is not good for those who have ignored God and lived their lives denying His existence.

Someday we will all stand before Him. Someday we will all answer to Him (Revelation 20:11–12). And it will break His heart when He has to tell many of us that we are not worthy to stand in His presence. *"Enter by the narrow gate; for wide is the gate and broad is the way that leads to destruction (hell), and there are many who go in by it. Because narrow is the gate and difficult is the way which leads to life (heaven), and there are few who find it"* (Matthew 7:13–14).

The misconception by so many people is that, because they are basically good and kind, they deserve to and will go to heaven when they die. But this is simply not the case. It takes much more than being a decent human being to get into God's perfect world. The Bible tells us, *"For it is by grace you have been saved through faith, and that not of yourselves; it is the gift of God, not of works, lest anyone should boast"* (Ephesians 2:8–9).

If you didn't choose God before you died, why should He recognize you on Judgment Day? Good deeds or works on earth won't count in your favor. Helping others, giving to charities, or just being kindhearted will not get you into heaven. Neither will just believing in your mind that God exists! You need to believe in His Son, Jesus Christ. You need to know without a doubt that Jesus hung from the cross—beaten, bruised, bloodied, and betrayed—and the blood He shed was for you. Jesus died so that you could live! Every drop of blood that oozed from His torn and tattered body was your sin… falling to the ground and erased forevermore! *"For God so loved the world that He gave His only begotten Son, that whoever believes in Him should not perish but have everlasting life"* (John 3:16).

If you are one of these people who has neglected God over the years, it is never too late to turn your life around. Don't make any more excuses. It will cost you more than you know…

Dave Sanders

Fire Captain Dave Sanders was considered a local hero, especially after the events of September 11, 2001. In fact, every fireman in America became a hero after the terrorist attack. Dave was proud to hold the title, although he never thought of himself as one. He was just doing a job he loved to do.

Since he was a young boy, Dave had always dreamed of being a fireman. It gave him a deep sense of purpose along with an incredible feeling of power to know that he was in charge. Dave knew that no matter how hot the fire burned or how long it took, he would not give up until the last flame was out and the last red ember had cooled.

Dave Sanders was a decent man, with high morals and a caring heart. He was loved and respected by all of his colleagues. Over the years, he had spent a great deal of time with the men in his unit, and he considered them his family. Dave was always willing to lend a hand to anyone in need. He liked the way it made him feel. Though Dave regarded himself agnostic on the subject of God or the existence of heaven and hell, he knew he was born for a reason. But the dedicated firefighter never gave death or the afterlife much thought. Even when he helped save that apartment building from burning to the ground the month before, and managed to get out all the families inside, Dave never let his mind go beyond what he could see and touch. He believed when someone died that there wasn't anything else to be said. They were gone, end of story. If there was something or someone else out there, he wanted proof.

It never once occurred to the 42–year–old fireman that he could be wrong. Dave was not the least bit prepared when his life suddenly and drastically changed that Saturday evening after Christmas. His unit was called out to a deserted building downtown that was burning out of control. It went up so fast that when the firefighters arrived on the scene, there wasn't much left to save except the structures that surrounded it.

Dave was the first one out of the truck. As soon as his boots touched the ground, he began shouting orders to his men. No one knew about the gas containers inside the building until it was too late. The explosion was heard for miles. Flames shot up in the air, high enough to be seen from every direction. Dave was standing in front of the burning building and was the only one seriously affected by the blast. Suddenly, he felt himself being lifted off the ground and then tossed like a rag doll into the field across the street.

In a matter of seconds, the skeptic about God and all that He represented had all the proof he needed, but it was too late. Dave found himself on the edge of eternity, and in a brief but memorable moment, he was in the presence of an incredibly awesome Being who was very real and so much larger than he could have ever imagined…

Chapter One

The bell sounded louder than usual at Engine Company Number 9. Dave woke from a sound sleep and quickly jumped into his gear. It seemed like he had just closed his eyes. In under five minutes, his unit was driving through the late night traffic on its way to the scene.

"I could have done without one of these calls for the rest of the year," Dave commented to his good friend, John Bailey, who sat in the driver's seat. They had been partners for more than fifteen years.

"I know what you mean. A house in flames with children trapped inside. No matter how you look at this one, it just can't be good," John replied sadly.

"You got that right! It's times like this when I wished all we had to do was put out forest fires or hose down vacant buildings."

"Me too, Dave. But we wouldn't be very heroic if all we saved were trees and structures. Besides, somehow it just wouldn't be the same," his friend told him honestly.

"No, I suppose you're right. We got to take the good with the bad, I guess. I just hope this one has a happy ending."

"So do I, Davey. So do I."

Their unit was the first to arrive. When the fire engine pulled up in front of the house, flames were already shooting out from the roof. Screams were heard, but Dave couldn't tell whether they were coming from somewhere inside or from the crowd that had gathered on the sidewalk.

Dave jumped out of the truck. He immediately began shouting orders to the other firefighters as they all donned their masks.

"Johnny, the hydrant is over there on the edge of the driveway. Get that hose hooked up quick! Phil, you stay here and help Johnny. Harvey, come with me. We're going in," he yelled above the noise, relieved to hear the sounds of sirens nearby, from other fire engines, trucks, and ambulances on their way to assist.

As they entered the burning structure, Dave and Harvey immediately found the source of the screams. It was coming from a young father who was caught under a beam in the living room. He was holding an infant in his arms.

"Please, help. My son needs help. Please get us out of here!" the man pleaded.

"It's okay, mister. I'll have you out before you know it. Stay calm and don't move. I am going to take your son first and give him to my partner. Then we'll get you out," Dave promised.

"You don't understand. This is my daughter. My son is still in his room. He's only two. Please help him. He doesn't know how to open the door!" His voice cracked as he explained.

"Which way?" Harvey asked.

"Over there by that wall," he pointed. Dave quickly took off in that direction, leaving Harvey with the father.

"Is there anyone else in the house?" Harvey wanted to know.

"No. My wife went to visit her mother. It's just my children and me. Please hurry. My son needs help!"

"It's going to be okay. My partner is already working his way over there. Just hang on. We'll get you all out of here, I promise," he said, handing the baby over to another firefighter at the entrance. Then a muffled voice was heard in the distance.

"I found him, Harvey, and he's okay. I'm bringing him out now," Dave yelled.

After the little boy was safe, Dave and Harvey worked quickly to lift the beam that trapped the young father, while several other firefighters were attending to the flames outside, and to make sure the surrounding houses were not burned. Minutes later the beam came loose, and he was free. All three of them got out just before the back of the roof collapsed. As the trio made their exit, the spectators began to scream and applaud.

A short time later, the crowd thinned out and only a few of the firefighters remained.

"Chalk up another one for the boys!" John said, pleased with their victory.

"How I love happy endings! Now, let's get the heck out of here!" Dave replied, giving John a high–five.

"Right behind you, buddy. Say, I believe it's your turn to make breakfast, right?" John asked jokingly. He knew all too well that it was his turn to whip up the morning meal, which was just fine with him. John Bailey was a big man. And when he was hungry, there was no one who could fill that need except for John himself. But Dave continued to play along.

"Sure, big guy. I'll make you breakfast. How's about a Pop Tart or a nice bowl of Fruit Loops?"

"Yeah, right!" he said sarcastically. "Well, thanks anyway, but I'll pass. The breakfast I'm making will be fit for royalty, so you better be hungry."

"You better know it! Hey, before we head back to the station, why don't we swing by the hospital and check on those kids and their dad? I just want to make sure they're okay."

"Good idea. I only wish I had thought of it first! It would make me look a whole lot nicer!" John laughed. "I'm sure Phil and Harvey won't mind, will you guys?" he asked into his headset, directing his words to the men in the back

"Not at all! We were just wondering ourselves how they were doing," Harvey answered.

The hospital was only a few blocks out of their way. John and the others waited in the truck while Dave ran inside. Less than ten minutes later he was back.

"Good news, guys! The nurse at the front desk said the kids are doing really great, but the dad is a little more serious. He'll have to stay a while, but he's not critical. The little ones can go home with their mom in a few days. Now, let's go eat! I'm starved."

A short time later, they were all sitting around the kitchen table at the fire station sharing in small talk. Dave glanced at his watch and noticed he had a little over three hours before he was off duty…for three whole days! He was anxious to go home and get cleaned up. He had another date with a very special lady. Her name was Kathleen Chambers, and this would be their fourth date together. Dave met Kathleen two weeks before at their annual fireman's picnic. She had been hosting one of the bake–sale booths, and he couldn't keep his eyes off of her. He smiled as he remembered.

Chapter Two

"Who's that?" Dave asked John, more than just a little curious about the petite blonde who stood in the distance attending to the bake stand.

"Oh, she's Harvey's little sister, Kathleen. She moved here about six months ago after her divorce. Quite the knockout, huh?"

"That's putting it mildly. So, she's single now, huh?"

"Yes, that would make her available, Davey, my boy. Why not go for it? Get over there and talk to her before someone else does," his friend encouraged.

"I think I will," Dave told him and left abruptly.

Kathleen was quick to notice Dave, too. It was a mutual attraction that had them both in a tailspin. She was suddenly feeling giddy like a teenager, and he was smitten like a schoolboy. It was definitely a first for both. She had been married right out of college, but Kathleen never remembered feeling so vulnerable, or so attracted to a man. She tried not to let it show, but she was too honest to pretend otherwise.

As Dave approached the young beauty, she turned and smiled.

"Hello…" was all he could say.

"Hello to you, too," she responded, a little shier that normal.

"I couldn't help but notice that you were all alone over here. I thought I could buy a cake or something from you." Dave didn't know what he was saying, but the words continued to come. "Do you have anything in chocolate or banana? I like the chocolate better, but I'd take banana if that was all you had. Did you bake all these?" he rambled.

"I baked some of them, but not all of them. Good grief, I would have been in the kitchen for months had I done them all!" she laughed, and Dave was hooked. "Yes, I do have a wonderful chocolate cake, with custard filling. It's my favorite."

"Then it will be mine as well. I'll take it. And your phone number, too, if I can be so bold to ask."

"Well, you seem harmless, so okay. Besides, Harvey already told me you were one of the good ones. I guess I need to start listening to my brother more often," she said sweetly.

"You'd better. He knows his stuff!" Dave smiled and took the cake from Kathleen. Their hands touched and their eyes locked, but neither one pulled away. The moment seemed to last forever. Before he turned to leave, he told her he'd call her that evening, and he did. It was the beginning of their fairy-tale friendship and love.

Even though both Dave and Kathleen had been hurt in previous marriages, they never shied away from the new relationship they had begun to form. Dave had been married when he was in his twenties, but it had only lasted a couple of years. When he found out that his wife had been unfaithful, Dave was hurt, but not surprised. She left shortly after, claiming irreconcilable differences. They had no children, but he did get to keep his dog, Norman. Kathleen's six-year marriage had produced two young girls, six-year-old April and four-year-old Ciera.

As Dave waited for his shift to end, he noticed the clock on the kitchen wall at the fire station seemed to be hardly moving. As the hands rounded the hour for the last time, Dave gathered his belongings. Then it was time. Dave found himself running to his truck, his feet barely touching the ground. He couldn't wait to see her again. It had been almost 36 hours since they had talked, and nearly three days since their last encounter. He had almost kissed her then, but had changed his mind at the last minute. There would be plenty of time for that stuff later. Right now he just wanted to be with her.

Chapter Three

Over the next several months, Dave and Kathleen were inseparable. They discovered many things about one another, sharing what they believed to be their greatest accomplishments, their worst fears, and their hopes and plans for the future. Dave's list was simple as he told her of his dreams of being able to travel the world when he retired. But he never once mentioned anything about religion or about God. This concerned Kathleen, and she decided one day to just ask him about it.

"You know, Dave, we've spent a great deal of time together, but I've never once heard you say anything about God. Do you believe in Him?" she boldly asked.

"Wow, that came out of nowhere!" he said, feeling somewhat uncomfortable. "To be honest, Kathleen, I can't tell you that I do or don't. I won't say that God doesn't exist. I'm just one of those that needs proof. It's hard to believe in something that isn't right here and visible."

"But how can you say that?" she responded quickly. "Look around you, Dave. What do you suppose this world would look like if God were not real? There would be no sky or oceans or mountains. Not to mention that you and I would not be sitting here having this conversation if there were no God!" Kathleen defended her faith and wanted so much for Dave to see the possibilities, if he could only understand. But no matter what she said, it didn't change his mind.

"Honey, if this is the kind of thing you need to believe in, then I am fine with that. But I don't think hearing it is going to change my mind. If God is real, let Him come down and show me. I don't think it's too much to ask. Let me see one of His miracles. Then He will make a huge believer out of me, as well as many other people around here! If God can do all things, like I've heard, it shouldn't be that difficult," he told her.

"God could perform miracles if He thought it was necessary. But He asks us to live on faith, knowing that He can do anything and everything that is within His will for us. That's what having faith is all about: trusting and knowing that God will be with us and protect us no matter what!" she explained.

"Really? Then why do we continually have to attend funerals for the young? Why do my men and I have to fight fires and save lives if God is there to protect us?" Dave said, trying to keep his emotions intact.

"I could try to explain, but I have a better idea. Why don't you come to church with me? Harvey set me up in his church, which is just down the street, and I love it. Please, Dave, won't you come with us and just listen? You'll learn a lot, I promise. And you may even learn some of the answers to these questions you have. I'm not saying it will change your mind or your heart, at least not right away. But at least give it a chance. For me?" she asked sweetly.

"I've been to church before, Kathleen, and nothing made me change my thinking. But because it's so important to you, I'll give it another try. I'll show you that I'm not completely against religion, or God, for that matter. I just want to be more realistic about this whole concept of there being a higher power who looks over the entire universe and has so much say so over it. It's pretty bizarre when you think about it. The idea of that is so futuristic and so Hollywood, like right out of a Steven Spielberg movie! But I will go with you, I promise."

"When?"

"How about this weekend? I have the next couple of days off, and we could take the girls and then go to breakfast afterward, if you want," he suggested.

"That would be great, and the kids will love it, too!" she said hugging him tightly. Kathleen just knew Dave would come around eventually, and her heart soared with hope.

That weekend the couple made their way to the entrance of Hope Community Church. Staff members and volunteers were at the door to greet and seat everyone. Kathleen dropped the girls off in their classrooms. Then she and Dave made their way into the sanctuary. She normally sat in the front row, but because she wanted Dave to feel comfortable, she let him lead.

They ended up in the very last row, closest to the exit. But for Kathleen, it was perfect.

Pastor Gabriel McKenna approached the pulpit and led the congregation in prayer. Then he opened his Bible to the Book of John.

"We're doing a message today called 'From Survival to Significance.' So let me ask you. What is significance? I once saw a postcard that read: 'All I ask of life is a constant and exaggerated sense of my own importance.' Is this significance?

"Turn with me to John 10:10 in your Bibles. If you didn't bring one, I am sure there is someone who will share. The Scripture reads '…I have come that they may have life, and have it to the fullest.'

"Significance is more than breathing and taking up space. It's more than monotonous routine, more than possessions, status, power, acting important, and more than rushing everywhere. Significance is becoming what God intends for you to be! Significance is being in a fruitful relationship to God. In John 15 verses 4 and 5, it says, 'Remain in Me, and I will remain in you. No branch can bear fruit by itself; it must remain on the vine. Neither can you bear fruit unless you remain in Me. I am the vine; you are the branches. If a man remains in Me and I in him he will bear much fruit; apart from Me you can do nothing.'

"Now go to verse eight, where it says, 'This is to My Father's glory, that you bear much fruit, showing yourselves to be My disciples.' Also John 15:16 tells us, 'You did not choose Me, but I chose you and appointed you that you should go and bear fruit, and that your fruit should remain, that whatever you ask the Father in My name He may give you.'

"So, let me ask all of you, if significance equals a fruit-bearing relationship to God, where do you start?

"There are three questions you need to ask. First, am I wanted? This is a question all of us struggle with. How does a person know if he or she is wanted? The answer is simply this: Are you being pursued? The key word here is 'pursued.'

"For those of you who are married, did you get married because you had a chance meeting and found your way to the altar? Let's read Isaiah 43:1–3. 'But now, thus says the Lord, who created you, O Jacob, and He who formed you, O Israel: "Fear not, for I have redeemed you; I have called you by your name; you are Mine. When you pass through the waters, I will be with you; and through the rivers, they shall not overflow you. When you walk through the fire, you shall not be burned, nor shall the flame scorch you. For I am the Lord your God, the holy One of Israel, your Savior..."'

"God has completely pursued you in the relationship!" Pastor Gabe went on. "'For the Son of Man has come to seek and to save that which was lost.' That's from Luke 19:10. Perhaps the greatest imagery in Scripture of the pursuit of God is the imagery that He is the Good Shepherd and we are the sheep!

"During the recent uprising in the Middle East, Ron Jones, who serves with the Christian and Missionary Alliance in Israel, communicated the following in his prayer letter:

'The result of the fighting and killing has left a profound sense of discouragement that hovers over the country. Several times we have come into closer contact with this conflict than our comfort zone allowed. Yesterday, a friend shared with me something she observed that was a delightful reminder of God's care for us. She watched a shepherd caring for his flock near the area where guns are fired. Every time the shots rang out, the sheep scattered in fright. The shepherd then touched each of them with his staff and spoke calmly to them, and the sheep settled down immediately because they trusted the shepherd. And then another shot sounded, and the same routine happened again. Each time, the sheep needed the shepherd to reorient them and reassure.'

"Am I wanted? Yes!

"The next question is: Am I accepted? Young people today are asking themselves: Who am I? Who do I want to be? At the heart of these questions is the desire for acceptance. They are bombarded with messages that tell them that worth and acceptance are given conditionally—that you have value, if... and you are accepted, if... Well I am here to tell you all that nothing can be further from the truth!

"God's love is based on who we belong to, not what we do! His acceptance is based purely on the fact that we are His…nothing more, nothing less. Romans 15:7 says, 'Accept one another just as Christ has accepted you in order to bring praise to God.' How did God accept us? Unconditionally! No one's acceptance is based on performance! God's economy is different than man's! Most of what we call love is really infatuation.

"Infatuation is thinking he is as sexy as Brad Pitt, as smart as Bill Gates, as noble as Jimmy Carter, as funny as Woody Allen, and as athletic as Mike Tyson! Love is realizing he is as sexy as Woody Allen, as smart as Mike Tyson, as funny as Jimmy Carter and as athletic as Bill Gates! And he is no Brad Pitt, but you will take him anyway!" Laughter filled the room. When it died down, Pastor Gabe continued.

"Ephesians 1:6 tells us, 'To the praise of the glory of His grace, by which He made us accepted in the beloved.' In a book called *Connecting*, Larry Crabb writes, 'A friend of mine was raised in an angry family. Mealtimes were either silent or sarcastically noisy. Down the street was an old-fashioned house with a big porch where a happy family lived. My friend told me that when he was about ten, he began excusing himself from his dinner table as soon as he could without being yelled at, and walked to the old-fashioned house down the street.

'If he arrived during dinnertime, he would crawl under the porch and just sit there, listening to the sounds of laughter. When he told me this story, I asked him to imagine what it would have been like if the father in the house somehow knew he was huddled beneath the porch and sent his son to invite him in. I asked him to envision what it would have meant to him to accept the invitation, to sit at the table, to accidentally spill his water, and hear the father roar with delight, "Get him more water! And a dry shirt! I want him to enjoy the meal!"'

"Crabb goes on to say that 'we need to hear the Father laugh!' Change depends upon experiencing the character of God.

"So, I ask you again. Are you accepted? The answer is yes!"

As Gabe spoke, Dave watched, fascinated by the man's teachings and how naturally he spoke to his audience. He seemed to reach out and touch everyone, keeping them in his grasp and them holding on to his every word. But the pastor still had a long way to go before Dave was convinced. He continued to listen.

"Now the third and last question is: Am I needed? For this, turn with me, if you would, to I Corinthians 12, verses 15–19. It reads, 'If the foot says, "I am not a part of the body because I am not a hand," that does not make it any less a part of the body. And if the ear says, "I am not a part of the body because I am only an ear and not an eye," would that make it any less a part of the body?' Suppose the whole body was an eye—then how would you hear? Or if your whole body were just one big ear, how could you smell anything? But God made our bodies with many parts, and He has put each part just where He wants it. What a strange thing a body would be if it had only one part!'

"Now look up on the screen. Here are a few typical reasons that people don't serve God. They think they can manage without Him. They don't have any talent. They don't have any time!

"Three things you need to understand: You can make a difference in the present! You can make a difference in eternity! And a small ministry can make a huge difference!

"D.L. Moody once said, 'If this world is going to be reached, I am convinced that it must be done by men and women of average talent. After all, there are comparatively few people in the world who have great talent.'

"A while back, in what the news called 'a miracle,' nine miners were trapped for three days, 240 feet underground in a water–filled mineshaft. They decided early on that they were either going to live, or die, as a group.

"The 55–degree water threatened to kill them slowly by hypothermia, so according to one news report, when one would get cold, the other eight would huddle around that person and warm them, and when another person got cold, the favor was returned.

"Everybody had strong moments. But at any certain time maybe one guy got down, and then the rest would pull together. And then that guy would get back up and maybe someone else would feel a little weaker, but it was always a team effort. That was the only way it could have been.

"They faced incredibly hostile conditions together—and they all came out alive—together! What a picture of the body of Christ! A miracle indeed! But did they need each other? Yes! Am I needed? Absolutely! Let's pray.

"Father, we are so humble for Your gift of life. Please let us all be aware that we are significant in this world, but we cannot do anything without You. Give us the grace and mercy to follow Your will and to be all that we can be, making us good servants in Your purpose and plan for us. Lead us down the path of righteousness and allow us to do all we can to serve You better. In Jesus' name. Amen.

"Thanks for coming today, everyone. See you next week."

As soon as the pastor left the stage, Dave and Kathleen stood.

"So, what did you think?" she asked anxiously.

"I think your pastor is a great speaker. I also think he does a wonderful job in his field, and he seems to know his stuff. But is it for me? I don't know. It's just too soon to tell. I might have to come back a few more times," he told her honestly.

Though it wasn't exactly what Kathleen wanted to hear, she was more than pleased that Dave said he wanted to come back. "Thank You, Lord," she said silently.

She and Dave became regulars, as often as his schedule would allow. He even looked somewhat forward to their outings, not necessarily for the message, but for the company of the woman he had come to adore.

Chapter Four

As the weeks grew into months and the trees began to shed their autumn leaves, the couple grew more in love. By this time, they both knew they wanted to spend their lives together. Kathleen had only one problem. She knew that she was not supposed to enter into a relationship with a non–Christian. The Bible was quite clear on this, as it warns of the dangers of becoming unequally yoked to a nonbeliever. It was often said to be spiritual suicide. Kathleen turned to her pastor and asked his advice.

"I'm just so flustered. I know in my heart that this is real and right, but I just don't know what to do. I love him, and I want us to be together, but I don't want to do this if it doesn't have God's blessing," she told Gabe honestly.

"Kathleen, from what I can tell, Dave seems like a wonderful man. He will no doubt provide for you and the girls very nicely. He also appears to have strong morals and values. But he doesn't believe in God, and he doesn't have a clue who Jesus Christ is and why He died. And you do! No matter how hard I try with the messages at church and in spite of all the one–on–one conversations I've had with him, I can't make him understand how important all of this is. What's really sad is that Dave doesn't even know what he's doing to himself and to you, too, if you marry him. In his line of work, he could be killed at any time whenever he leaves the station. How would you handle that knowing that he won't be where you are someday? And worse, that he will forever be separated from God, living out his eternal days in the absolute worst environment never before imagined by man!"

"Oh, Gabe, I fear for him so much. It's all I think about whenever I hear sirens and see the trucks. I don't know what I'll do if he dies before he knows Jesus. And you're right, he doesn't have a clue what that means! Sometime before Christmas, maybe you could do a message for people like Dave. I'll make sure he comes and maybe, just maybe it will open his eyes. If not, I'll just keep praying for him. If it is God's will that Dave be in His Book of Life, then his heart will open and he will know what to do. If not, God help me to get through the pain and the anguish that I know Dave will have to suffer for the rest of his eternal days." Just saying the words made Kathleen wince with pain.

"I have to tell you that I don't agree to this relationship. But it seems to me that you already have your mind set on being with him. This is entirely your choice, Kathleen. I just hope you can handle it. I was already planning to do a message next month on Jesus. It would be great if Dave could be there. I think he'll learn a lot. Whether he comes to know Jesus as his Savior after he hears it is an entirely different thing. I will pray that his heart be opened to the words. I hope you know what you're doing with all of this, Kathleen. I will pray for both of you," he told her.

For the next few days, Kathleen prayed harder than she had ever done before. She knew God was listening, but she had no idea what His plans were for her or for the man she had grown to love more than anything else in this world.

"Father God, I am so confused. You have been here for me for so long, and I am so grateful for Your blessings. But I've come to a very poignant time in my life. I have found a wonderful man, who is kind and so loving to my daughters and to me. He is able to provide for us and take care of us like no one else has ever done before. I know You have certain commandments that I must follow, especially when it comes to choosing a mate. I know that he must be a believer in the Word and that we must start our relationship with You as our foundation. But as You are well aware, Dave doesn't know You yet. And right now, I am not sure he ever will. But I am drawn to him like a magnet, Father. My heart cries out to know him better. Help me, Lord. Help me to choose wisely and know that my choice has Your blessing. I don't want to be disobedient, but somehow this feels so right. Please put Your hand on us and guide us to know You better together. Thank You for all Your grace and mercy that You so lovingly provide for all of us. I am so grateful for Your presence. Don't ever leave me." When she was through, she felt relieved to know she had put her heart and hope in the hands of God.

And like he promised, Pastor Gabe had a message in early December called "Who is This Jesus? Jesus, the Living Explanation of God." Kathleen begged Dave to go to church with her.

"Please come, honey. Gabe is doing this for people like you who are having trouble understanding. I want you to go with me. It's important, not only for us, but for you, too. I am so afraid that if you don't understand this soon, that something terrible could happen to you before you do, and it will be too late," she said with tears in her eyes.

"Oh, Kathleen. Please don't cry. I'll admit I don't know what all the fuss is about, but I will go with you if it's that important," Dave promised, and she rewarded him with a kiss.

That next weekend, as the family drove down the main street to the church, Dave noticed an older man on the corner selling newspapers. He pulled into the parking lot and got out of his truck. Then he proceeded to walk over to the man.

"Say, buddy, how's it going today? You selling lots of papers?" he asked curiously, while Kathleen and the girls listened.

"Not too many yet, but maybe if it gets a little warmer, I'll have some customers!" the stranger replied, shivering from the dampness.

"How many do you have left?" Dave wondered. After a short pause, the man answered.

"I have around twenty–eight."

Dave reached into his pocket and pulled out two twenty–dollar bills.

"Here, take this, and give me all you have. I really only want one copy, so you can leave the rest or just toss them. Now go home and get warm!" Dave scolded the man jokingly.

"Oh, thank you, sir. I will. Thank you so much!" With that the man was gone. Dave climbed back into the truck and closed the door without a saying a word.

"Well, that was about the nicest thing I have ever seen anyone do! You are so thoughtful and kind, Dave. You never cease to amaze me!" Kathleen said proudly, and Dave just shrugged.

"Hey, it's the least I can do. It's way too cold out there for anybody! Now let's get to church before we're late. I'm sure God wouldn't like that at all!" he said smiling.

After they took the girls to their Sunday school class, the couple seated themselves in their usual spot, which had now been moved to the center of the sanctuary. It seemed that each time they went to church Dave got more comfortable and moved them closer.

When the music had ended, Pastor Gabe led them in prayer.

"Father, we come before You today and ask, in light of the season, that we be filled with Your Spirit today and that You would speak through the message that I am about to give. Let unknowing hearts be opened and give way to understanding how important these words will be for them. Thank You for Your guidance and love. In Your Son's precious and holy name, I pray. Amen.

"Just a few days before Christmas, two ladies stood looking into a department store window at a large display of the manger scene with clay figures of the Baby Jesus, Mary, Joseph, the Shepherds, the Wise Men, and the animals. Disgustedly, one lady turned to her friend and said, 'Would you look at that! The church is trying to horn in on Christmas!'" Gabe sometimes liked to begin his message with a little humor. It seemed to help make everyone more comfortable and to make him appear less threatening. The audience burst into laughter, knowing that some people truly felt this way about Christmas! When the laughter dwindled, the pastor continued.

"Who is Jesus? Will the real Jesus please stand up?" he asked his congregation. "What do you think men saw when they looked at Jesus, when they heard Him teach, when they followed Him, and when they lived with Him?

"A great many images of Christ today are far removed from the biblical picture of Him. They range all the way from 'Gentle Jesus, meek and mild'—a sort of harmless, gentle spirit whom no one need take very seriously—to a fiery-eyed radical, all set to burn everything to the ground and overthrow the establishment.

"In the midst of these contradictory images, our heart longs sometimes to say, 'Will the real Jesus please stand up?' Why do you suppose people have such a hard time recognizing who Jesus is?

"A young man who worked for an armored–car company tells the following story: 'One day we got a call from a Bank of America in downtown San Bernardino, and they were in a panic. "We've got to have some coin within the hour," they said. Well, all the armored trucks were gone, and so Larry, my manager, backed his Ford pickup into the bay. We loaded $25,000 worth of coin in the pickup. That thing was dragging! That's over a ton. Larry said, "Hop in. We're going up to B of A." And so I hopped inside. I'm in my T–shirt and blue jeans. We drove up to the front of the bank, parked the truck, and Larry said, "Hang on. I'll go in and get the dolly, and we'll haul this stuff inside." I'm whistling, standing against this truck for twenty minutes. I don't have a gun or any protection whatsoever. I thought, if anybody notices what is in this common looking pickup truck, I'm dead! Oh, the treasure that people were walking by! But they didn't see it for the commonness of the delivery system.'

"That, my friend, is the story of Jesus!" the pastor announced, raising his voice, while making eye contact with many of the people in the audience.

"John begins his Gospel with an 18–verse introduction, the theme of which is the question, 'Who is Jesus…really?' These first 18 verses contain a summary of John's most profound convictions about our Lord.

"Number one is the confirmation. This morning we are going to call to the witness stand several witnesses to testify as to the identity of the real Jesus.

"Witness number one. I call to the stand God Almighty! My question to You, God, is simply this: Do You have a relationship to this Jesus of Nazareth? John 1:1–2 reads, 'In the beginning was the Word, and the Word was with God, and the Word was God. He was in the beginning with God.'

"This expression 'in the beginning' does not refer to a particular time, but assumes a timeless eternity. Literally it would read: 'In beginning…' There is no definite article—meaning not a time, but a condition!

"In what beginning would the writer be talking about? It is the beginning that antedates all beginnings. It is the beginning of beginnings that never began! The word 'was' is the imperfect tense and would be best translated 'was continuing.' The Word existed eternally! The Word had no beginning. What is the Word?

"It is the Greek word 'logos.' This is a common Greek word that usually means word, speech, or account. About 500 years before Christ, Greek philosophers began to use it to signify 'that which gives shape, form, or life to the universe.'

"To the Jew, the word, 'dabar' was associated with the reason, the mind, the will, or the power of God. Who or what is the 'logos'? Go to John 1:14. 'And the Word became flesh and dwelt among us, and we beheld His glory, glory as of the only begotten Son from the Father, full of grace and truth.' The Word is Jesus, as unfolded in the rest of John. The Word was 'with God' ('pros ton theon'). The preposition 'with' (pros) carries two ideas with the accusative: continually toward—that is, face–to–face—and nearness!

"This is to say, God and Jesus experience deep equality and intimacy! When nothing but God had being, the Word enjoyed an 'I–Thou' relationship. God and Jesus are eternal in relationship! Jesus is God in essence and character: separate in personality, but equal to the Father!

"Witness number two is creation. In John 1:3 it tells us that 'All things came into being by Him, and apart from Him nothing came into being that has come into being.' Wow, that pretty much says it all. Everything by Him, nothing without Him!

"Think about this: the average galaxy contains about 100 billion stars, and there are at least 100 million galaxies that we know about. Scientists believe that there are at least 10 octillion stars. To put this into better perspective, just in case you don't know what an octillion is, an octillion equals 1000 septillion, a septillion equals 1000 sextillion; a sextillion equals 1000 quintillion; a quintillion equals 1000 quadrillion; and a quadrillion equals 1000 trillion. That makes my head hurt! But Jesus created them all! And so, you have creation.

"Witness number three: I call John Q. Sinner to the stand. In other words, man. Go to John 1:4–5. 'In Him was life, and the life was the light of men. And the light shines in the darkness, and the darkness did not apprehend it.' What relationship does Jesus play in men's lives? He creates conflict! Jesus is the mediator of two things: life and light. The term 'life' is 'zoa.' This represents spiritual life, or eternal life. Eternal life is life characterized by God! The closest definition we have of it would be in John 17:3. 'And this is eternal life, that they may know You, the only true God, and Jesus Christ whom You have sent.' This verse does not seem to suggest a time relating to eternal life, but a quality of life enjoyed by God. The term 'light' represents revelation!

"In other words, eternal life rested in Him, and He came to reveal to men that eternal life. But when the quality of life men have intersects with the quality of life God has, there is inevitable conflict. In fact, there is a collision! John introduces a subject here, which is a theme all through the Gospel of John: the conflict between light and darkness!

"The world lies in the realm of darkness, but God is light. Jesus comes to bring light to a very dark place. The conflict alone testifies to who He is. He comes from a wholly other world and represents a wholly other kingdom. And frankly, it steps on the toes of those who walk in darkness. Even as an unbeliever: 'Just the mention of His name made me uncomfortable!' You are dismissed, Mr. John Q. Sinner. Thank you for your testimony.

"Next up is witness number four, John, also known as the Baptist. 'There came a man, sent from God, whose name was John. He came for witness, that he might bear witness of the Light, that all might believe through him. He was not the Light, but came that he might bear witness of the Light.' This is from John 1:6–8.

"For four hundred years there had been no prophet, no message coming from God. This man, John, was no half-baked prophet! He was greater than Solomon, according to Jesus, written in Matthew 11:11, 'Assuredly, I say to you, among those born of women there has not risen one greater than John the Baptist; but he who is least in the kingdom of heaven is greater than he.' The greatest prophet of the Bible declared Jesus to be the Light!

"Now we have witness number five, truth! In John 1:9 it reads, 'There was the true light which, coming into the world, enlightens every man.' Jesus is true as opposed to deceiving, in contrast to all the false lights! True, as opposed to dim; all the prophets were but dim lights! True because He is the source, not merely a reflection! And true, in the sense of supernatural. In other words, Jesus Himself is a credible witness.

"Which brings us to our last witness, Jesus. Turn to John 1:11–13. 'He came to His own, and those who were His own did not receive Him. But as many as received Him, to them He gave the right to become children of God, even to those who believe in His name, who were born, not of blood, nor of the will of the flesh, nor of the will of man, but of God.' These same verses in The Living Bible, which make this Scripture a little easier to understand, read this way, 'Even in His own land and among His own people, the Jews, He was not accepted. Only a few would welcome and receive Him. But to all who received Him, He gave the right to become children of God. All they needed to do was to trust Him to save them. All those who believe this are reborn! —and not a physical rebirth, resulting from human passion or plan—but from the Will of God.' Jesus' authority to grant the right to become children of God testifies to who He is!"

There it was, plain as day, the way to become a child of God and have the gift of eternal life in heaven, spoken by Pastor Gabe and written in God's own words. Kathleen listened carefully and hoped that Dave was as well. "Please make him understand, Father," she prayed silently.

"Now let's move on. There are three charges laid against Jesus. The first charge is that He is the God/Man! In John 1, verse 14, it says, 'and the Word became flesh, and dwelt among us, and we beheld His glory, the glory as of the only begotten of the Father full of grace and truth.' Again, to make it easier for some of you to understand, here is the same verse in The Living Bible. It says, 'And Christ became a human being and lived here on earth among us, and was full of loving forgiveness and truth. And some of us have seen His glory—the glory of the only Son of the heavenly Father!'

"In the Old Testament, where did people see the glory of God? It was associated with the tabernacle. That is the same word! If you have seen Jesus, you have seen the glory of God! The logos became flesh. Humanity was added to Christ's deity!

"Let me see if I can illustrate this. C.S. Lewis wrote, 'Lying at your feet is your dog. Imagine, for the moment, that your dog and every dog is in deep distress. Some of us love dogs very much. If it would help all the dogs in the world to become like men, would you be willing to become a dog? Would you leave your loved ones, your job, hobbies, your art and literature and music, and choose instead of the intimate communion with your beloved, the poor substitute of looking into the beloved's face and wagging your tail, unable to smile or speak? Christ, by becoming a man, limited the thing which to Him was the most precious thing in the world: His unhampered, unhindered communion with the Father!'

"Notice the phrase the 'Only begotten,' from John 3:16. The One and Only. Who is Jesus Christ? The unique, One of a kind! God/Man.

"The second charge laid against Jesus is that He offered inexhaustible grace! John 1:16–17 reads, 'for of His fullness we have all received, and grace upon grace. For the law was given through Moses; grace and truth were realized through Jesus Christ.' The construction here would lend itself to translating the phase 'grace upon grace' as inexhaustible grace! Martin Luther said, 'Even if the whole world were to draw from this fountain… still it would not lose as much as one drop.'

"The third charge against Jesus is that He is the ultimate explanation of God. 'No man has seen God at any time; the Only Begotten God, who is in the bosom of the Father, He has explained Him' (John 1:18). The word 'explain' can be translated 'exegesis'! Jesus is the ultimate explanation of God!

"Folks, Christianity is not a religion! It is not a philosophy! It is about the person Jesus, the unique Son of God. To take Jesus out of Christianity would be like taking numbers out of mathematics, like taking doctors out of medicine, or like trying to think of daylight without the sun. Jesus is absolutely central to the Christian faith!

"Now for the challenge. Every human being sooner or later must deal with Jesus—who is the Logos! He is the ultimate crisis in every human life. Who do you say that He is? I challenge you to give your life to Christ. He gave His life for you. Give your life to Christ this Christmas as your Christmas gift to Him. You will be eternally grateful that you did. Let's give thanks and pray.

"Father, we are so grateful for Your gift of life. We ask You today to touch the hearts of those who don't know Your love and mercy, and who don't understand Your ways but want to. We ask that You bring them to Yourself, Lord, so that they can feel the joy of love from the One true living God of all

Creation. Thank You for all You do and all You continue to do in us. We are so blessed. In Jesus' merciful name, I pray. Amen."

After the service, Dave took Kathleen and the girls out to brunch. When their stomachs were full and the air had warmed a bit, they went to the park so the girls could play on the swings. While they watched them frolic in the sunshine, the couple talked about the message, which was still unclear to Dave.

"I'm not so sure I am a candidate for all of this Christian stuff, Kathleen. I don't get it, and I don't know if I ever will. Your pastor seems to know what he's talking about, but what is he talking about? It all sounded Greek to me and made absolutely no sense, except maybe here and there!" Dave said, trying not to offend her or her pastor.

"What is it that you're not getting?" she asked curiously.

"Well for one thing, I don't understand the whole concept behind God becoming Jesus. As Jesus the Man, He puts Himself through all these tests and trials here on earth when it doesn't seem necessary. Then, as if that isn't enough, Jesus ends up on a cross and dies and then miraculously comes back to life! Now, we're supposed to believe that He did that to save us! What exactly is He saving us from? And if God can do all of this stuff, why can't He just come down here and show us? He talks about miracles all the time, yet would it be so hard for Him to just perform one so we doubters won't have any reason to doubt? It would be like a magician saying that he can do all this magic and then not show us any of his tricks. Like we're just supposed to take his word for it. How can the magician think we will believe that he can, if he doesn't demonstrate what he knows? It's the same with God!" The more Dave talked, the more confused he got.

"Oh, dear. You do have a way of putting things, don't you?" she laughed, feeling a bit uncomfortable. Just then, April came running toward them.

"Mommy, could you help me with my shoes? They keep coming untied," the child asked sweetly. Kathleen bent down and tied them, then sent her daughter off to play once again. "Be careful," she said, as she watched April rejoin her sister on the merry-go-round. Then Kathleen's attention turned back to Dave.

"Look, sweetheart, I'm not real knowledgeable with of a lot of areas in the Bible. Some things are still unclear to me, especially in the Old Testament. But I learn something new every time I read it. However, there are a few things I do know! I can tell you that what Jesus saved us from is death: not a physical one, because we all have to die, but a death of our spirits. Let me try to explain in a way you might understand." Kathleen glanced out at her daughters to make sure they were still in sight. Then she looked at Dave.

"When we die here on earth, our spirits go on into another life, where they will live forever. That's how God made us. If, while we're here on earth, we choose to know God and believe that He sent His Son to die on the cross for us, then our spirits will go to heaven. I want you to believe this because I don't want you to spend your eternity forever separated from God. It would mean you went to hell, Dave. What the Bible says of hell should scare most people into believing and doing whatever it takes to keep them out of there! But too many of them spend their days here thinking this is all there is and that because God is good, that when they die they will someday live in heaven. Well, they are right about God being good, but He is also fair and just. If they ignore Him in this life, how could anyone think that they deserve to be with Him when they die, when they never gave Him a thought while they were alive? It doesn't work that way!"

"Okay, let's say that all you just told me is true. How can God send us to hell if He wants us to believe that He loves us?" he asked curiously.

"It's called having free will, Dave, the right to makes our own choices. But for genuine choice to exist, good and evil have to be allowed to co–exist. God loves us so much that He allows us to choose. That's what fathers do. Let's say you're a father, and your child was misbehaving. You tell him over and over that he will be punished if he doesn't stop, but the child doesn't believe you. Eventually, the consequences of his choice to misbehave result in you punishing him. You couldn't make him believe that there were going to be consequences for his actions, but you warned him and allowed him to make the choice to continue to misbehave. He made the decision not to listen on his own. God works in the same way, only on a higher level. He gives us the Bible to read and churches to attend and pastors to teach us. He basically gives us all the information and tools we need to make the right choice, but it's still up to us to take that leap of faith. He warns us that if we choose not to believe in His Son, that there will be consequences for our actions. Unfortunately, many people choose not to listen." Kathleen looked out at her children again. She noticed they had moved from the merry-go-round to the monkey bars.

"You girls be careful!" she warned them.

"We will, Mommy," Ciera yelled back.

"Watch us jump down, Mommy," April hollered, just as they both let go.

"That was really good! Just don't get hurt," Kathleen told them. "Sorry, Dave. I didn't mean to get sidetracked."

"That's okay. I was just going to say that when you put it that way, it's a little easier to grasp. But the Bible is still so confusing. I haven't read much of it, but I've heard from other people and sources that it's contradicting and everyone has their own interpretation of it. If God would just show us some of His stuff now, while we're all still here, many people who are skeptical, like myself, would surely be more apt to believe in Him."

"He tried that already, Dave, and still people did not believe. Throughout the Bible, Jesus did many miracles, and yet men had a hard time believing, even when they witnessed one. There will always be someone who doubts and who puts his own theory on whatever God does. You talk about magic! Don't you think that the people today would think that was all it was? They would come up with some lame reason how Jesus could heal the sick or turn water into wine or part the sea or calm the storm, not even coming close to what it really was, a miracle!"

"I don't know. I think if I saw any of those things that it would sure help me believe!" he told her.

"But that's why we call it faith, Dave. We live on the faith that God can do anything and everything. Having faith is believing in something we can't see or touch, like the wind. We can't see or touch it, but we know it's there, because when it blows we can feel it. We can't see or touch God, but when we believe in Him, we feel Him in our hearts and we know He is there. Come on, let's walk over by the girls. I can't see them any more, and I want to make sure they're okay," she said, as she grabbed his hand.

"Well, I'm still not sold on the whole idea, but don't give up on me. Maybe somewhere down the road I will feel the urge to know more. It may take a while, but stranger things have certainly happened. I just don't want to be pushed. I will do it in my time and in my own way."

"Whenever you're ready, I'll be here. But remember, honey, life is so short. You just never know what can happen. Please, don't wait too long. Maybe we could start by reading the Bible together. Do you think you could…for me?" she asked.

"I would do anything for you, Kathleen. If you don't know this by now, shame on you!" Dave said sincerely. "I know all of this stuff means a lot to you and you mean a lot to me. I promise I'll try to understand, and hopefully one day I will. I want you more than anything in the world, but for now, I am what I am."

With the exception of Dave not knowing God's grace, Kathleen wouldn't take him any other way. She knew this man was good and kind and that had to count for something. And though their relationship was not biblically correct, she was so sure that Dave would come around someday that she eagerly accepted his proposal of marriage the following weekend during dinner. Six months later they were married.

After a short honeymoon to Mexico, the couple settled in their newly purchased four bedroom ranch–style home near the edge of town. There was plenty of yard for the girls to enjoy and plenty of space in the house for additional children, which they hoped to have one day soon.

Then lo and behold, after five months of trying, Kathleen discovered she was finally pregnant. Soon they were blessed with a beautiful son. They named him Brandon Joseph. And life was good for a while.

Chapter Five

Over the next few years, the couple never had any major disagreements. Dave was content and happier than he had ever been before. He was eager to please and so much in love that whatever his wife wanted, they did. It wasn't until their third year of marriage that they experienced their first serious conflict.

The girls were visiting their dad for the weekend, and Dave was at work. Kathleen and Brandon were at home by themselves. At 2:00 a.m., Kathleen woke to the sound of a muffled cry. It was coming from her son's room. She immediately jumped out of bed and threw on her robe. When she opened Brandon's door, it hit her hard. The room was filled with a vaguely familiar smell. She couldn't put her finger on it at first, but soon she knew. It was the same odor she smelled as a child in her grandparents' house, a few days before her grandmother died. It was the smell of death.

Kathleen rushed to Brandon's bed. She knew instantly that something was wrong. She bent down to shake him and was startled when she felt his body. He was burning up! His eyes had rolled back in his head as he convulsed and gasped for air. "Oh dear God!" she screamed, and ran quickly to the phone to call her husband. The rescue unit was dispatched to the house within moments, and Dave followed closely behind. He was the first one inside.

"Kathleen!" Dave called out.

"In here, Dave! Please hurry. I don't know what to do!" she wailed.

All three men sprinted to the back bedroom, where they found a small, unconscious child in bed and a distraught mother in tears on her knees, praying with all of her heart.

"Kathleen, what are you doing?" he screamed and pushed her aside. "Brandon needs a doctor, not a figment of your imagination! We need to get him to the hospital, now! Get dressed, and we'll meet you there!" It was the first time Dave had ever raised his voice to her.

Moments later they were gone and Kathleen was all by herself. She quickly changed from her nightgown into a pair of jeans and a sweatshirt. As she drove herself to the hospital, she turned to the only One she knew who would be listening.

"Oh, Father! Please don't take my child. He's just a baby. We need him, Lord. We want to see him grow into a man and have children of his own. Please don't do this. I don't know if Dave will ever be able understand Your love if You take him from us, Lord! You may lose my husband forever. I just can't take that! Please, Father, help Brandon to get better and let Dave see what a true miracle is really all about. Show him, Lord. Please show him!" she begged out loud.

By the time Kathleen walked through the entrance to the emergency room, Brandon was still very warm and struggling for air. He looked so small lying there in that big white bed. Kathleen knelt down and reached for her son's limp hand. She felt the sudden urge to talk to him and to tell him not to give up.

"Please, honey. Don't leave me. Hang on. God will make sure you're back home soon. Look up and see Him watching you, Brandon. He's there right now. He has His angels all around you, protecting you. He loves you, honey. He loves you, and so do Daddy and Mommy. Don't give up. Hang on, hang on, hang on," she whispered over and over again, as she stroked his hair and kissed his cheek.

Almost a half an hour had passed and still there was no improvement. Dave and Kathleen didn't know what to think. Brandon seemed a little fussy when he went to bed, but it wasn't that unusual. He was getting his two–year molars, and he was always cranky when he was teething. There didn't seem to be any reason for concern. But how quickly all that had changed. Brandon was barely hanging on to life—the short life he had only known for a little more than two years.

Dave was beside himself with grief. His wife did her best to comfort him, but it was hard. He refused to believe that if there was a God and He was good, He would ever do this to them.

"See, this is exactly what I mean!" Dave whispered loudly. "How can there be a God when these things happen all the time? What if he dies, Kathleen? What if our little boy dies? How would you explain that one to me? How could you tell me that there is a God who loves me and then takes away the only thing, besides you, that matters to me? How? Why? What have I done?" he cried out to his wife in painful sobs.

"Dave, don't say that! God is not going to allow anything to happen to Brandon. We just have to be strong and pray," she told him, but she wasn't quite sure if she believed it herself.

"Baloney! How can we sit back and do nothing, and as you say, 'pray?' How does that resolve or fix anything? It's just talk, Kathleen. Words that are meaningless if they don't work!" Dave tried to hide his anger, but it came anyway.

"Please, don't talk that way. You know how important God is to me. I know He has His own plan and purpose, and if this is all part of it, then we will just have to accept it, no matter what happens! If you want to know the truth, right now I feel as though my heart is being ripped out of my chest. Losing Brandon would destroy me beyond anything I could ever imagine! But it would not destroy my faith, Dave!" Kathleen walked around the edge of the bed, being careful not to disturb any of the cords and equipment. She then took her husband's chin and forced it up so that his eyes met hers. "Look at me when I tell you that nothing or no one will ever do that! I don't know how nonbelievers go through this stuff all by themselves, dealing with sickness and death. Tell me how you do it, Dave! Tell me! Because you can't possibly have any hope. And that is exactly what I have…hope, trust, and faith! I know that God will do whatever it takes to open your eyes and mine, too, if that is what He is trying to do, and let us know that He is and will always be in charge. If God takes our son, then we will have to try to understand. We have to get on our knees and beg Him for the strength to go on. But I am not ready to just give up. God has to make Brandon better! He just has to," she whimpered softly. Dave walked over to her and held her close.

"I'm sorry, honey. I am so sorry. I just don't know if I will ever be able to believe in God if He takes our baby away. I'm not that strong. I'm not that faithful, and I am certainly not that forgiving."

"Dave, please. Won't you just pray with me? Pray like you have never done before! Then just see what happens," she suggested, trying to stay strong.

"If you want to know the truth, I have prayed," he admitted. "I said a prayer all the way to the hospital and even before you got here. But, look! Brandon's condition hasn't improved one bit! And do you know why? Because God either doesn't care, He isn't listening, or He doesn't exist! If He did, He would put His hand on my son and give Him back to me! End of story. I need to get some air. I'll be back." And with that he was gone. But within moments everything changed.

Suddenly, Brandon took a turn for the worse. Dave wasn't there when his son stopped breathing; he wasn't there to see when his child was rushed into surgery; he wasn't there to witness his wife on her knees begging for God to show mercy and grace to her baby, and let him live. No, Dave Sanders missed it all! And the one thing he asked God to see most of all was a miracle, but he missed that, too.

Kathleen stood and waited by the entrance to the operating room, with hope in her heart. She refused to give up, even when it looked as though her child would be with God sooner that she had ever imagined. As her head rested against the back of the wall, she watched the automatic doors, willing them to open. Then suddenly they did! The doctor rushed through with tears in his eyes, meeting Kathleen's gaze straight on.

"Oh please, no," she whispered, thinking the worst. Her knees nearly buckled beneath her.

"I have to tell you, Mrs. Sanders. For a while there, I didn't think your son was going to make it. But something or someone had other plans. Brandon is going to be just fine," Doctor Henry Bennett announced.

"He is? Oh, thank you, thank you!" Kathleen cried. "I can't even tell you what a blessing you have given to us, that God has given to you to give to us! Thank you, doctor! Thank you so much. Can I see him?" she asked hopefully.

"He'll be on his way to recovery in a few minutes. You can see him then. He's still a little groggy, but he'll be fine. He's a tough kid and a very lucky little boy."

"Luck doesn't have anything to do with this one! It is only by the grace of God that Brandon made it through. Our prayers were answered. Do you know what was wrong with him?" she questioned.

"Well, the best I can figure is that Brandon has a flu virus of some sort. We think that's why his fever was so high. We finally got that down and stabilized, and he's doing a lot better. However, there was something else. I don't know why we didn't see it sooner, but evidently your son was chewing on a tiny plastic piece of a toy or something. He probably had it in his mouth when he went to bed, and it was still there when they brought him here. No one knew it was there. But when he started choking and couldn't breathe, we had to rush him into surgery. That was when we found it. If you hadn't discovered Brandon's fever, he probably would have choked to death during the night. It really is a miracle! The nurse will come and get you as soon as they get him situated," he told her.

"I can't imagine what was in his mouth, but I am so grateful that you found it when you did. I don't even want to think about what could have happened if you hadn't. Do you know how long he'll have to stay?" Kathleen asked, trying hard not to expect too much.

"I think if he continues to heal at a rapid rate that you should be able to take him home by the end of the week. If you have any other questions, you can call my office," he said and handed her his number. "His throat will be tender for a while, but little kids bounce back so quickly. Your son should be back to normal in no time. I'll be back later to check on him," he told her, with a comforting pat on the arm.

"Thank you again, Doctor Bennett. Thank you so very much!"

As Kathleen sat there and waited for the nurse to come get her, Dave walked in. He was unaware of anything that had happened.

"The emergency room nurses told me they had to take Brandon to surgery. What happened? Has anyone let you know anything yet?" he asked his wife through blood–shot eyes. It was evident that the pain and suffering had taken its toll. Tears filled Kathleen's eyes.

"Oh, Dave," she said running into his arms. "I told you that God would intervene. I told you He wouldn't let anything happen to our little boy. Dave, Brandon is going to be fine! He wasn't, but he is now. And you know what else? The doctors are calling it a miracle! So there you have it! You asked for one and God provided. If this doesn't make you a believer, then nothing will!" she said matter–of–factly.

"I don't understand. What happened?"

Kathleen then explained to her husband what the doctor had told her only a few minutes before. When he heard that Brandon had teetered on the edge of death, his heart dropped to his stomach.

"You mean he really could have died?"

"He stopped breathing, Dave! But he's a fighter, and for reasons only God knows, it wasn't His will to take Brandon right now. I hope someday you'll realize that no matter what happens, God will always see us through, if we trust Him. Even if we had lost our child, Dave, God would have been here for us. He would have held us and given us the strength we needed to endure the loss." Kathleen tried to explain, but it was no use.

"Well, I'll give Him credit that this was truly something special, and I will forever be grateful that He didn't take Brandon. That is, if He is really the One who makes the ultimate decision about this stuff. But I'm still not completely convinced. I really do hope someday that I'll understand. It would be a great feeling to know that we are being watched so closely, by Someone who says He loves us so much. However, I'm not ready to make a full commitment to all that just yet. Besides, honey, I've got lots of time! I'm barely in my forties, remember?" Dave reminded her. He smiled at his wife, and she smiled back. Then Kathleen walked into his arms and silently thanked God once again for all He had done.

It was a weekend that neither of them would ever forget. But, as miraculous as it was, it was still not enough to change Dave's mind or heart.

As hard as Kathleen tried, she couldn't get her husband to see the truth. Dave refused to be persuaded or pushed into believing something he didn't understand. It was his choice, and he believed what he wanted to believe.

Dave thought like many other people in the world that he had plenty of time to decide. But too soon his time ran out. In the end, Dave Sanders, respected citizen, fireman, hero, husband, and father would ultimately suffer the consequence for his choices.

Chapter Six

The next two years seemed to fly by. Before long it was Christmas time again. The decorations went up quickly and in mass quantity. The downtown area was brimming with anxious shoppers hurrying to get the best buy on all the things on their list. Snow covered the ground, and holiday music filled the air.

But after weeks of celebration, everything went back to normal as the season once again came to an end. But this year's end would remain in the minds of many as a time to reflect, a time to remember not in joy, but in heartache, sorrow, and inconceivable disbelief.

It was Saturday night at the Sanders' home. Kathleen struggled to get four–year–old Brandon ready for his sisters' performance in the auditorium at school. Ciera was playing the lead role in *Annie*, and April was in the choir. It was an annual play that the kids put on the same time every year—the first weekend after Christmas.

"Please, Brandon. Let me put your new pants on you. They look so cute. And look, you can even wear this tie, like Daddy does when he goes to church," she begged the little tyke foolishly, but to no avail. Brandon was not going for it.

"No! I don't want to wear those pants. I like these," he said, holding up the powder blue snow pants he had worn earlier that day.

"Honey, you can't wear those to the play. You need to look special, like when we go to church. Please, just put these on and you can wear those pants when we get home!"

"But, I like these, Mommy! And they're special, too. Please, can't I wear them?" His eyes were so big and blue, and his voice was so sweet and innocent, Kathleen could not resist.

"Okay, you can wear them. Just hurry, please. We're going to be late!" She zipped his pants and helped him with his white shirt and tie, which didn't go with anything. But it didn't matter anymore. It was just a little play and Brandon wanted to feel special. And he did!

The girls were driven over to the school two hours before so they could rehearse for the last time. They were a little nervous, but both were such hams that neither of them gave any thought to the crowd gathering outside. By the time Kathleen arrived, there was hardly a vacant seat in the house. Dave was supposed to meet them when he got off work, providing there were no emergency calls before he left.

The curtain rose on cue and the players took their places on stage, just as the sirens wailed loudly outside. The familiar sounds of distress filled the auditorium. Kathleen knew immediately that her husband would not be joining them that night. It was his unit that was called. It was the closest one around.

Several minutes passed and Kathleen could no longer stand the suspense. Before the second scene, she took Brandon's hand and went outside to see if she could see anything that resembled a fire in the surrounding neighborhood. She never expected it to be just down the street, about two miles away. Flames shot up over the two high–rise apartment buildings that were near the school. They weren't in any danger, but it was a sight to be seen.

"See that over there, Brandon?" she asked pointing in the direction of the blaze. "That's where your Daddy is. He is making that fire go away. That's why he can't be here with us right now, but he'll be home by the time we get there," she assured him. But no sooner had the words left her mouth than the ear–piercing blast filled the air. It happened so quickly that it caught her completely off guard, and she grabbed her son and ran inside. The explosion shook the auditorium slightly and made the lights flicker. But it lasted only a few seconds. The play continued and the children scattered across the stage to the next scene. Kathleen tried her best to put it out of her mind as she watched her daughters' performance, but something wasn't right. She could sense it.

Immediately after the blast, Dave felt himself being lifted high in the air, and then crashing down on the pile of rocks in the field across the street. He could smell his flesh burning from the intense blistering heat that covered his body. Loud, tormented screams filled the air, though Dave had no idea they were his. The experienced fireman knew it was bad, but he didn't realize how bad until later, when he was on his way to the hospital. In the far distance, he heard voices.

"Get him hooked up or we're going to lose him. Hurry! Turn on the oxygen," John Bailey shouted to the rescue unit as they drove up. "Oh God, he's not breathing. I can't find a pulse. Get back. Give him some air. He needs CPR. Come on, buddy. Don't give up. You can't let go. Hang in there, Davey. Please, don't go!" the firefighter screamed as the emergency medical technician thrust down hard on what was left of his friend's chest.

By that time there were plenty of other firefighters on the scene, and John elected to ride along in the ambulance. When they reached the hospital, Dave was still unconscious and could no longer breathe on his own. The machine had to do it for him. His vital signs were scarcely registering. The explosion had ripped away much of his protective gear. Dave's face and torso had suffered the most damage, and some areas were grossly disfigured, almost completely covered in third–degree burns. He was barely recognizable. It was a blessing that Dave was not conscious, for the pain would have been too excruciating for him to withstand.

Kathleen's cell phone vibrated in her pocket.

"Hello," she whispered, trying not to disrupt the production. "What? I can't understand you. Hold on, Johnny. I need to go out in the hallway," she told him. Then turning to her son, she said, "Stay here and watch your sisters, honey. I need to see what Uncle Johnny wants. I'll be right back." Kathleen excused herself and made her way down the aisle and out the door.

"Kathleen, are you there?" John asked her.

"Yes, finally. I'm sorry. I'm over at the school watching the…" but he wouldn't let her finish.

"You need to get over to the hospital, Kath. It's Dave. He's been hurt really bad. You need to hurry!" he told her.

"I'll be there in less than ten minutes!"

Kathleen refused to think the worst. She made her way back inside the auditorium and grabbed Brandon.

"Come on, honey. We need to take a ride really quick," she said, as calmly as she could.

After leaving instructions for her neighbor to take the girls home with her when the play was over, Kathleen and Brandon ran to the car. The hospital was only ten blocks away. After parking in front, they rushed through the emergency entrance and found John sitting in the waiting room, covered in ash, with tears smeared on his blackened face.

"What happened, Johnny? Is he okay? Is Dave going to be okay?" she asked fearfully.

"Oh, Kathleen, I'm so sorry." John jumped to his feet as soon as he saw Kathleen come through the door. "We tried our best to get him here as soon as we could. But he isn't doing very well. He was walking toward the building when it exploded into a fiery ball. It was so powerful that it threw him at least 20 yards. He's burned really badly and is having trouble breathing, or at least he was when I left him a few minutes ago. He had to be put on a ventilator," he told her regretfully.

"Oh, dear God. How can this be happening? Dave can't die! He isn't ready yet, Johnny. Oh, please, God, don't take him, not yet! Let him find You first! Save him, Lord! Please!" she begged out loud, grabbing John by his jacket.

"What are you talking about?" he asked, looking very confused.

"Johnny, if Dave dies now, he won't go to heaven because he isn't saved!"

"You're not making any sense, Kathleen. What does that have to do with anything? Dave's been a great husband and the best friend anyone could ever have! And look at all the stuff he's done for everyone. He'd give the shirt off his back, even if it were the last one he had! What do you mean, he's not going to heaven? How could he not?" the fireman asked.

"Because that isn't how it works, Johnny. You have to believe in Jesus and know why He died before you can go heaven! I've tried to tell Dave this for years, but he never understood. And if he dies now, he never will! Please, God, don't let him die! Not yet! Please, not yet!" she begged out loud.

Kathleen's heart ached to even think of what her husband's eternal future would be like if he were taken too soon. The thought of him writhing in pain and torment forevermore made her stomach turn and her body tremble. Even in his current state of painful disfigurement, what Dave would undergo in the next world would be a million times worse than anything he had ever suffered in this life.

Several hours later Kathleen was finally allowed to see Dave. John stayed in the waiting room with Brandon, who had fallen asleep on the couch. When she walked into the small sterile room, she gasped. It was obvious even to her that her precious husband was hanging on only by the grace of God. Parts of his upper body and face were nearly seared to the bone, and the only sounds in the room were coming from the machines nearby. As she neared his bed, tears filled her eyes once again, and a sob escaped her lips.

"No! Oh, no!" she cried, barely above a whisper. Kathleen stood in front of the grossly deformed figure that had once been her husband. Then she carefully reached for his bandaged hand. She knew immediately that Dave could not possibly survive his injuries. Though she believed with all of her heart that God could do anything and everything, if it were His will, she was still realistic enough to know that her husband was all but dead. Only the machines were keeping him alive. She didn't want him to live the rest of his life grieving and suffering, with scars that would never heal and anger in his heart that would never go away, but she was also painfully aware of the alternative.

She did the only thing she knew how to do. Kathleen dropped to her knees, folded her hands in front of her, and turned to her Father in heaven.

"Almighty God! I need You now more than I've ever needed You before. I know that You must have Your reasons for all of this, and I promise to do my best to understand. But, Lord, I can't take the thought of Dave not being in heaven with You, and with me, too, when it's my time. I've tried so very hard to make him understand Your Word, but he wasn't ready to accept it.

And now if You take him, Lord, he never will! Please let him hear You! Don't let it be too late! And if all that we are going through now is to help others know You before their time runs out, then help me to spread Your Word, Father. Help me to say the right things for You. Let me use this incredibly painful experience to make others aware that their time on earth is short and that they need to know You as the One True God of all the universe before it's too late. Please don't let my words fall on deaf ears like they did for Dave. And, Lord, if there is any way that You can save my precious husband from the horrifying grave of eternal hell, please, I beg You to do it! Please, Father. He's a good man and a wonderful husband, father, and friend. Please, Lord, give him another chance to choose You."

Kathleen knelt for a few minutes longer, remembering her husband as she knew him to be… vivacious, kind, loving, and honest. But was that enough to get him into the streets of heaven for all eternity? Kathleen knew better than to even ask.

Early the next morning, Dave Sanders took his last breath. Kathleen chose to disconnect the machines that were keeping him alive. It was her husband's desire not to remain on life support. The doctors had told her that his brain was dead, and she could find no other reason to prolong the inevitable. She bent down and tenderly kissed him for the last time.

"I love you, Dave. I will always love you," she whispered. "Think Jesus, honey. Jesus is the Light! He's there if you look for Him. Jesus loves you, and He died for you. You must believe this, you must! Please, Dave. The kids and I want to be with you in heaven. Look for Jesus. He's there if you would only believe! This is your last chance, my love. Please, please, believe!" she sobbed, begging him to understand. Then Kathleen gently held his hand until he was gone. But Dave couldn't hear her anymore.

Chapter Seven

As Dave's spirit left his body, it gravitated upward into another dimension where time had all but vanished. Dave could feel that what he was going through was not of the world he had known. Then without warning, it happened. A light appeared before him that was brighter than anything he had ever seen or any fire he had ever fought. Being in the presence of such wonder should have been peaceful, calming, and serene, for it was pure love! Dave had never known anything like it before. But no matter what he did or how hard he tried, he couldn't make himself move toward it. Dave had no idea where he was or how he had gotten there, nor what the unbelievably brilliant mass was that glowed in front of him. But before his thoughts were answered, the light disappeared, and he was swept away.

Suddenly, everything became all too clear and Dave knew without a doubt. The illuminating light had been that of God. The same God he rejected on earth, whose promise of wondrous unconditional love he had forfeited for his own selfish desires. Dave had been presented with many opportunities to become a follower of Christ, opportunities that would have secured him an eternal life in heaven—but he ignored them all.

God had sent him Kathleen—sweet, wonderful, Kathleen—but he ignored all that she had to say. She continuously gave him incredible words of wisdom and had even taken him to church with the hope that he would grasp the understanding of what he had to do. Yet he still refused. Even when his son, Brandon, became deathly ill, he should have realized that it was a sign from God for Dave to put his faith where it was meant to be—in God and God alone! And God had healed the child, just as Dave had prayed. But once again, the sign that was crystal clear to his wife fell on the blind eyes and deaf ears of Dave Sanders, who had his own way of dealing with life's bumps, trials, and roadblocks. And never once did it include his Father in heaven.

Before long, Dave was whisked away once again into yet another realm, one that was filled with complete and utter remorse. Pains of regret encompassed what was left of his dying spirit. Agony permeated his soul. No matter how much he begged, it would not go away! The core of his being continued to fall, crushing any signs of love and life from his memory.

Anguish ravaged his heart. Where once was laughter and happiness, all that was left was the shell of a man he would never be again.

The devoted husband, loving father and friend, and sometimes hero, who had been worshiped by thousands, soon grasped the realization that this was the beginning of his long eternal existence—an existence without even a glimpse of anything godly, righteous, or good ever again.

Dave screamed out in painful regret and disbelief, but no one heard. No one, that is, except for the myriad of others doomed to this black bottomless abyss with him. And come Judgment Day, there would be nothing but weeping and gnashing of teeth for all eternity.

Taylor Morgan

"This is the last time, I promise," Taylor said for at least the tenth time that week, to the pale reflection in the mirror. "I just need one more. Then I swear I'll stop." As the words left her lips, her hand trembled and she reached for the bottle under the bed. Her palms grew moist with excitement as she tilted the bottle upward. The warmth of the liquid stung her throat at first and then did its magic as it flowed through her veins. Her body felt instantly relieved and renewed. "How can something that makes you feel so good be so wrong?" Taylor wondered and replaced the cap. She smiled to herself and got out of bed. It was Tuesday morning, and sixteen–year–old Taylor Morgan had to get ready for school.

Young Taylor had been drinking since she was in the fifth grade. She started out experimenting with all the different colored bottles in her parents' secret cabinet, shortly after the death of her precious Nanny—the only person who ever cared about her. That first sip tasted terrible, but the feeling it gave her inside was something quite unique. She instantly felt more confident. It gave her power. That's how her habit started. Once a week she treated herself to a small sip or two. "What could be the harm?" she thought. But soon it grew to twice a week, then three times a week. Each time the sip got bigger. She can't remember the exact day it happened, when she could no longer go to school without having at least one full glass to start her day. By the time Taylor left her house, she was in the familiar, clouded state of mind, ready to conquer the world.

Taylor had been a straight–A student. She never let her secret pleasure get in the way of her studies. At least she tried not to. But after several years of daily indulging, Taylor was finding it harder and harder to concentrate. Her A's became C's, and her desire to go to college suddenly became not as important. Her parents didn't have clue. They were too busy caught up in their own social status just as they had been since she was an infant. Her friends knew, but they were not about to tell. After all, Taylor was their ticket to all their party weekends, with her providing much of their entertainment.

No one noticed when she changed. It seemed to happen overnight. But with her mounting depression and feeling of worthless incompetence, the only thing the teenager had any interest in was death...hers. Suicide had to be the answer. Taylor thought it was the best way to escape and put an end to her miserable existence. She believed that her death would reunite her with her sweet Nanny in heaven. But Taylor found out too late that her bad choices had caused her to make the worst mistake of her life.

Chapter One

Taylor was born in the early spring to Tom and Anna Morgan. They were slightly less than thrilled with their new arrival and had little time to spend with her. She was handed to the nanny when she was only three weeks old. The woman's job was to clean the house and tend to all of Taylor's needs, including love. Nanny, the name Taylor gave her as soon as she could talk, had no children of her own, and she knew she never would. Nanny was well past the age of childbearing, but not too old to care. And she was delighted to be a part of the Taylor's world.

Tom was a stockbroker, and his wife a successful attorney. Neither one had planned for a family. In fact, they assumed that after eight years of marriage Anna couldn't get pregnant. But they quickly discovered how wrong they had been. They made the best of the situation for themselves and were rarely home before the child was put to bed for the night. Then conveniently, by the next morning, they were both gone when she woke up. Most weekends were spent out of town, mostly on business or sometimes for pleasure, but always without Taylor. This went on for the first ten years of the little girl's life.

When Taylor was a toddler, she had always assumed that Nanny was her parent. She really didn't know who Tom and Anna were, although when she saw them she called them Mother and Father, at their insistence. But it was Nanny who taught her to ride a bike and tie her shoes. It was Nanny who read her stories at night and kissed away her tears when she fell down. It was Nanny who took her to school for the first time. It was Nanny who was always there for her, no matter what.

Nanny was also the first and only one to tell Taylor about God. She took the child to church with her when she had an occasional day off. For Nanny, or Beth Moore, as her friends knew her, she considered a day off to be some form of punishment. She loved being with Taylor as much as Taylor loved being with her. She felt lost without her. From the beginning, Taylor was her whole world.

On those special Sundays when they would go to church together, Nanny always dressed up. Taylor wore her good clothes, too, and sometimes they sat in the sanctuary together. Other times, Taylor would join her Sunday school class for special teachings about Jesus and heaven. It was on one of these days when Taylor had just turned six years old, that she left the classroom in tears. It was the very first time the young girl had ever heard about death.

Nanny didn't see her until she came outside and found her on the steps of the church entrance. Taylor was sobbing.

"Child, what's wrong? Did someone hurt you? Did you fall? Tell me where it hurts, honey. Let me fix it for you!" she said with great concern.

"I didn't fall, Nanny. But I hurt inside where my heart is. My teacher told me that people die! They go away and never come back!" Taylor said with her eyes drenched in tears.

"Yes, honey. I'm afraid that everyone has to die. But it doesn't mean it has to be bad. For those people who put their trust in Jesus, they get to go to heaven and be with God!" the woman tried to explain.

"But, it means that we can't see them anymore. Right?" Taylor's lip quivered as she spoke.

"No, we can't see them again down here. But we can when we are all in heaven."

"But that could be a long time, couldn't it?" the child asked.

"Sometimes it is. It just depends on what God's plan is for them," Nanny answered.

"But I don't want you to die, Nanny. What would I do without you? I would miss you so much. Please don't leave me here by myself!" Taylor wrapped her little arms around the woman who had become the most important person in the little girl's life.

"Oh, you sweet little thing. You are such a good girl, Taylor, and you will never be alone! I promise. I will never leave you. I will always be right here for you, no matter what! Now you dry those tears and let's go get some ice cream! How about a sundae with lots of whipped cream and a cherry on the top? Does that sound good?"

Beth knew that someday the child would grow up and maybe forget all about her when she was no longer needed. But for now, it was the most pleasing thing in the world to her that she had such an important role in Taylor's life. She wouldn't trade that for anything.

"Okay, Nanny. Let's go! I'll race you to the car," the little girl squealed with delight. Though she was crushed at the news that people had to die someday, Taylor was able to put it out of her mind temporarily.

Chapter Two

Christmas was just around the corner, which was by far the favorite time of the year for both Nanny and Taylor. Nanny always made the holiday special as she put up the decorations and had the tree all prepared to trim and light when Taylor came home from school.

They spent hours putting the hundreds of lights on the branches and each ornament in its place. When they were through, Taylor climbed the ladder and placed the angel on the top. Then she climbed down the ladder, walked over to the wall, and flipped the switch. The lights glowed brightly and the angel moved its wings as if it were about to ascend into the heavens. Several presents in beautiful wrappings and bows were already under the tree. The biggest one was Taylor's. The two smaller ones were for Nanny. As they did each year, Tom and Anna spent Christmas in Hawaii. But this never bothered Taylor. She had all she wanted right there—just her and Nanny.

On Christmas morning, Taylor got up early and turned on the coffee, so it would be ready when Nanny woke up. To the woman's surprise, Taylor had also put together a Continental-style breakfast for them, with orange juice and cinnamon rolls, then served it all on an elegant tray from her mother's best china. The tray was too heavy for her small hands to carry, and Nanny came to the rescue once again.

"Little one, this is so lovely," the older woman commended. "But you're going to get us both in trouble if your mother finds out we're using these dishes! Let's hurry and eat. Then we'll put them back, and she'll never know. It will be our secret. Thank you so much, Taylor, for making this day so special. And thank you, too, for my beautiful scarf and sweater. I'm going to wear them to church on Sunday so everyone can see!" Nanny told her young friend, and Taylor beamed with pride.

On Sunday, Taylor decided she wanted to stay with Nanny in the sanctuary, instead of going to her Sunday school class. She loved the music and moved in perfect rhythm to every beat. When the music ended, Pastor Jacob Forman, who was the senior pastor at Lord of Life Church, came to the center of the stage.

"Before we begin our service, let's give thanks to a wonderful God". He bowed his head in prayer. "Father, you are such an awesome God. You care so much for us, and we are truly humbled by Your grace and mercy. Let us have an incredibly powerful week, Lord, by growing in Your Word and letting each of those words draw us closer to You. Thank You for Your love. In Jesus' name. Amen. You may be seated.

"Today we're going to continue our series on 'The Future: Discovering God's Plan and My Destiny!' Part 9 is called 'What in the World is God Doing?'

"A little girl was walking with her father in the country. As she looked up into the star–studded sky, her eyes were filled with wonder. Turning to her father she asked, 'If the wrong side of heaven is so beautiful, what do you think the right side will be like?'

"What an incredible way to describe heaven! Everyone dreams of Utopia. What is your Utopia?

"For some, it is relaxing with a fishing pole by a lazy river. For others, it is a permanent residence in Hawaii! And for many of us, it is inheriting a million dollars! We are all victims of utopian fantasies! But soon we come back to reality…and dismiss our thoughts as delusional.

"But according to the Bible, Utopia is more than a delusion: it is a promise of God! And its fulfillment will exceed your wildest imaginations! God has promised the earth a time of glory that will far exceed anything you can imagine. It rests in the biblical promise of Christ's return to earth to complete His prophesied program!

"You see, for the believer our best days are yet to come! Here's another touching story for you. Some of you may have heard it already, but it's worth repeating.

'There was a woman who had been diagnosed with a terminal illness and had been given three months to live. As she was getting her things in order, she contacted her pastor and had him come to her house to discuss certain aspects of her final wishes. She told him which songs she wanted sung at the service and what Scriptures she would like read. The woman also requested to be buried with her favorite Bible. Everything was in order, and the pastor was preparing to leave when the woman suddenly remembered something very important to her.

'There's one more thing,' she said excitedly.

'What's that?' came the pastor's reply.

'This is very important,' the woman continued. 'I want to be buried with a fork in my right hand!'

The pastor stood looking at the woman, not knowing quite what to say.

'That surprises you, doesn't it?' the woman asked.

'Well, to be honest, I'm puzzled by the request,' said the pastor.

The woman explained. 'In all my years of dinners, I always remember that when the dishes of the main course were being cleared, someone would inevitably lean over and say, "Keep your fork." It was my favorite part of the meal because I knew that something better was coming, something wonderful and with substance…like velvety chocolate cake or deep–dish apple pie! So, I just want people to see me there in that casket with a fork in my hand, and I want them to wonder, "What's with the fork?" Then I want you to tell them: 'Keep the fork…the best is yet to come!'"

The congregation broke into happy applause and laughter, with tears of joy rolling down their cheeks. The story touched everyone's heart! Then, as the noise died down, the pastor went on.

"Now you know why I said it bears repeating! When Jesus taught His disciples to pray, He taught them to pray 'Thy kingdom come.' What does that phrase mean? From Genesis to Revelation, the kingdom of God is described. Remember back in the beginning of our studies of things to come, we stated that God is doing two things? He is reclaiming His kingdom and He is redeeming His people!" Pastor Jacob said excitedly, as he walked from one end of the stage to the other, making eye contact with everyone in the first few rows.

"Let me give you just an overview of the kingdom of God on earth. It began with a theocracy: the direct rule of God! He chose out a nation... Israel. He led that nation in a direct, visible way. In Exodus 19:5–6a it says, 'Now then, if you will indeed obey My voice and keep My covenant, then you shall be My own possession among all the peoples, for all the earth is Mine; and you shall be to Me a kingdom of priests and a holy nation.'

"The problem was that Israel didn't want a theocracy. They wanted a king to be over them so they could be like all the rest of the nations! Turn to 1 Samuel 8:4–7. 'Then all the elders of Israel gathered together and came to Samuel at Ramah: and they said to him... "Now appoint a king for us to judge us like all the nations." And the Lord said to Samuel, "Listen to the voice of the people... for they have not rejected you, but they have rejected Me from being king over them."'

"They traded a theocracy for a monarchy, and they paid the price! That decision eventually led to the nation's undoing, but God, who is rich in mercy, sent His Son with an offer of the kingdom. But the Jews rejected and crucified the Son! At this point, a mystery form of the kingdom was inaugurated. Someday Jesus is coming back to set His kingdom up physically on planet earth, and His reign will be seen by all. Today, however, His throne is in the ear of every believer, and His reign is an invisible one today as opposed to a visible one that will be established upon His return.

"Today, between the First and Second Coming of Christ, the kingdom of God is being lived out in the life of the believer! Colossians 1:13–14 reads, 'For He delivered us from the domain of darkness, and transferred us to the kingdom of His beloved Son, in whom we have redemption, the forgiveness of sins.'

"How does a person become a part of that kingdom today? The answer is found in John 3:3–5. 'Jesus answered and said to him, "Truly, truly, I say to you, unless one is born again, he cannot see the kingdom of God." Nicodemus said to Him, "How can a man be born when he is old? He cannot enter a second time into his mother's womb and be born, can he?" Jesus answered, "Truly, truly, I say to you, unless one is born of water and the spirit, he cannot enter into the kingdom of God.""" Several 'Amens' were heard from different parts of the room as the pastor continued.

"God's rule today is through the Holy Spirit in you! But there is coming a time when Jesus Christ will physically rule on planet earth! Go to 2 Timothy 4:1. 'I solemnly charge you in the presence of God and of Christ Jesus, who is to judge the living and the dead, and by His appearing and His kingdom.' The kingdom is physically tied to His appearing.

"Is there a reign of Christ on this earth? I believe so without question! In 2 Samuel 7:12–13, it says this, 'When your days are complete and you lie down with your fathers, I will raise up your descendant after you, who will come forth from you, and I will establish his kingdom. He shall build a house for My name, and I will establish the throne of his kingdom forever.'

"In Psalm 89:3–4, this is a covenant that God entered into with David: 'I have made a covenant with My chosen; I have sworn to David My servant, I will establish your seed forever, and build up your throne to all generations.' Selah.

"Why then doesn't the seed of David reign over Israel today? Hosea 3 says that it is because Israel committed adultery against the Lord. In verse 4 it reads, 'For the sons of Israel will remain for many days without king or prince, without sacrifice or sacred pillar, and without Ephod.' Then in verse 5, 'Afterward the sons of Israel will return and seek the Lord their God and David their king; and they will come trembling to the Lord and to His goodness in the last days.'

"Jesus Christ, being the seed of David, is the heir to the throne! Turn to Luke 1:31–33. 'And behold, you will conceive in your womb, and bear a son, and you shall name Him Jesus. He will be great, and will be called the Son of the Most High; and the Lord God will give Him the throne of His father David; and He will reign over the house of Jacob forever; and His kingdom will have no end.'

"When will that happen? Turn to Revelation 11:15. 'And the seventh angel sounded; and there arose loud voices in heaven, saying "The kingdom of the world has become the kingdom of our Lord, and of His Christ; and He will reign forever and ever.'" Pastor Jacob noticed nods of approval and agreement from as far back as he could see.

"Its duration is one thousand years, then comes the new heaven and the new earth! At the end of the thousand years, Satan will be released and he will deceive once more and lead a rebellion against God! People will be born during this time and just like today, they will need to be born again! And even with Christ reigning on earth personally, many will refuse the new birth, which demonstrates the sinfulness of man!

"What's it going to be like during that time? Well, let me tell you… happy days are here to stay! First Satan is bound and sealed for the greatest of that time. There will be a great increase in knowledge, and freedom from violence, poverty, and fear. Man will be living in abundance. Ezekiel saw it as a restoration of the Garden of Eden (Ezekiel 36:35). Death will be there, but not the norm. A death at one hundred years of age will be considered a youthful death. Perfect justice and equity will prevail, for the Lord will judge. No rebels will be allowed to enter. And the most important thing of all… Jesus Christ will be there!

"Before we close, I just want to read one passage of Scripture that I found in Isaiah 11. It goes from verse one to twelve. 'Then a shoot will spring from the stem of Jesse, and a branch from his roots will bear fruit. And the spirit of the Lord will rest on him, the spirit of wisdom and understanding, the spirit of counsel and strength, the spirit of knowledge and the fear of the Lord. And he will delight in the fear of the Lord, and he will not judge by what his eyes see, nor make a decision by what his ears hear; but with righteousness he will judge the poor, and decide with fairness for the afflicted of the earth; and he will strike the earth with the rod of his mouth, and with the breath of his lips he will slay the wicked. Also righteousness will be the belt about his loins, and faithfulness the belt about his waist. And the wolf will dwell with the lamb, and the leopard will lie down with the kid, and the calf and the young lion and the fatling together; and a little boy will lead them. Also the cow and the bear will graze; their young will lie down together; and the lion will eat straw like the ox. And the nursing child will play by the hole of the cobra, and the weaned child will put his hand on the viper's den. They will not hurt or destroy in all My holy mountain, for the earth will be full of the knowledge of the Lord as the waters cover the sea. Then it will come about in that day that the nations will resort to the root of Jesse, who will stand as a signal for the peoples; and his resting place will be glorious. Then it will happen on that day that the Lord will again recover the second time with His hand the remnant of His people, who will remain, from Assyria, Egypt, Pathros, Cush, Elam, Shinar, Hamath, and from the islands of the sea. And He will lift up a standard for the nations, and will assemble the banished ones of Israel, and will gather the dispersed of Judah from the four corners of the earth.'

"But so what? There are two facts here: The first one is God keeps His promises! The second one is God's timetable isn't always ours! Timing is everything and God's timetable is almost never ours.

"My final thought here is to be a seeker! If you came here seeking, but don't know Christ, look on the screen with me at this verse. 1 Corinthians 6:9–11, 'Or do you not know that the unrighteous shall not inherit the kingdom of God? Do not be deceived; neither fornicators, nor idolaters, nor adulterers, nor effeminate, nor homosexuals, nor thieves, nor the covetous, nor drunkards, nor revilers, nor swindlers, shall inherit the kingdom of God. And such were some of you; but you were washed, but you were sanctified, but you were justified in the name of the Lord Jesus Christ, and in the Spirit of our God.'

"If you are a believer, you are admonished in Matthew 6:33–34, 'But seek first His kingdom and His righteousness; and all these things shall be added to you. Therefore do not be anxious for tomorrow; for tomorrow will care for itself. Each day has enough trouble of its own.'

"Don't be consumed with materialism but be consumed with seeking the kingdom of God! Life is tragic for the person who has plenty to live on, but nothing to live for. But how do you seek the kingdom? By abounding in the work of the Lord. By building on the foundation of Jesus Christ. By persuading men and by seeking God! It should produce in you a victor's mentality, not a victim's mentality.

"For this last story, let me take you back. On Palm Sunday in 1981, millions of Americans shared a great sense of anticipation as they awaited the liftoff of the manned space shuttle Columbia. The media billed the event as 'the dawn of a new age.' More than 80,000 people were crowded into Florida's

Kennedy Space Center to witness the launching of the nation's first real space plane.

"Hundreds of thousands drove to nearby roads for the best view they could get. And countless numbers watched in front of their television sets. As the countdown reached the last ten seconds, the nation counted down in unison. Then at 7:00 a.m. Eastern Standard Time it happened.

"The great flying machine rose…straight up! Orange flames and vapor engulfed the launch site, as sound and shock waves thundered through the air and ground. The hopes of all future–manned space flights seemed to focus on the success of that long–awaited mission.

"As promising as that event was though, it's nothing compared with another event… the countdown of which may already be taking place in heaven. It is the return of the Lord Jesus to the earth. Oh what a day that will be! Let's bow our heads in prayer.

"Father, thank You for this time together. We are so grateful for all You continue to do in our lives. Lord, we try every week to bring a special message to those who may not know Your glory and love yet. But try as we may, someone always gets left out. I ask You now, Father, to bring us those people. Let us show them what they need to do, to dwell in the house of God forever and to bring You the glory and honor You so richly deserve. Keep us safe, Lord, and bring us back next week. I ask all of this in Your precious Son's holy name. Amen."

On the way home, Nanny and Taylor were mostly silent. Nanny was deep in thought about the message and how she could be a better servant to God. Taylor was troubled and needed to ask Nanny a question.

"I liked the message today, Nanny. But I was wondering what that word crucified means? Pastor Jacob used it when he was talking about Israel and Jesus, and said that they crucified Him," the child asked. Even as young as she was, she seemed to know what was going on, at least in most of the services.

"Crucified means they put Jesus on a cross. You've seen that picture before, like the one in my room over my bed. They put nails in His hands and in His feet, and then He hung there until He died," the woman told her, as tears formed in the corner of her eyes.

"Did it hurt Him?" Taylor wondered.

"Oh, yes, my sweet child. It hurt Jesus very much."

"But He could have gotten down, couldn't He? He did all those miracles and stuff. He didn't have to be up there! He could have just climbed down if He wanted, right?"

"Yes, if that was the way it was supposed to be, He could have. But He needed to die. He came to earth to die, so that you and I and everyone else would be forgiven of our sins and be able to live with God someday in heaven. When Jesus was on the cross, He took all our sins with Him. That is what I was trying to tell you that day you first heard about death. Remember when you were so upset a few years ago? Well, people who hold Jesus in their hearts and treat others with love will have a place in heaven someday. All they have to do is believe that Jesus died for their sins. Do you believe that, Taylor?" Nanny asked.

"I believe what you tell me, Nanny, because I know you would never lie. But I don't understand how Jesus can stay up in heaven without falling out!" she replied innocently.

"Because Jesus can do anything, Taylor. He lives somewhere past what we see as the sky. Heaven is past the clouds, and even farther than the sun, moon, and stars. He can't fall because there are streets in heaven. And do you know what else? They are made of gold! It is the most beautiful place in the entire universe." Nanny wasn't sure if her answer was any help to the child, but Taylor seemed satisfied for now.

"Wow, heaven sounds really pretty. I'd like to go there sometime. Are you going to go there, Nanny?" Taylor wondered.

"I sure hope so, honey."

"Will you have to die first?"

"Yes, we have to die here first. But then we can live forever in heaven with Jesus."

"Okay. Then I will go with you," she told Nanny matter-of-factly.

Taylor seemed to understand, at least mentally, who God was and that Jesus was His Son, but she didn't know how to trust her life to Him nor did she ever ask Him to forgive her sins. Because of this, Taylor always felt spiritually empty.

However, by the world's standards, Taylor was said to have it all! She had the best clothes, games, toys, and anything else she desired. She lived in the biggest and best house in the community, with sprawling hills for her backyard and a swimming pool and tennis courts, too. The house was so big that when Taylor was little she often got confused as to where she was going. She wasn't allowed in the far side of the house, but occasionally she took a wrong turn and ended up there. Finding her way back to the main part of the house usually took her awhile, but she always made it out. However, as Taylor got older she would find that there were some things that she could not get out of on her own.

Chapter Three

When Taylor turned ten, Nanny had a surprise party for her in the backyard. Her parents were out of town, as usual, but all her friends from school were there, all thirty–two of them. There was plenty of room for everyone. Nanny had rented a clown and several ponies. The children spent the day riding, swimming, and laughing in the warm California sunshine.

Later that evening, after Nanny cleaned up the dishes from the party, she told Taylor she needed to rest.

"I think I overdid myself a little today, honey. I am exhausted. I'm going to go to bed early tonight, so you need to get into your pajamas and stay in your room until it's time for you to go to sleep," the woman explained.

"Are you okay, Nanny?" Taylor asked.

"Oh, my Lord, yes! I just need to get off my feet. Now you run along and get your teeth brushed and your pajamas on, and I will be in there to tuck you in."

"But who will read to me?" she wondered.

"I think just for tonight you can start where we left off last night and read to yourself for half an hour or so. Then it's lights out, okay?" This would be the first time in all of Taylor's life that Nanny hadn't read her a story.

"But, Nanny. You always read to me. Are you sure you're okay?" Taylor was deeply concerned and didn't like how she was feeling inside.

"Now don't go and worry yourself. I'm fine. I just need to get some rest. It's been a very long day and a long week, too. Now stop fretting and get yourself ready for bed. I'll be up directly to kiss you goodnight. Go on, scoot!" Nanny said, lightly shoving her out of the room.

Nanny gave Taylor about twenty minutes to get herself into bed. Then she made her way up the stairs and down the hallway to the girl's room. She was nearly out of breath when she reached for the door.

"All ready?" she asked the child.

"All ready, Nanny!" Taylor told her as she sat propped up in bed with her book.

"Now promise me you'll go to sleep right after you read this chapter. I don't need your parents bawling me out because you stayed up too late on a school night. They should be home shortly, so lights out when you're done!"

"I promise. I'll go to sleep as soon as I am through," she agreed.

Nanny leaned over and kissed Taylor on the forehead as she had done every night since she was just a baby.

"Goodnight, my sweet little girl. I love you. Never ever forget that!" she told her again.

"Goodnight, Nanny. I love you, too. See you in the morning."

For Taylor, the warmth of that kiss lingered on until she fell asleep. And for Nanny, all the kisses she had ever given her little friend and companion stayed with her forever.

The next morning, Tom and Anna were getting ready to walk out the door, when they noticed that Nanny was not in the kitchen as she always was before they left. It seemed odd because Nanny never slept this late, so they decided to go to her room and check on her.

Anna reached the closed door first. She lightly tapped and called out her name, but no answer was returned. So she tried again.

"Nanny! Can you hear me? Tom and I are leaving and we want to make sure you're up!" she said, getting louder this time. She tried the door but it was locked.

"Let me try," Tom interrupted, and moved in beside his wife. "Nanny, open the door!" he insisted.

"What do you suppose is going on, Tom?" Anna asked, more annoyed for the inconvenience than concerned for the person inside.

"I don't know. But you know how reliable Nanny is. This isn't like her at all. Something must be wrong." Tom once again banged on the door, but still it went unanswered.

"Don't we have an extra key around here somewhere?" Anna asked.

"In my office. I'll go get it. Maybe you should wake Taylor and get her ready for school," he suggested.

"Let's see what's going on with Nanny first. I don't want to assume the worst until I have to. Taylor is awfully attached to that woman. She'll fall apart if there's anything wrong, and I'm not prepared to handle it!" Anna's patience was wearing thin. It was bothersome to have to deal with all of this right now when she was trying to prepare for one of the biggest cases of her career.

"Yeah, maybe you're right. I'll be right back."

His office was on the opposite end of the house of Nanny and Taylor's rooms so it took him about ten minutes to return. Anna paced the floor until she heard his voice.

"I found it. Stand back so I can see if it works."

It took a few seconds for it to connect, but then they heard the click. The door was finally unlocked. They opened it slowly and walked inside together.

"Nanny, are you in here?" Anna whispered. But there was no answer. As they moved closer to the bed, they saw why. Nanny was face–up and her eyes were stone cold and wide open. It appeared that she had been dead for several hours.

"Oh no! Poor, Nanny," Tom said sadly. "This is going to crush Taylor.

What are we going to do?"

"Let's not make this complicated or create a big scene. Taylor doesn't need to hear sirens or anything like that. Neither do our neighbors. Just call the coroner's office and tell them we had an elderly person who died during the night and she needs to be removed. I am sure you can get one of your buddies over there to come out without a hassle," his wife told him without emotion.

"Anna, you sound pretty coldhearted. I thought you liked Nanny!" he stated.

"I did like her. She was great to have around and great for Taylor. But now what do we do with our daughter? I hate to have to try to find someone else. Taylor's nearly old enough to take care of herself. To bring someone else in for a few years doesn't seem logical to me. What do you think?"

"Well, she's what…ten now? I think she could stay alone as long as we aren't going out of town. Then maybe we could just hire someone from the agency to stay with her those weekends we had to leave. I guess, worse case scenario, we could even take her with us if we had to," he commented.

"I suppose that could be an option. But I'd rather have her just stay here, with school and all." Anna hadn't ever been alone with Taylor and she wasn't feeling very comfortable with the whole prospect of it. She wondered what on earth would they ever talk about and what would she do with her?

"Well, first things first. I'll call and get Nanny taken care of. One of us is going to have to tell Taylor what happened. Do you want to, or should I?" Tom asked his wife.

"I think you're closer to her than I am. You should probably be the one to break the news. I'll go get her up while you make the phone call. She can still go to school, right?" Anna wondered.

"Well, you know Taylor will be crushed. Nanny was all she has ever known. But I think she's tough enough to go to school even with this. So, why don't you get her going, and I'll be there in a few minutes to tell her what happened." Anna walked out of the room, and Tom headed to his office to call for the pick up of their longtime housekeeper, babysitter, and the only companion their daughter had ever known.

Chapter Four

Taylor was just beginning to stir. The sun was shining through her window telling her the day had begun without her. She knew it was time to get up, but she wanted to put it off as long as possible. She was sure Nanny would be up there to get her soon, and she sometimes stayed in bed on purpose just to see her friend come through the door. But it wasn't Nanny who came. It was her mother.

"Come on, get up! It's time for you to go to school," Anna said in a stern voice.

"Mother! Where's Nanny?" the child ask curiously. Something had to be wrong. Taylor could feel it.

"Just get up. Your father will explain what is going on when you get downstairs. Now hurry. You'll be late for school." And with that she was gone.

Taylor couldn't stop thinking about Nanny. Why wasn't she the one to wake her? Was she sick? Did she quit? Taylor was beside herself with worry. She rushed to get dressed. Then she brushed her teeth, grabbed her books, and ran downstairs as quickly as she could.

Tom was waiting in the kitchen for her when she walked in.

"Sit down, Taylor. I made you some cereal."

"Father, what is going on? Where is Nanny? Is she sick?" his daughter asked, more concerned than she had ever been before.

"Taylor, something terrible has happened. Nanny passed away last night. We found her in bed this morning," he explained.

"What do you mean by 'passed away'?"

"She died last night, Taylor. She must have had a heart attack or something," he told her sadly. Even though Tom rarely conversed with his daughter, he felt some sympathy for what she had to be feeling.

"She died? But she can't be dead. She promised. Where is she? I want to see her!" the girl screamed.

"You can't see her. She's gone, Taylor. She's never going to come back, so you need to just get over it. I know you cared for Nanny a great deal, but there is nothing else to do now except move on." Tom's words were cold and harsh, but he was late and there was no time to mourn. "Now eat your breakfast, and I'll drop you off at school. I'll arrange for someone to come and get you afterward. Next week you will have to start taking the bus. Your mother and I have decided that you're probably old enough to stay alone during the day. There will be plenty of food in the freezer so you can make yourself your own meals in the microwave from now on."

The news hit Taylor so hard she could barely comprehend what her father was saying. She moved in slow motion as she ate her cereal and cleaned up her breakfast dishes. Then she followed her father out the door and into the waiting car.

As she rode the three miles to school, Taylor's thoughts went back to last night when Nanny wasn't feeling well.

"She was sick last night," she said out loud, directing her comment to no one in particular.

"What? Speak up, girl. I can't hear you when you mumble." Her dad was on his cell phone and was irritated when she interrupted.

"Nothing. I just said that Nanny didn't feel well last night and she went to bed early. She couldn't even read me a story," Taylor told him.

"Well, you're getting too old to be read stories. You need to read for yourself. Someday you're going to have to do that anyway. You may as well start now." That was the last time either of her parents spoke of the incident, and the last time they ever mentioned Nanny's name. The woman was cremated two days later, without a memorial service or recognition of any kind.

Taylor barely made it through school that day. When she got home, she crawled into bed and hid. It was Friday, and the beginning of a long holiday weekend. Taylor didn't move for the next four days although no one ever noticed since there wasn't anyone around to check on her. By the middle of the next week, Taylor had cried her eyes bloodshot and screamed out in anger and in pain, hurting more than she ever knew she could. And the pain never subsided. She eventually pushed it down far enough not to be noticed, burying it deep inside, along with all the memories of her beloved Nanny. After awhile, Taylor sank into a world of deep, chronic depression and would never be the same.

That's when her addiction began. She was just barely ten years old. It wasn't planned; it just happened. She was roaming around the house one night when she came upon the decorative cabinet next to her father's gun case, which was in a room that was completely off limits to her. Her parents had left strict orders about what she could do and where she could go, and this room was not on the list. But that didn't matter. Their rules meant nothing to her.

While exploring through the drawers and cupboards of the cabinet, she found a collection of bottles. There seemed to be two of every color, some in fancy bottles and other ones in just plain brown or clear. Taylor had no idea what was in the bottles, but she quickly found out! And it was the beginning of a very long and lonely relationship that the young girl chose to carry with her throughout the rest of her elementary school days and well into high school.

The days of sharing and caring were gone. Those special outings to have ice cream and play in the park were in the past. Church and God were out of the question, and companionship was never to be shared with anyone ever again. Her precious Nanny was gone forever. Taylor was alone. The young girl decided from the beginning of her new life without her friend, that she didn't need anyone. The pain was too deep and hurt too much. The contents of the bottles seemed to ease the pain, if only for a while.

Chapter Five

Years passed and Taylor slowly went downhill. Though she made it into high school and was taking honor classes, no one ever knew about her addiction or cared when her grades slowly began to decline. Her parents had hired another caregiver. Her name was Sheila. She was nice enough, and she cooked pretty well, too. But she wasn't Nanny, and Taylor refused to let her into her heart. No one was ever allowed to dwell in that part of her again. The hurt was too deep and the pain never went away. "Don't let her get too close," a voice inside constantly warned. And she never did.

Her spiritual walk that began before Nanny died was all but gone. Once in a while, Taylor thought she heard voices, telling her to go back to church and that everything would be all right again someday. She heard the voice inside tell her to have faith and pray. But whenever this voice was heard, Taylor was always in a very confused state, and she pushed it away as quickly as it surfaced. She didn't need prayer. She didn't need God. She didn't need anyone.

In the summer of her junior year, Taylor had made a few new acquaintances at camp. She refused to think of them as friends because she knew she'd never let them get close enough to her. But they wanted something she had, and they were quick to bond. Taylor went to camp every year after Nanny died because there wasn't anyone to attend to her at home. It also gave her parents time to enjoy their vacations alone, not that Taylor was ever with them; they just didn't want to have to worry about finding someone to stay at the house through the summer. Once Taylor turned sixteen, Sheila had been dismissed. Her absence never bothered the teen, or so she let them believe.

That summer before she left her house for camp, Taylor stashed several bottles of liquor in her large overnight case. No one suspected or inspected her belongings once she arrived at camp. One night she was sitting by the fire with several other girls her age. They were talking about parties and boys and all the fun they would have once they got back home.

"Camp is for babies," one of the girls said.

"It used to be fun. But now it's different. I like being with my friends and partying. And I miss the drinking a lot!" another girl commented.

Taylor looked up and grinned mischievously.

"Well, I have something in my cabin, if you promise not to squeal," she told the girl to her right. Her name was Elle, and she swore not to say a word.

"If it makes us feel good, what are we waiting for? Let's go!" she said quietly so the others wouldn't hear.

"I don't mind sharing with those girls if they're your friends. There's plenty of stuff to go around," Taylor said proudly.

"Okay. As long as you don't care that it will probably all be gone by tonight!" Elle told her.

"There is no way that we could drink it all by tonight. Besides, when we do run out, I have my ways of having it delivered."

"No way! Who would do that for you?" she asked inquisitively.

"I never reveal my sources, but let's just say a very good friend who drives, and I pay very handsomely for his services." Taylor winked.

"Let's party!" Elle whispered loudly to the two girls next to her. They didn't want to draw any attention from the camp leaders, who were having their own party down at the next campsite.

Elle McDonald, Ginny Rafford, and Marissa Bingham were tight as thieves. They had been close friends since the fourth grade and spent every summer together at camp. The girls had a wild streak, and the older they got the wilder it became. They were all from well-to-do families whose parents would rather have them gone, than to spend any quality time with them and interrupt their summer plans. It gave the girls plenty of time to get into mischief. What one didn't think of, the other two did. Taylor had no idea how much they all had in common, nor would she ever know. For to inquire about the girls' private lives meant that she cared, and she refused to care for anyone.

All four girls made a quick dash to Taylor's cabin. She roomed alone and liked it that way. For the next few hours, the girls indulged in an assortment of beverages, from rum to vodka and then on to whiskey. They were feeling no pain within the hour. By sunup they were hugging the toilets and sick as dogs. They told the camp leaders that they ate something that didn't agree with them. All four of them spent the day in bed. That night, they did it again, but not as much, just enough to have a really good time.

And so, the superficial yet better–than–nothing friendships began for Taylor. She knew keeping company with the teens would never come close to what she had with Nanny, but it was better than being alone. Elle and Marissa went to the same high school as Taylor. Ginny went to a private school, but was close enough to drive to Taylor's house whenever the four of them got together—something they did at least twice a month up until Christmas.

Chapter Six

Soon the weather began to change. It was getting colder and it rained more often. Thanksgiving had just passed and the merchants were decorating the streets in the spirit of Christmas. Taylor's thoughts went back to the holidays, when she was younger, happier, much more content, and with the only person that she ever loved. She couldn't stop thinking about Nanny. For the years since Nanny's death, Taylor tried hard to forget her dear friend. But no matter what she did, nothing worked this time of the year, not even the alcohol. She was more depressed than ever before, and indulged more often. But it never satisfied her.

One night after her friends had left, Taylor decided to drive downtown alone. She had just enough liquor to keep her sane, but not enough to forget. As she slowly cruised through the streets, she began to hear the faint sounds of music coming from somewhere close by. Suddenly, from deep down inside, she heard a voice calling out to her. It was loud enough and clear enough for her to understand. It simply said, "Come!"

Taylor decided to investigate. As she got closer and the music got louder, she couldn't help but smile. It was coming from the Lord of Life Church, the church where she and Nanny had gone just before Nanny had died.

Taylor pulled the car over and parked. She walked the few blocks to the entrance of the church and opened the doors. Just being there again made Taylor feel closer to Nanny. Memories flooded her senses and nearly took her breath away. It had been nearly seven years since she crossed the threshold of the church's doorstep.

It was crowded inside, but she managed to slip in the back without disrupting the service. Pastor Jacob was preaching. He hadn't change one bit, except for a little graying around his temples. He had just ended a prayer and was beginning a message on "Tough Faith for Tough Times." Taylor listened carefully, or at least as best as she could in her clouded condition.

"Someone once said, 'Tough times never last, but tough people do.'

Someone else said, 'When the going gets tough, the tough get going.' But, when times get tough, what you and I need is a 'tough faith' that will enable us to go through those tough times.

"It's easy to trust God when all is well, everything is going the way we want it to go, and there are no battles to fight. But it's different when things fall apart and things aren't going the way we want them to.

"If there were ever a time to get close to God, it's when times are tough. We don't need to run from God in those times. We need to run to God! Last weekend, we looked at the huge discrepancy between what the Bible calls faith and what many of us immediately think of when we hear the words 'faith' and 'belief.'

"Today, we'll go a step further in our journey through Hebrews 11, God's Hall of Faith, as we explore three things we simply cannot do without faith. Let's review first. Biblical faith is trusting God enough to do what He says. It begins with a belief that God exists. It's based on a belief that God rewards. And it works when we trust His judgment more than our own." Pastor Jacob reached for his Bible and turned to the book of Hebrews.

"This weekend I want us to turn our attention to three things that you simply cannot do without faith. We need to rest confidently in God's promises! Hebrews 11:3 says, 'By faith we understand that the entire universe was formed at God's command, that what we now see did not come from anything that can be seen.'

"Here is the issue at stake: If God is the Creator of the universe, this verse says that He created everything you see from nothing! If that is true, He is the originator of history and the consummation of history, which means that He is in complete control of everything in the middle, including my life! If I didn't believe that, with what is going on in the world today, I would be a basket case!

"Just out of curiosity, how many people here saw the movie *Braveheart?*" More than half the room raised their hands. "Great movie, wasn't it? If you remember at the end, William Wallace, played by Mel Gibson, faces execution for leading a revolt against England. He is told that if he renounces his actions and begs for mercy, then he will receive a quick death instead of a torturous, agonizing death. He says, 'Every man dies; not every man truly lives.'" The pastor noticed many nodding heads. It was one of the most powerful scenes in the movie, and they remembered it well.

"The promises of God, if believed in and valued, allow us to truly live as men and women zealous for God's eternal blessings. The promises of God are based upon one simple fact: God is able!

"If we really want to know the omnipotent God intimately and experientially, we ought to think through some of the things He is able to do. When we read that God is able to do something, it means He has the power to do it. So unlike us! Once we were able, and now we're not. You know what you used to be able to do—and then age set in.

"Who do you say that God is? Let me illustrate this: An atheist had an old tree in his backyard. During a storm the tree fell on his neighbor's house. The atheist called his insurance company to see if he was covered. His insurance agent was a good, church-going man, and he knew about the atheist's lack of belief. With this in mind, he gave the following response to the atheist. 'If your tree fell over because it was dead, we cannot cover this expense; you will have to pay the repairs on your neighbor's home yourself. However, if the tree fell because of 'an act of God,' your insurance will cover it. So, which one do you consider it to be?'" The audience broke out in laughter. Taylor found it humorous as well and laughed right along with them. It felt good to laugh. She hadn't done that in a long time.

"Look at a few of the specific things the Bible says God is able to do. First, He is able to save us completely! 'Hence, also, He is able to save forever those who draw near to God through Him, since He always lives to make intercession for them.' That's in Hebrews 7:25.

"Secondly, He is able to keep us from sin! 'Now to Him who is able to keep you from stumbling, and to make you stand in the presence of His glory blameless with great joy.' That's out of Jude 24.

"Thirdly, He is able to supply our needs as it says in 2 Corinthians 9:8: 'And God is able to make all grace abound to you, that always having all sufficiency in everything, you may have an abundance for every good deed.'

"Fourthly, He is able to heal our diseases and deliver us from death! There are other references in Scripture to what God is able to do, but none more exciting than the one in Ephesians 3:20: 'Now to Him who is able to do exceeding abundantly beyond all that we ask or think, according to the power that works within us.'

"In the early days of our country, a weary traveler came to the banks of the Mississippi River for the first time. There was no bridge. It was early winter, and the surface of the mighty stream was covered with ice. Could he dare cross over? Would the uncertain ice be able to bear his weight?

"Night was falling, and he desperately needed to reach the other side. Finally, after much hesitation and with many fears, he began to creep cautiously across the surface of the ice on his hands and knees. He tried to distribute his weight as much as possible to keep the ice from breaking beneath him.

"About halfway across, he heard the sound of singing behind him. Out of the dusk came a man, driving a horse-drawn load of coal across the ice and singing merrily as he went on his way.

"Here he was—on his hands and knees, trembling lest the ice not be strong enough to bear him up! And there, as if whisked away by the winter's wind, went the man, his horses, his sleigh, and his load of coal, upheld by the same ice on which he was creeping!

"Some of us have learned only to creep upon the promises of God. Cautiously, timidly, trembling, we venture out upon His promises, as though the lightness of our step might make His promises more secure. Be bold in what God has promised!

"There is something else that I cannot do without faith: Be in a relationship with God! Turn to Hebrews 11:4. 'It was by faith that Abel brought a more acceptable offering to God than Cain did. God accepted Abel's offering to show that He was a righteous man. And though Abel is long dead, he still speaks to us because of his faith.'

"Abel's faith led to three progressive things: true worship, true worth, and true witness! 'It was by faith that Enoch was taken up to heaven without dying—suddenly he disappeared because God took him. But before he was taken up, he was approved as pleasing to God.' That is from Hebrews 11:5.

"Genesis 5 tells us that Enoch walked with God all of his life. That walk with God, which Enoch experienced, was one of deepening intimacy. A walk implies a journey in a certain direction, at a measured and regular pace.

"Enoch's faith flourished as he walked, and God bore witness to him that his daily life was pleasing in His eyes. Enoch is an example of what we should long to see happen to us: a steady, daily growth in grace achieved by the inner resources which God supplies to those who take Him at His Word and act in faith on what He has said.

"Enoch enjoyed the continuous presence of an unseen Person and related his life daily to that Person. The result was a fellowship which death could not interrupt. He was translated to glory!

"Max Lucado, one of my favorite pastors and authors, says, 'There are many reasons God saves you: to bring glory to Himself, to appease His justice, to demonstrate His sovereignty. But one of the sweetest reasons God saved you is because He is fond of you. He likes having you around. He thinks you are the best thing to come down the pike in quite a while—if God had a refrigerator, your picture would be on it. If He had a wallet, your photo would be in it! He sends you flowers every spring and a sunrise every morning. Whenever you want to talk, He'll listen. He can live anywhere in the universe, yet He chose your heart. And the Christmas gift He sent you in Bethlehem? Face it, friend, He's crazy about you!' What great words to ponder.

"But that can only be realized by faith! List some problems in your life that seem to be impossible to solve. Now, fully yield your will to Him, commit the problems to Him in prayer regularly, and then believe with all of your heart that He will solve them in His own perfect way! Let's pray.

"Father God, You are such an incredible Father to us. You are always there when we call and always bring comfort when we are hurting or confused. Lord, I ask You now to reach out to the hearts of those who seem to be struggling more than normal. Help them to hear Your voice through their pain, Lord, and give them the faith they need to see it through. Let them know they can't get through it without You. Show them where You are, Father. Comfort them and keep them safe. In Jesus' name, we pray. Amen. Thank you all for being here. Have a wonderful and safe Christmas. See you next week."

Taylor left the church and walked the streets for over two hours. Nothing the pastor said had fazed her in the slightest. She hurt inside, but her pain went too deep to reach. She was sure not even God could help. As she strolled along, a thought came to her mind. She was so tired of struggling, so tired of hurting, and so tired of being alone in a place full of too many painful memories. She just couldn't bear it any longer. She missed Nanny and she wanted to be with her more than anything else in the world.

Suddenly, Taylor remembered a conversation that she had with Nanny one day after church when she was just a little girl. Nanny told her that they could be in heaven together someday, and in Taylor's still somewhat foggy frame of mind, she believed all she needed to do was die and they would be together again, forever. She wondered why hadn't she thought of that before. She had wasted so much time trying to cope without her precious Nanny here with her, and all this time they could have been together.

Taylor's mood changed immediately. She felt instantly renewed. She had joy in her heart and wanted to shout to the world. She was actually happy for the first time in very long time.

"Nanny! I am coming to see you! I love you, and I have missed you so much! I'll be there soon," she cried out to the stars that seemed to shine brighter than ever. Then she ran to her car and drove home. Her parents were still in Hawaii and would be through New Year's Day. Taylor was certain that neither of them would ever miss her.

Chapter Seven

She waited until the Sunday morning after Christmas. Sitting on a stump in the middle of the grassy knoll, Taylor realized for the first time in a very long time that she was finally at peace. She had begged for the confusion and pain to end, and it was finally going to happen. Looking up into the cloudless sky, she placed the gun in her mouth feeling the bitter taste of cold medal against her teeth. Her finger slowly reached for the trigger. With only the slightest hesitation, she pulled. Suddenly, the ear–piercing blast echoed throughout the canyon.

Within what seemed like seconds, the spirit of the young life torpedoed through the light, never slowing, never stopping. In an instant, the distress she felt prior became more intense, more vicious, and much more ferocious, as she cried out into the darkness. The pain went beyond excruciating, tormenting her more than she had ever known. The deafening screams grew closer and louder. Taylor soon realized that the outcries of agony she heard were not just hers and that they would never go away.

After Nanny's death, Taylor never found the tough faith she needed to keep her strong enough to go on, but God still held her accountable, according to His will. God had a plan and purpose for Taylor when He brought her into the world, as He does for everyone. But instead of turning to God when she lost the only person who mattered, Taylor turned to alcohol, and it destroyed her. God tried a few times to reveal Himself to her, but she refused to accept Him. It was her choice.

Nanny had also tried to open the door to God for her when she was a child, but when Nanny died, Taylor turned away. She chose to never go back, until that last night when God made way to give her one last chance and guided her to church. But Taylor's state of mind was too fogged, and she neither understood the concept of the message nor heard it clearly. Unable to withstand the pain any longer, she decided instead to end her life. She missed Nanny and wanted to be with her in heaven, but she never made it there. Once again her choice cost her dearly.

In the end, Taylor never grasped the concept of eternity. Even though as a child Nanny had tried to explain that heaven and hell were very real and that to get to heaven Taylor needed Jesus. In the end, she was still not sure how it all worked, but then she never tried to find out. Again, it was her choice. Taylor didn't fully understand that with death, another life began. As God promised, it would be an existence that would last forever.

Too late, the young girl realized the terrible and very permanent mistake she had made, by never experiencing saving grace while she was alive. She never imagined that the pain she suffered on earth would be nothing compared to the agonizing torment and sorrows that were waiting for her in the fiery walls of damnation where she was doomed to exist.

In a darkened evil world, full of broken dreams and endless terrifying nightmares, the screams of hopelessness were louder than she ever thought possible, and were the ones that Taylor Morgan would endure for the rest of her eternal days.

Mary Burgoff

Mary Burgoff crawled into an over–stuffed chair and poured herself a small glass of wine. She glanced at the clock on the wall and sighed. "Is it really only four o'clock?" she asked herself. Daylight had always been the worst for her, but lately it didn't matter what time it was. Her pain seemed to grow with each sunrise.

The young mother tried hard to pull herself out of the daily depression that she had sunk into since the loss of her two young daughters, four–year–old Skylar and little Amy, had been just barely two. It hardly seemed as though any time had passed since that morning when Mary got the phone call from her estranged husband telling her there had been a horrible accident. But six very long and pain–filled months had slowly crept by, and there was still no comfort in sight.

"Tell me, Lord, if You're such a good God and You love me so much, how could You do this to me? Is this how You show Your love? By taking away my little girls? They didn't need to die!" she screamed out. "And why both of them? Couldn't You have left me one? What am I supposed to feel now, God, if it even matters to You? I'm not a wife anymore. And, thanks to another one of Your brilliant decisions, I'm no longer a mother! My babies will never call me Mommy again! What am I, God? Can You hear me? What am I now?"

Mary spent the next several weeks struggling with her anger and grief. Some days she never made it out of bed. She desperately tried to move on, but found it much too hard, much more than her heart was willing to allow. Mary knew she would never be able to forget her little girls. She could still smell them as if they were in the room with her. She remembered their touch, the warmth of their breath when they slept by her side, their innocent smiles and infectious laughter, and the joy they gave her in such a short period of time.

All during her time of need, Mary never realized how much God really loved her. That day when Skylar and Amy were killed, He saw her tears and felt her pain, and He never once left her side. But she didn't know that until much later, until that Sunday morning after Christmas when she took her last breath on earth. With open arms and a very humble heart, Mary adoringly and willingly welcomed the awesome, forgiving, and very loving presence of God as she stepped over the threshold into eternity.

Chapter One

"It's almost over, honey," Justin told his wife lovingly, as he wiped the sweat from her beaded brow. "Just one more big push."

With one last breath, Mary pushed with all her might. Suddenly, there was great relief. The excruciating pain that had ripped throughout her entire body for the past several hours had finally stopped. Her legs were shaking uncontrollably, and tears spilled from her eyes. A few minutes later, her infant daughter was placed on her chest.

"So it was you who was causing all that commotion inside. You aren't so tough now, are you, little one? How could someone so tiny cause so much pain?" Mary asked the newest member of her family as the child's eyes tried hard to focus on her new surroundings. "Justin, look at her. Isn't she the most beautiful little girl in the world?"

"Well, she's certainly tied for it!" he told her. "If I remember correctly, you said the same thing when Skylar was born!"

"You're right. I did say that. Speaking of which, where is Skylar? I want her to meet her new baby sister, Amy."

"Amy, huh? I like it. Skylar is in the waiting room with our parents. You wait here," he joked, knowing full well she couldn't get up, "I'll go get her."

Mary watched her tall, ruggedly handsome husband walk out of the room. It was all she could do not to go after him. She had been crazy in love with Justin Burgoff since she was just the gawky kid next door. Back then he was always friendly, but because of the age difference, he didn't have too much to say except to offer a "How are you?" now and then. After all, she was five years younger and at that awkward stage that little girls go through when they're only twelve…too tall, too thin, and with a mouthful of braces.

Her thoughts suddenly went back to those memorable days, not so long ago, when Justin Burgoff was king of the neighborhood and prince of her heart.

Chapter Two

"Say, Mary," her young neighbor yelled from across the yard. "How's it going today?"

"Oh, it's okay. How about for you, Justin?" she yelled back, extremely self–conscious of her attire. Her hair was uncombed, her jeans were full of paint, and her T–shirt was torn in more places than not.

"I'm doing pretty good. How's your summer going so far?"

"It's going by too fast. My friends and I are going to the movie today, but we haven't decided what we want to see. Have you heard about any good ones lately?" Mary tried to keep the conversation going, but she knew he didn't really care. He was just being nice.

"I heard that new scary movie at the Grand is really good. You guys should check it out. Then you can let me know. Well, kiddo, I gotta run. I'll see you around," he said as he climbed into the cab of his brand–new, lifted truck.

"Yeah, maybe we'll check it out. Thanks, Justin. See you later." It was all Mary Griffin could do to stay focused. He was so good looking she could hardly retain her composure. He always made her feel so special when he took the time to talk to her. She was sure it was just a simple act of kindness, and maybe even a little pity on his part, but to Mary it was pure heaven.

Justin had just graduated from high school and was getting ready to leave for college. But Mary always made sure she was around when he came home for holidays and summer breaks. She'd sit for hours at her bedroom window waiting for him to drive up. When he finally did, she just sat there and stared, unable to move. The few times he noticed her watching, she nearly fainted from embarrassment. He always waved and smiled at her like it really mattered. And because she was caught in the act, she had no recourse but to wave back.

For the next five years, Justin came home each summer and on holidays to visit his family and friends. But he rarely noticed the little girl who sat in awe of him from the private world of her second story window. But all that changed one day when he returned home from college during her senior year of high school.

Justin pulled up in the driveway of his parents' home early one summer afternoon. The first thing that caught his eye was the incredibly striking creature standing on the front porch next door. She nearly took his breath away. Her white shorts and halter top showed off her long legs and tanned midriff, and the sunlight caught the highlights in each strand of her long dark hair as it blew softly in the breeze. Justin walked over to introduce himself. When she turned around, he nearly fell off the porch.

"Justin!" Mary squealed with delight. "When did you get home?"

"Mary, is that really you?" he asked, taking a closer look just to make sure.

"Of course it's me, silly. How have you been?" Mary immediately noticed the difference in Justin's attitude. She was thrilled to be finally getting the attention she had craved from him for years. He seemed to be looking at her for the first time, and she wanted the moment to last forever.

"I—I'm okay. I guess I don't need to ask how you are, do I?" It was the only time in his life that Justin was at a loss for words.

"When did you get home?" she asked ever so sweetly.

"Just now. I can't believe how much you've changed, Mary. It's like a moth to a butterfly—no offense." He didn't mean to dwell on the subject, but he was so surprised.

"None taken. And thank you."

"I need to go change and say hi to my mom. But if you're not doing anything later, can we go for a ride or something?" Justin knew it would be fine with Mary's parents. After all, they had been neighbors for years and their families were close friends.

"I'd like that a lot, Justin. I'll go change, too, and meet you in an hour if that's okay?"

To Justin Burgoff, it was very okay. And for Mary, it was a dream come true. The twosome spent the rest of the summer hanging out together, either with his friends or just by themselves. They enjoyed boating, skiing, wake boarding, and four–wheeling, as well as several private picnics spent down by the river. Mary was on cloud nine.

When the summer ended, Justin left for his last year of law school. He managed to get through his schooling early by taking summer school classes and several correspondence courses as well. It was hard for both of them to say good–bye, but they managed to keep in touch nearly every day with cards, letters, and long–distance phone calls.

Mary finished high school and waited for Justin's return. She busied herself with night classes at the college, trying to take as many courses in interior decorating as possible. It would mean less for her to take when she enrolled at the university the following fall semester.

The year slowly dragged on for both of them, but they remained positive about their future. They knew the separation wouldn't last forever, and they managed to enjoy their final Christmas and spring breaks together, knowing that the time spent alone in between was the last they would ever have to spend apart.

Two years later, Mary and Justin were married in an elaborate church wedding celebration with more than 350 guests in attendance. She was the most beautiful bride that anyone had ever seen. Three months later, Mary rushed home with the most exciting news. She could barely keep it to herself.

She made a special dinner for her and Justin. Then Mary took a little extra time to apply her makeup and redo her hair. She wanted to look her best when she made her announcement. She bought a brand new dress for the occasion and put it on just before Justin walked in. When he saw her standing in front of the doorway looking a bit smug, yet ever so appealing, his heart jumped in his chest.

"What's going on here, Mrs. Burgoff?" he asked curiously, noticing the elegant table setting.

"I just thought I would fix my husband his favorite meal because he works so hard. And even though you are so handsome, I think you'd better leave before he gets home," she teased.

Justin's smile broadened as he walked toward her and took her in his arms. They stood there for several minutes before Mary broke away. Walking over to the table, she reached for their wineglasses.

"I have an announcement to make," she said holding her empty glass, then lightly touching it to his. "To our future, my incredibly wonderful husband, and also to the father of my baby!"

"Wh—what…? We're having a—a baby? Are you sure?" Justin stuttered. "I can't believe it. When did you find out?"

"Just today," she told him. "I thought I had a touch of the flu because I was feeling nauseous all the time. But I found out it wasn't the flu at all. It's a baby, Justin. Our baby."

"How are you feeling? Maybe you should sit down, honey. I'll get you some water," he said concerned for her well being.

"Don't be silly. I'm fine. I'm not sick, and I'm certainly not an invalid. I'm just having a baby. Wow, I don't think I will ever get used to hearing that—we're having a baby," she repeated.

Skylar Anne Burgoff was born seven months later and right on time, weighing in at a whopping eight pounds, fourteen ounces. Mother and baby were sent home the next day…and so their life began.

It was a never–ending fairytale. Justin was her prince, and she turned out to be all he ever wanted in a wife. The surprise, but very welcome addition of their first–born child, was the perfect end to one segment of their lives, and the beginning of a promising future, full of immeasurable hope and very reachable dreams.

Chapter Three

As she remembered every detail of their life together, Mary's thoughts were interrupted by the cry of an infant. It immediately brought her back to the present. Amy was hungry and she let her mother know it. Unlike her sister, Amy weighed a little less than seven pounds, but it didn't stop her from eating. With the first taste of her mother's milk, the child ate nonstop and surpassed her older sister's birth weight within the first five weeks.

Mary and Amy were released from the hospital the following morning. Her life was finally complete. She had married the man of her childhood dreams. She had two precious little girls and lived in a beautiful house on the outskirts of the city. "Does it get any better than this?" she wondered.

The girls were happy children and very easy to care for. Mary spent hours playing with them either in the nearby park or in their spacious backyard. Skylar was a beautiful little girl, very petite, with bright blue eyes and strawberry blonde hair. She was the complete opposite of Mary and Justin. But somewhere down the genetic line, light complexions and towheads ran in the family. Amy favored her parents with olive skin and big brown eyes, but her hair was lighter, though not as light as Skylar's.

Skylar loved to play peek–a–boo with her little sister, which made Amy squeal with delight whenever Skylar jumped out from behind her. Being a parent was very fulfilling, extremely rewarding, and much too easy. Mary wondered what she did so right to have it so good all the time.

The young mother's indescribable bliss lasted for several years. Every day she had to pinch herself to make sure she wasn't still dreaming, like she so often did as a teenager. It wasn't until the winter of their fourth year as husband and wife that Mary discovered something was very wrong. Skylar was three and Amy had just turned one.

Justin had been spending far too much time at the office, though in the beginning she really didn't mind. His new but flourishing career as a lawyer was starting to grow, and Mary knew this was part of being his wife: staying home and taking care of the children. She tried to understand his constant absences, and made the necessary excuses when she showed up at family gatherings alone, with only the little ones in tow. But even after his business had settled down into some sort of routine, Justin was still gone more often than not. Whenever she asked him about it, his answer was always the same.

"Mary, you knew it would be like this. I have to build this practice now while it's ripe for the picking. The competition around here is brutal, and I need to get the word out and make us known. Then later, I'll cut back and spend more time with you and the girls," he explained for the third time that night.

"It's been three years, Justin. You have plenty of clients now. And you're never here! The girls and I miss you. Don't you want to see them grow up? Skylar asks about you all the time, and poor little Amy doesn't even know who you are! She took her first step today. Do you even care?"

"Of course I care. I just know I need to do this right now. Then in another few months, or maybe a year tops, I can cut back. I am bringing in another partner next month and trying to get some financial backing, too, which will take some of the load off. Please, try to be patient a little longer, for me… for us!" he begged, sounding extremely sincere. He leaned over and kissed her gently on the cheek.

"You're just missing out on so much, and you can't get these years back, Justin. I don't want you to regret any of this. Please don't wait too long." Mary turned and walked back to the kitchen to finish fixing dinner. It was only a matter of minutes before she heard the front door close. Justin went back to the office, and once again Mary sat alone at the table with only her babies to keep her company.

Chapter Four

Several weeks later, Justin was once again working late, and Mary decided to surprise him with a picnic basket full of treats. It would be like old times when they were young and carefree, spending all their time in his truck or on the rocky shores of the riverbank.

Mary had fried chicken earlier that afternoon and had also whipped up a batch of potato salad and homemade biscuits. To top off their meal, she grabbed a good bottle of wine from the cellar. After checking herself in the mirror, Mary turned her attention to the babysitter.

"Here's the office number where I'll be, Tanya. If there's no answer, you can call my cell phone. The number is right here next to the other numbers on the list. I just checked on the girls, and they are already asleep. They didn't have a long nap today so they should sleep all night. If Amy wakes up before I get back, just give her a bottle. There's one in the refrigerator. She should go right back to sleep. Skylar will sleep through an earthquake, so I don't think you have to worry about her. Call me if you need me. We shouldn't be too late."

Mary couldn't believe how nervous she was. She felt like a schoolgirl sneaking out of her own house. It was just after nine. The streets were dark and deserted. As she got closer to Justin's office, Mary checked her makeup in the rearview mirror one more time. She wanted to look irresistible.

There was a parking space right in the front. She quietly and carefully pulled in and turned off the lights, not wanting to bring any unnecessary attention, in case Justin heard any disturbances outside. Mary grabbed the basket and slid across the seat to the other side. When she got out, she adjusted her short skirt and loosened the top button of her lacy blouse. Not only did she want to look irresistible, she wanted to knock her husband's socks off. With the three-inch heels she was wearing, it would be hard not to notice her. When she passed the large window of Justin's building, she saw her reflection and smiled. "This ought to do the trick," she said, pleased with the results.

The main door was still unlocked, which indicated that there were other people in the building. Mary started to have second thoughts that maybe this wasn't such a good idea after all, but they didn't last. "What could be the harm?" she thought. She was only bringing her husband the dinner he missed that evening, along with every other dinner for the past two months! "Don't get angry," she whispered. "This is not the time. Think good thoughts!" she said out loud, as she pushed past the wooden door that led to Justin's private office.

His door was closed. Mary stood there for a moment trying to catch her breath when she thought she heard voices inside. She started to move closer but hesitated. Then she heard the distinct sound of a woman's voice and stopped in her tracks.

"Please, Justin just let me stay here with you this one time. I promise, no one will ever know. It will be our little secret," the woman begged.

"No, Brenda, I can't. You have to go home tonight. If you don't show up there pretty soon, he'll wonder where you are. If he looks here and finds you, we could both lose our jobs—yours as his wife and mine as a financial partner. I can't afford that. I've worked too hard."

"Come on, please? It won't matter if I go home or not. Paul never even looks to see if I am in my room. All he cares about are his precious money and cars. He doesn't care about me at all anymore."

But before Justin could respond, Mary had heard enough. She charged her way through the door, coming face to face with both of them. The two very surprised people jumped when they heard the commotion, but the damage was already done. What Mary saw when she burst through the door left her feeling nauseous. She couldn't believe her eyes. Standing with Justin at his desk was a young, attractive brunette, holding steadfast to his body. In fact, they were so closely entwined that not even a sliver of light stood between them.

Mary dropped the basket of food and darted quickly out the door. Justin pushed Brenda aside and ran down the hall after her.

"Wait, Mary. Please. It isn't what you think!" he pleaded as he ran faster. Even with Mary in her high heels, he couldn't catch up. She was out the door and in her car before Justin got outside. Mary sped quickly away, not once looking back. She could barely see the street signs through her tears.

"Oh, dear God, what an idiot I am," she cried, "to think he loved me enough. I should have known better than to think I could be the one he wanted. I am such a fool!" Mary had to pull over. She needed to think fast and to try hard to cry it all out before she went home.

Justin walked quickly back into his office. Brenda was still there waiting for him.

"Gee, Justin. I'm really sorry. I had no idea your wife would come down here and spy on you. What's the matter? Doesn't the little lady trust you being here at night?" She moved closer and tried to put her arms around him again. But this time he pushed her away. He was furious, and he let her know.

"Look, Brenda, I know your husband neglects you, and I feel sorry for you, I really do. I've tried to be nice to you, but you take it all out of context. I don't want you! I'm sorry I have to be so blunt, but you just don't get it. I can't give you what you want. I'm married. And I'm happy. I've been working late for months to get this business off the ground. I had high hopes that your husband would want to finance me, but not at the expense of my marriage. I don't want you, Brenda. I love my wife! Now I have to go home and try to convince her that what she saw was not real. I pray to God that she'll believe me. Now go home! Leave me alone. For the last time, please just leave me alone!" Justin cleared the papers from his desk and threw them in his briefcase. Then he pushed Brenda out the door and locked his office.

"But Justin, I love you. Please let me show you," the buxom brunette begged and whined pathetically.

"For heaven's sake, get out of here! Go home where you belong!" he told her. And with that, he was gone.

All the way home, Justin prayed for a miracle. He never really prayed before, but he thought he needed all the ammunition he could get. He knew it would take some explaining, but he was confident that Mary would listen and forgive his stupidity and neglectful ways. He had never cheated on her in the whole time they had been together, ever since that summer day when he saw her on the porch. He knew from that day on that she was exactly what he wanted. “What a complete moron I am!” he said to himself. “How could I put my work so far ahead of what is really important?” Justin drove faster. He needed to tell his wife how much he loved her and how sorry he was. “Please don’t let it be too late!” he begged out loud to whomever it was that was supposed to be listening.

When Justin pulled into the driveway, Mary’s car was nowhere around. His heart sank. He ran quickly up the walkway taking three steps at a time. He reached for his key and was just getting ready to unlock the front door when it opened. Tanya stood there with Amy in her arms.

“I’m so glad you’re here. I’ve been trying to call Mrs. Burgoff for the past hour. She didn’t answer her cell phone, and I was getting worried. Where is she?” the young girl asked, looking behind him.

“She said she had to stop by the store, so she sent me home to relieve you,” Justin lied. It was none of the young girl’s business anyway, so he didn’t feel too guilty. “She should be here shortly. How much do I owe you?” he asked, digging into his pocket for his wallet.

“Oh, it’s only been two hours, so $12 should cover it. Amy woke up a little while ago. I think she had a nightmare.”

“I’ll take care of her,” he said and took the child from her. “Here you go, Tanya, and thank you,” he said handing her the money.

Before Justin closed the front door, he looked down the street for any sign of his wife’s car, hoping that she wasn’t far behind. But the street was dark, and there were no headlights anywhere.

He held his daughter tightly as he walked into the unfamiliar room where Mary had redecorated just three weeks before. It was beautiful, but he never noticed. All her intricate details and special-order materials blended well into the large, rustic room. She did it for him, and he never even thanked her.

Justin sat in the over–stuffed chair by the fireplace and held Amy close. She rested comfortably on his chest. He waited there all night for Mary to return, but she never did. By morning he was frantic. He had no idea where she would go. He didn't want to alarm either of their parents, so he didn't call. Besides, he knew if she showed up at either place, they would call him immediately.

Justin needed to get ready for work, but was afraid to wake his daughter. After another half an hour, he took a chance and slowly slid out of the chair. Amy slept through the transition. Justin put her in her crib and checked on Skylar. She was uncovered and at the bottom of her bed, but she was sound asleep. He adjusted her back to the top and covered her. Then he quickly jumped in the shower.

The phone was ringing when he got out. Oh please let it be Mary, he said to himself.

"Hello!"

"What time are you leaving?" his wife asked coldly.

"Mary, oh thank God. I've been worried sick. Where are you? Are you all right?" Justin asked with a sigh of relief.

"I asked you a question, Justin. I will be coming home to be with the girls, but not until you're gone. So please tell me when you're leaving," she asked again, with no emotion in her voice.

"Please, Mary. Let me explain last night. It isn't what you think. Brenda is married to Paul, the man that is giving us the money to secure our business. She's been hitting on me for months. But nothing happened, not last night or ever. I swear. Please, you have to believe me!" he begged.

"You're forgetting that I saw you, Justin. And what I saw didn't look like 'nothing' to me. I don't want to discuss this over the phone. In fact, I don't want to discuss this at all right now. You'll be hearing from my attorney in the next few days. Now please, tell me when you're planning to leave so I can come home to be with the girls. Then you'll have to figure out another place to stay. I won't share our home with you anymore. Please pack your stuff and leave us alone! I'm sure the kids won't miss you. I don't think they'll know they're supposed to. You haven't been around anyway. So what's to miss? I'm sure they will be fine." Mary was trying hard to be tough and uncaring, but deep down inside she was falling apart.

"Mary, for the love of God. Please don't do this! I love you. I need you and the girls. I know I've been at the office too late for too long, and I promise to stop. You've been so patient with me and I don't deserve you, but I'm begging you not to throw this marriage away. I need you!" Justin could not imagine what his life would be like without her.

"It's too late, Justin. I've put up with a lot. Then when I saw you and that woman last night, I can't even tell you how it made me feel. In fact, I feel numb. I have nothing in my heart for you, like you were never there. So, please make this easier on both of us and just get out and leave us alone. After we get adjusted, you can see the girls, and they can come over and visit as often as you want. I'll be there in less than half an hour. Please be in your truck and ready to leave," she said and hung up the phone.

Mary had spent the entire night in her car. She cried until there wasn't a tear left to shed or an emotion left to feel. She looked in the mirror at what used to be a very happy woman. What a change from the reflection she saw last night. Her eyes were red and nearly swollen shut. Her makeup had run everywhere, leaving dark streaks down her cheeks, and her once neatly–kept hair fell straight around her face. The clothes she had on, the same ones she took such pride in the night before, were wrinkled beyond recognition.

"How can life be so cruel?" she asked herself out loud. "God, if you're there, please help me to hear You. I need some peace and some answers, and I need to know what I am supposed to do now." But silence filled the car. Mary nearly gave up hope of ever feeling love and happiness again. All she had left were Skylar and Amy. Mary knew she needed to stay strong for them.

She pulled up in front of her house just as Justin was getting into his truck. He tried to wave, but she turned away. Mary went inside and closed the door behind her. After checking on the girls, who were still sound asleep, she headed for the bedroom. The first thing she noticed was that the bed was still made from the day before. For a brief moment Mary wondered why Justin hadn't slept there, but was too tired to care. She threw the covers back on her side and crawled in. Within minutes, Mary was sound asleep.

Chapter Five

Justin reached for the key to his office. When he opened the door, he was surprised to see Paul Mason waiting for him inside.

"How did you get in here?" the young attorney asked curiously.

"The doorman let me in. He heard what went on last night with Brenda and knew we needed to talk," the older man responded.

"Paul, I am so sorry. I don't even know what happened or why. I just know that my wife saw something that wasn't real and now she has kicked me out of our home and wants a divorce."

"I'm the one who's sorry, Justin. I don't blame you at all. This has nothing to do with anything that you've done. Brenda has been hitting on all my clients for the last several years, and I just ignored her, thinking it was harmless and would go away. But she has gone too far this time. I told her this morning that I've had enough and that she has to leave. I just can't jeopardize my position any longer by allowing her to go around making a complete fool of herself. And me, too, for that matter! I am really sorry about your wife. I'll talk to her if you want," Paul told him sincerely.

"She won't listen to anyone, I'm afraid. I think this is the end of us. For the last year I've been putting in a lot of hours after work to get this company off the ground and to make it look good on paper so you would want to invest. But with what happened last night, I don't know if you still want to, and at this point I am not sure if I even care any more. I can't lose her, Paul. She is my whole world." Justin tried hard to hold back his tears.

"This doesn't change anything between us, Justin. I promised to invest and I will. In fact, I want to draw up the final papers today. This has gone on too long, and I apologize once again. I have this nasty habit of making the client sweat a bit before I actually commit. But it isn't right. I know that now. I've known for several months that I was going to be a financial partner in your firm. Had I just done that even last week, none of this would be happening now. I owe you a lot more than an apology. I hope you can forgive me, Justin." This pleasant, caring demeanor was not what Justin had known Paul to be in the beginning. For the past year, Paul came across as an arrogant snob and a bit of a bully, someone who demanded respect if only for the size of his bank account. With his enormous yet classic physique, this persona suited him perfectly.

"I can't tell you what this means to me, Paul. I know this should be the happiest moment of my career, but it's hard to feel joy when I know I have to celebrate alone. I can say that I am very relieved to have it over. Let's go upstairs and get this finalized so we can move on." The two men shook hands and walked to the elevator.

Within minutes, the long–awaited deal was complete and the stress was gone. All Justin had to do then was go find another place to live. He spent the next few hours looking for a small house to rent.

Mary slept until almost ten that morning, when her slumber was interrupted by the familiar sounds of her daughters playing in their room next to hers. Tiptoeing her way down the hall, Mary quietly opened the door and peeked inside. A smile tugged at her lips.

Skylar was sitting in the crib with Amy, pretending to read her favorite story. She couldn't really read the words, but Mary had read her the book so often that Skylar was able to tell the story from the pictures on the pages. Amy sat and listened as if she understood every word her sister said. Mary's heart swelled with love and pride as she watched her precious daughters. And for a brief few moments, she was even able to forget the aching and emptiness inside of her.

While the girls sat at the table and ate their breakfast, Mary called her dad. She tried to explain what happened the night before, though she was still confused herself as to how it all came about.

"But Mary, this just doesn't sound like something Justin would do. Are you sure he was cheating with that woman? Or was he just being too nice to make her leave?" her father asked. His wisdom never ceased to amaze her, but she didn't want to hear it.

"He knew exactly what he was doing. I heard them talking, Daddy. She even asked if she could stay with him 'one more time.' That means it happened before. How plain can it be?"

"I think you're making a huge mistake, honey. I'm sure there is a perfectly good reason why that woman said that. Maybe she was lying, did you ever think of that? Or maybe you heard wrong. There was a solid wood door between you, remember? Why not just let things cool off a bit and then talk to him. He's a great man and a wonderful father, even though he hasn't been around a lot in the last few months. He wouldn't throw all that away for one cheap thrill! He has way too much to lose. I suggest that you take this a step at a time, even if it means you don't live together for awhile." Dennis Griffin knew how stubborn his daughter could be once her mind was made up, and he felt that the time spent apart might be a good thing for both of them.

"Maybe you're right, at least about us not living together. But I don't think my heart will change. I am just too hurt. I will never forgive him for what I saw, even if he was totally innocent. He knew better than to have that woman in his office, especially at night when they were alone. What was he thinking?" Mary asked, more confused than ever.

"He wasn't, Mary. He wasn't thinking at all or he wouldn't have done it. But you need to talk to him. It isn't right to just have an attorney show up at his office. You can talk to one and even arrange for a legal separation if you feel it's necessary, but don't do anything stupid or permanent right now. You're not in the right frame of mind to make that big of a decision based on your hostile emotions. Give it a few months. In fact, take all the time you need. I'm sure Justin will be there when you're ready to work things out."

"I don't know how you can be so sure that things can be worked out, but I will let Justin know what is going on and that he will have to get his own place for the time being," she replied firmly.

As it turned out, Justin found a cute little house a few blocks from Mary and the girls. It was a three–bedroom, brick house with a white picket fence around the front yard and was fully fenced in the back. It came totally furnished. All Justin had to do was move in his clothes and a few other personal belongings, which Mary left on the front porch for him to pick up after work the next day. His only purchase was a television and a DVD player for the living room so the girls could watch their Disney movies when they came over.

This arrangement worked out nicely for both of them for a while. They managed to talk a little, just enough to put together a visitation schedule for the girls. But Mary was far from ready to forgive, and she knew she could never forget, no matter how much Justin begged. She harbored anger that she had never felt toward anyone before, and it was eating her alive.

Chapter Six

Within a short period of time, Justin's law firm was booming. He had already surpassed all his expectations for what he needed to make it run successfully, and it was still growing. There were nine associates on staff and five more ready to come on board. Paul Mason was thrilled that his investment was finally making money. He and Brenda had ended their marriage shortly after the incident that left Justin somewhat of a bachelor again. Brenda took what money Paul had given her and moved back home to Iowa.

Mary continued to feel lost and confused. She didn't quite know which way to turn, so she started praying, like she used to do when she was younger. As her prayers increased, so did her need for answers, and the logical place for answers had always been church.

Before the weekend began, she drove by the church near Justin's office to see what time the services started. As she read the sign out front, she noticed the title of the message that week was "Reaching for Heaven." Heaven had always intrigued Mary. She wanted to learn more and decided that this was a good time to start. It was Justin's weekend to keep the girls, so Mary went alone.

She sat near the back and listened carefully. Pastor Mike Greene talked with a great deal of knowledge as he spoke passionately on the subject of the existence of heaven. Every eye in the room was on him as he preached to the more than eight hundred people in attendance, but Mary didn't notice anyone else. Her eyes and ears were focused only on him. It was as if he knew her heart.

"There are many misconceptions about heaven. Many of them we have from childhood. Maturing believers are greatly motivated by the hope of heaven. What can you know for certain about heaven? It is called 'gain.' Look in your Bible at Philippians 1:21–23. 'For to me, to live is Christ and to die is gain. If I am to go on living in the body, this will mean fruitful labor for me. Yet what shall I chose? I do not know! I am torn between the two: I desire to depart and be with Christ, which is better by far…'

"Now turn, if you will, to John 14:1–3. Follow along as I read it. 'Let not your heart be troubled; you believe in God, believe also in Me. In My Father's house are many mansions: if it were not so, I would have told you. I go to prepare a place for you. And if I go and prepare a place for you, I will come again and receive you to Myself; that where I am, there you may be also.' This passage gives us great hope and assurance that there is a heaven and Jesus is preparing it for us.

"In the Bible, heaven is spoken of as a city, a country, and a house. All of these analogies have location in common! What will the conditions of heaven be like? According to Psalm 16:11, heaven will be a life of fulfillment. 'You will show me the way of life, granting me the joy of Your presence and the pleasures of living with You forever.'

"For starters, we get a new body, a custom–built house, and a perfect world! Not only that, the Bible says that we can store up treasures in heaven by serving God on earth. Listen to what it says in Matthew 6:19–20. 'Do not store up for yourselves treasures on earth, where moth and rust destroy and where thieves break in and steal. But store up for yourselves treasures in heaven where moth and rust do not destroy, and where thieves do not break in and steal.' Heaven will be emptied of everything that brings sorrow! Revelation 21:4 says, 'And God will wipe away every tear from their eyes; there shall be no more death, nor sorrow, nor crying. There shall be no more pain, for the former things have passed away.'

"No one really knows what heaven will look like, but it will be beautiful beyond description. Turn to 1 Corinthians 2:9. 'But it is written: Eye has not seen, nor ear heard, nor have entered into the heart of man the things which God has prepared for those who love Him.' Revelation 21:10–11 reads, 'And he carried me away in the Spirit to a great and high mountain, and showed me the great city, the holy Jerusalem, descending out of heaven from God, having the glory of God. Her light was like a most precious stone, like a Jasper stone, clear as crystal.'

"Heaven will be completely different than earth. For example: take us! Philippians 3:20–21 says, 'For our citizenship is in heaven, from which we also eagerly wait for the Savior, the Lord Jesus Christ, who will transform our lowly body that it may be conformed to His glorious body, according to the working by which He is able even to subdue all things to Himself.'

"What makes a house a home isn't the address or the lot or the garage or the architecture. What makes it home is the people. And what makes heaven heaven is not streets made out of gold, great fountains, lots of fun, and no smog. That all may well be. Actually, I think that heaven is far greater than our wildest imagination. The same God, who designed the best of everything in this world, also designed heaven, only He took it to a far greater extent than anything we've ever seen. What makes heaven heaven is God. It is being there with Him. With His presence comes peace and contentment, a fulfillment, a sense that all is well. That is also a contentment that bubbles over into the rest of life. We can anticipate this future in the presence of God. We can be with Him in a place where everything He wants happens the way He wants it to happen. And that affects this life as well.

"Do you know for certain where you are going? According to Revelation 22:17, the invitation is open to all. 'The Spirit and the bride say, "Come!" And let him who hears say, "Come!" Let the thirsty ones come… anyone who wants to. Let them come and drink the water of life without charge.' This invitation by the Spirit remains open to anyone who will come by faith to Christ to accept the Lord's gracious offer of eternal life.

"In John 3:16, Acts 4:12, and again in Romans 10:9–10, it says the only way to get to heaven is through Jesus Christ and knowing that He is your Savior. He died for your sins, and if you believe this, you will have eternal life in heaven. This doesn't mean that you will never face challenges or crises in your life; it does mean that when you do, you can rest assured knowing that God will never leave you. In fact, you should rejoice during hardships because it means you're probably disrupting Satan's plan for you! John 10:10 tells us that Satan came to kill, steal, and destroy! It's the only reason he came here. Think about it this way: if Satan isn't bothering you, then you're probably not doing anything to bother him!

"If there are people here who don't know Jesus or who aren't quite sure if they do, but would like to have a personal relationship with Him, please come forward now and we will say a special prayer together."

Dozens of people stood and moved forward to the front. Mary was one of them. When they were all in place at the bottom of the stage, the pastor began a prayer of forgiveness and they repeated his words.

"Father, please forgive my sinful ways and let me have another chance at this life with You being the center. I come to You today humbly asking for Your mercy, forgiveness, and grace. I know that Your Son, Jesus, died for me on the cross and was resurrected again so that I may have eternal life with You someday in heaven. Please come into my heart and my life and lead me down the path that You want me to go, to fulfill Your plan and purpose for me. Help me to know You better, Lord. Thank You for this chance to start over again. In Jesus' precious name, I pray. Amen."

The pastor came to a close in his message by saying, "Folks, it isn't my job to change your heart. This is a divine work that only God can accomplish. I am just an instrument to reach out and touch you. To tell you how much God loves you and that there is everlasting life through Jesus Christ. He wants you to know that no matter what you are going through, the answers you are seeking are found in Him. I hope I did my job and that you will know Him now or better than you ever have before. Have a great afternoon, and may God be with you all."

Mary left the service feeling as if a heavy load had been lifted from her heart. She still had a long way to go before she could understand all that had happened between her and Justin, but for the first time in a very long time, Mary was willing to let the hurt go and at least try to bring in what God wanted for her.

Justin began to notice the change in his wife. She was softer and kinder when they spoke. Although Mary still had a great deal of resentment, she seemed to be more open to hear what he had to say. Justin knew she was attending the church next to his office. Because he saw positive results from her being there, he thought it might be a good place to start his new life as well.

Chapter Seven

Over the course of the next several months, Skylar and Amy adjusted nicely to their weekly visits with their dad. It became an event they all looked forward to. After all, even though Justin only saw his daughters once a week and kept them overnight twice a month, he was still spending more time with them than he had in the two or three years prior. The girls were finally able to get to know him, and they adored him.

Justin was thrilled that his little girls were part of his life, but he missed his wife and wanted her back. He tried on several occasions to tell her, but she still felt very bitter and betrayed.

"Mary, please can we talk? Let me make it up to you. This isn't the way it's supposed to be, with you over there and me here," he murmured into the phone. "I miss you. I miss us. Won't you please just let it go? It was a mistake, and I am more sorry than you will ever know, but I didn't cheat on you. I swear." Justin inhaled a needed breath, as he frantically continued to explain. "Brenda tried for months to get me to leave with her. She knew I worked late, and she made it a point to show up almost every night. I didn't think anything of her being there again because she was always there. But she wasn't a threat! Good heavens look at what she was! Compared to what I had at home, she was a zero! Why would I ever jeopardize what I had with you for her, or with anyone else? It doesn't even make any sense. Please, Mary. Please let me come home," Justin begged once again, but his words fell on deaf ears.

"I can't, Justin. I'm trying really hard, but it isn't working yet. I need more time. Don't you think I want to forget that whole incident and start over? But I just can't. That image will be burned into my memory until the day I die. I trusted you with my life. How can I ever let you come home, knowing that you were with that woman? Whether or not anything happened isn't even the point any more. You were both so entwined that it makes me sick to even remember. You're a married man, Justin, and you had no business being there like that!" she yelled.

"I know. I was wrong. I admit it. But you have to forgive me, Mary. It isn't fair that we live like this with the girls having to go back and forth. We're a family and we belong together. I know you need time, but it's been almost a year. How much longer do you need? I can't live like this forever. It isn't fair to any of us."

"I don't know how much longer it will take. It sure doesn't feel like it's been a year, but I guess it has," Mary said, remembering the celebration of Amy's second birthday the week before. "Just be patient with me, Justin. Please, give me that much. I am trying. I promise. I still care so much for you and what we had, but I don't want to try this again if I can't let go of the memory of what you did. It wouldn't be fair to you or to me if I kept throwing it in your face. I don't want to live that way. Please try to understand. I just want to be sure that the time is right when it does happen."

"Okay, honey. Let's not discuss it anymore tonight," Justin told her. As he thought about the hope–filled words she just said to him, he couldn't help but smile. "I'll pick up the girls after I get off work tomorrow, then keep them for the weekend. If you want to join us, we'll be around. I bought them a sandbox and put it in the front yard so they could play while I pull some weeds. And don't make any smart remarks. I know what you're thinking—and yes, I do know how to pull weeds!" he joked.

"I wasn't going to say anything. It didn't even cross my mind," she fibbed. "I knew you could be domestic if you really put some effort into it, though I would love to see it for myself. I may just have to come over and sneak a peek. I'll see you tomorrow. Good night," she said and hung up the phone. She was surprised when she felt the smile spread across her face. It seemed that with every conversation, her heart began to soften just a little.

The next evening the girls sat on the porch and waited for the sound of their father's truck coming up the hill. Mary knew exactly when Justin arrived. Their squeals were heard throughout the house and probably halfway down the street as well.

"Daddy's here! Mommy, Daddy's here!" Skylar screamed and jumped with delight.

"Daaaddee!" Amy yelled, watching his truck pull into the driveway.

Mary stood in the doorway and waited until she saw Justin nearing the steps. Her heart still leaped in her chest whenever she saw his face. The girls were already hanging on his legs, which made it difficult for him to walk. But he didn't complain, nor did she. The gratifying scene was one that Mary had longed to see for many years. She allowed herself to dwell in it for as long as it lasted.

"Okay, guys. Let me get your things and talk to your mom for a minute. Then we'll go have some pizza. Would you like that?" he asked.

"Yeah, pizza. I like pizza," Skylar told him excitedly.

"Peesa, yay. Me peesa, too," baby Amy said, clear enough to be understood.

"I can't believe how much they can do now. I am enjoying them so much, Mary. Even though I hate being away from you, I think this separation has done me a lot of good, especially when it comes to the girls. I've really learned a lot since I've had them this past year. And I can't even begin to tell you what they mean to me. I would like it more if we could do all of this together, but at least I know some good has come out of it," Justin said sincerely.

"Well, I'd never go through this again in a million years, but I am really happy that you've gotten to know your daughters better and that they bring you so much joy. They are pretty special kids. I'm going to miss them tonight." Mary usually stayed home to read, but for some reason she was restless this evening and needed more than a book to satisfy her needs.

"You could always come and have pizza with us, if you wanted," her husband casually mentioned, trying not to get his hopes up too high.

"Yeah, Mommy, come have pizza with us!" her oldest daughter screamed out.

"Oh, I don't think so. It's your night to have them, and I don't want to intrude. Besides, I was going to take a long hot bath and finish my new book."

"Mary, you won't be intruding. And you can always take a bath. Please join us." Justin tried not to beg, but his voice had the distinct sound of desperation, even to him.

"Maybe tomorrow night. I'll let you have tonight with them, then how about I come over tomorrow night? I could make your favorite… lasagna! The girls like that, too, and it might be fun to all be together."

After Mary told Justin her idea, her heart began to stir. Excitement filled her mind and heart at the prospect of them all being together again. It would be the first time in a more than a year, but she realized that she was looking forward to the next day with great anticipation. The message in church the week before was on forgiveness, and she felt she was ready to give it a try.

"Okay, then it's a date. I'll call you tomorrow and we'll make plans," Justin said, leaning over to kiss his wife on the cheek. "And thank you, Mary. I don't know what this all means, but I promise not to read anything into it that I'm not supposed to. However, it is the first time that you've wanted to be a part of us again, and I can't help but be a little more than just casual about it all."

Justin walked down the steps with one girl on each arm. Then Mary heard them drive away. She didn't know what was happening inside of her, but she knew it was the right thing to do. And for the first time in a very long time, Mary felt truly happy.

Chapter Eight

The sounds of the sirens interrupted her sleep. They seemed too close, and it made her feel a little ill at ease. Mary looked at the clock on the nightstand. It was just past nine thirty in the morning. She couldn't shake the feeling. She was nervous, and she didn't know why. Mary reached for the phone to call Justin.

"Busy? How can a phone be busy in this day and age?" she wondered out loud. She hung up and tried again. "Still busy. Get off the phone, Justin. I have to talk to you," Mary said trying to send him a mental message. As soon as she put the receiver down, the phone rang. She nearly jumped out of her nightgown.

"Justin? I've been trying to call you." Mary knew it was Justin because she saw his name on the caller ID.

"Mary! Oh my God, Mary, I'm so sorry," he wailed, sounding more frightened than he had ever been in his life.

"Justin, what is it? Is it the girls? Where are they?" But he didn't respond, and Mary yelled in the phone, "Justin, for the love of God, tell me the girls are okay, please!"

A sob rang out on the other end of the line, and Mary screamed.

"Oh God, no..."

She remembered very little of what happened next. There was a voice on the phone, but it was one she had never heard before. He said he was with the police department and he was on his way over to the house to pick her up.

Mary quickly pulled on her jeans and threw on a baseball cap. Though she felt like she was moving in slow motion, she was waiting at the door when they pulled up. Justin got out and ran to her. He fell to his knees sobbing hysterically.

"Our babies, Mary. Our poor little babies. Oh Lord, help us!"

"Justin, you're scaring me. Please tell me what happened. Where are they?

Where are Skylar and Amy?" She tried shaking him, but he just sat there with a dazed look on his face. Seconds later, the policeman who was with her husband walked up.

"Mrs. Burgoff, please. There is no time to waste. You need to come with us. The girls have been in a very bad accident, and they were taken to the hospital. We need to hurry!" he told her as calmly yet firmly as he could.

"Accident? But how? When?," she begged to know. Mary got in the back seat with Justin, and they held hands and prayed all the way to the hospital.

As they rode, Officer Williams explained what happened. Justin couldn't find the words, nor could he relive what he saw his little girls go through.

"From what your husband told us, Mrs. Burgoff, the girls were outside playing in the front yard. Your husband explained that he walked to the side of the house for a minute to retrieve his rake and gloves. Within seconds after he went around the corner, there was screeching, then a very loud bang. Then came the screams."

"I was only gone for a second, Mary," Justin interrupted. "They were both playing in their sandbox near the front porch. I ran back as soon as I heard all the noise. The first thing I saw was the flatbed truck in the front yard sitting by the steps. It was right where the girls were playing. Oh God, I just can't believe it. I felt like I was dreaming. I kept hearing their cries, but I couldn't see them anywhere. Then I saw a little bundle in the yard next door. It was Amy. I ran over to her as fast as I could, but it didn't feel like I was running at all. When I bent down, I heard her making small whimpering sounds. Her eyes were open and she was looking at me. I wanted so much to pick her up and hold her. Oh, Mary, she looked so small lying there. Her little body was all torn and bruised and there was blood everywhere. I didn't want to move her for fear of hurting her more, so I covered her with my shirt and told her I'd be right back. I look around for Skylar, but I couldn't see her anywhere. I screamed her name, but she didn't answer. Then I ran in and called 9–1–1. When the fire truck and ambulance got there, I called you. I don't know who finally found Skylar or where, but I know someone did."

"One of the firemen found Skylar. The impact pushed her under the front porch. She was still inside the sandbox," Officer Williams told them sadly.

"Was she alive?" they both asked at the same time.

"They rushed her out so fast that I didn't have a chance to ask. Then I got busy talking to you, Mr. Burgoff, and we were trying to get a hold of your wife." The officer hoped he sounded convincing. He knew the status of their oldest daughter, but he knew, too, that it wasn't his place to inform them.

When they arrived at the hospital, four policemen, three doctors and Mike Greene, the pastor from Mary's church, were waiting at the door. It didn't take long for the distressed parents to put the pieces together. Pastor Mike approached them first. He put his arms around Mary.

"I'm so sorry to have to tell you, Mary, but..." Before he could finish, Mary collapsed in his arms screaming in disbelief.

"No! No! How can this be? Which one, Mike, which one is dead?" she asked barely recognizing her own voice.

"Mary, I am so sorry," the pastor said sadly. "But it's both of them. They're both gone."

"Both? How can that be? How can they both be gone? What kind of God would do that? I don't understand. I thought He was a good God, Mike. You told me He loved me! Is this some sort of sick joke or what? How can this be love?" Mary whimpered.

"God does love you, Mary. He didn't do this to you, or to them! He isn't that kind of a God. You know that. He is everything that is good, and He will see you through this, I promise. Don't lose your faith, not now, not when you need it the most!" Mike Greene tried his best to comfort his new Christian friend, but she was no longer able to hear him.

The lobby of the hospital grew still. Sounds of silence filled the air. Mary could no longer hold back the pain and anger that had built up inside. Suddenly, the most painful, pathetic, bloodcurdling scream that any of them had ever heard before echoed through the halls. There wasn't a doctor, nurse, patient, or employee on the main floor who didn't hear the mother's heart–wrenching cry. Justin rushed to his wife's side, but she pushed him away.

"How could you leave them alone?" she screamed at him. "I trusted you. How could you do that to them, Justin? How could you do it to us?" Mary pounded on his chest demanding answers, though she didn't expect him to have any. She realized she needed to get as far away from him as she could.

As she tried to stand, the walls grew close and the room began to spin around her.

"Help me, please. I can't…" Mary grabbed her chest, trying hard to fill her lungs with air, but her strength was gone. "I can't breathe. Please, help me," she murmured just before she lost consciousness.

"Please, Mary, don't...I need you. I didn't mean to hurt them. I didn't know. Please…" Justin watched in horror as his wife slid to the floor. "Mary!" he called out, but she could no longer hear him.

One of the attending physicians administered oxygen to the distraught mother and put her in a room. Then he turned to Justin.

"Sir, are you okay? Do you want me to find you a bed so you can rest?" he asked with great concern.

"I don't understand. How can both of my daughters be gone? They were playing together less than two hours ago. I heard them laughing. Do you know what the sound of a child's laughter can do to you? It grabs you by the heart and hangs there for weeks, sometimes months. You never forget. How am I supposed to just walk away from this place knowing that I will never hear that sound again?" As the reality of his words rang in his head, Justin fell to his knees and cried. "Oh God, help me. Help me please!"

Without much resistance, Justin was carefully lifted to his feet. He was admitted to the room next to his wife, where they were watched carefully for the next several hours. Both of them were sedated and slept until the next afternoon.

Mary woke up in a fog. She felt nauseous and dizzy. Her mouth was dry and her head was pounding. At first she didn't remember where she was, or why. Then it hit her. Once again her pathetic cry filled the hospital corridor.

"Skylar…Amy…no! Not my little girls! Please tell me it isn't true!" she begged out loud. Kelly Oliver, one of the young nurses on duty, came running to her room.

"Mary, please don't cry," she said sympathetically. "It will be okay. Your daughters are with God. They're safe now. Nobody can ever hurt them again. Everything will be okay, I promise," the young nurse said, feeling the mother's loss.

"Oh, really? And just how do you know it will be okay? Do you have kids? Have you ever lost one of them? Tell me, what makes you such an expert on the subject of death and children?" Mary had no idea what the young woman had been through, but she knew she couldn't possibly understand her pain.

"Yes, as a matter of fact, I have lost little ones before, Mary, and I know exactly how you are feeling. So I guess that makes me somewhat of an expert on the subject." The sting of Mary's words shot like arrows through Kelly's heart as the memory of her children surfaced. "It's been four years now, but sometimes it feels like only yesterday. I lost them in a fire. All three of them, twin boys and a little girl. I can still hear them screaming for me. I tried to get to them, but the fire was so hot." Her voice was barely above a whisper as the tears slowly filled her eyes. Kelly's hand immediately went to the fading scar on her right forearm, one of the many reminders of a day she would never forget.

Mary silently watched the young woman as she spoke. She looked like a child herself, nowhere near old enough to have had children already.

"Well, isn't life just grand?" Mary said sarcastically. "So tell me, Nurse Kelly, what's your secret? How do you survive the pain and go on? And why do you even want to?" Mary wailed, still unable to comprehend her loss.

"I don't know if you ever get over it, Mary, but surviving is something that you just make yourself do. You have to do other things to take your mind off your loss. Shortly after I lost the kids was when I decided to go back to school and get my nursing degree. Being around people who need me helps a lot. It takes my mind off of my own pain. But I couldn't have done any of it without my faith. God has given me the strength to get through each day and the peace I need to want to keep living. There is no way I could have gotten through it alone. If you don't know Him, Mary, now is a good time to start."

"I was just starting my walk with God because I thought He was the answer to what I was missing, but now I don't know. I guess my faith isn't real enough because He is the first one I want to blame. God is supposed to be good and kind and love us so much, but if He is and does, how can He let something like this happen to me, or to you?" Mary was so confused. Kelly decided this was a good time to take a break. She pulled up the chair next to the bed and the two of them talked for the next two hours.

"Mary, if God allowed this to happen, then there's probably a very good reason for it! Accidents are part of life, pain and suffering are inevitable, and death is a reality. God never once told us that life would be a bed of roses, whether we followed His ways or not. But I can tell you from experience that His ways are the only ways to get through all the stuff this world does to us. And we will all deal with some form of tragedy in our lifetime. This is for certain. God only promises never to leave us when things like this happen. I can't imagine how someone can deal with something like this without God's strength. It's such a wonderful feeling to know He is there holding us up and helping us to cope. Soon the pain will subside a little, but it's never completely gone. It will just be a different feeling than it is now. Your life will go on, Mary. Maybe you will even have other children to love, if that is God's will. But don't give up. It will be okay again, I promise. God has this amazing way of turning our heartache and pain into something incredibly good."

"I don't think I can be as confident or as strong as you claim to be, Kelly. I am not that secure in my faith and now I am not so sure I ever can be. I can't even imagine trying to replace my babies with another child. How could I ever love that way again?" she sobbed.

"Give it time. I know it doesn't seem possible, but it will get better," the nurse told her, holding tightly to Mary's hand. "My marriage didn't survive the loss. Though it was ruled an accident, my husband felt responsible for the fire. He had left the screen to the fireplace open, and one of the embers shot out and ignited the carpet. By the time we heard the alarm, we just barely got outside. That was when I heard my babies screaming. The twins were four and my daughter was only nine months old. I can still hear their cries even today. For several months afterward, my husband saw a therapist, but nothing they said worked. He just couldn't live with the guilt. He committed suicide three years ago this month."

The shock and surprise on Mary's face was obvious. But she was still so hurt and so very angry at God for what happened that she just couldn't bring herself to feel pity or compassion for the young woman who sat in front of her.

"Well, that's just great that you made it, Kelly!" Mary said with even more sarcasm. "But don't expect me to just roll over and think this is okay. I will not succumb to God's will. If this was all a part of His plan, then I don't want anything to do with it, or Him! And don't expect me to ever understand, because I won't!" Then realizing the harshness of her words, she softened slightly. "I don't know how you can be so positive, Kelly, after all you've been through. But if believing in God is really the answer, I hope He's still around if and when I feel the need to reach out for Him again," she said trying to smile.

"He will be, Mary, because He loves you."

"Kelly, do you mind if I ask you what your life is like now, today? How do you even want to get out of bed?" the grieving mother asked curiously.

"I've come a long way since that day. For a very long time, I had to force myself to get out of bed. Then the next step was leaving the house. But I knew I had to go on living even though it was the hardest thing I ever had to do. Then by the grace of God, I was blessed with another chance. God sent me an angel, Mary. His name is Dr. Keith Rubin, and we're getting married next year. I can't even tell you how wonderful my life is now. I can't have any more children because I had some trouble after my daughter, Janie, was born. I had to have a hysterectomy. But Keith is fine with it. He said there are plenty of children who need adopting. He is so sweet and so gentle. That's why I am telling you to never give up. You just can't! God has a plan for you, Mary, and He will reveal it when it's time. But you have to be ready when the door opens. You're allowed to grieve. You need to grieve. Take as long as necessary. Cry and be angry—it's okay. But in time, let the door close on your pain so another door will open, and it will be even wider and better than the first, I promise."

"I'm a long way from closing any doors! Right now I just need to be mad at something or someone. If that someone is God, then so be it. He made it happen, so He better fix it! I just want to get through it all as quickly as possible. I guess my first step will be going home. I don't know what it will be like there, but I know it will be hard. I have to go face an empty house full of memories of my children. I can't imagine what that will be like."

"I guess in that sense I was somewhat blessed because we had no home to go to after the fire. I never had to be back in a place where all their memories were, and it probably helped speed up the healing a little. Mary, when you get home, and if you find it too hard to cope, please call me no matter what time of day or night it is! I'll leave you my number. I really want to help you get through this," the young nurse said sincerely.

"Thank you, Kelly."

The two women held each other for a minute. Then Kelly excused herself and went back to work. Mary lay there for another few hours before she felt strong enough to leave. She knew that Justin would want to be with her when she went home, but Mary needed to be alone and told him so when he came for her.

"Justin, please let me have some time to think and to feel. I know you are hurting, but I need this time alone. I don't know how long it will take, but I just can't be with you right now. Try to understand," Mary said in a firm but gentle voice.

"They were my kids, too. I need to be with you again, Mary. I've waited so long. But I will give you the time and space you need. I just don't know how you will be able to go home to an empty world when it used to be so full of life and hope. Please, call me if you need company, and I will be there in a heartbeat. No strings attached," he told her honestly.

"Thank you, Justin. My mother is coming to get me. I will talk to you soon. We have to make funeral arrangements, and I guess we need to do that in the next few days," Mary said, barely able to comprehend her own words.

"Our parents said they would handle everything, so we don't have to worry about that. You just go home and try to rest. I will check on you later this evening." He leaned over and kissed her gently on the forehead. Then he was gone.

Over the next several months, Mary had many fits of anger, unbearable anguish, and never–ending grief. She didn't know how long she could go on in the state of mind she was in. It didn't seem to get any better. In fact, some days were even worse than when the girls first died.

Kelly came to her rescue many times, and for this Mary was very grateful.

The young nurse stayed with her on several occasions and slept on the couch. Kelly knew everything Mary was experiencing, and she wanted to help in any way she could. They quickly became friends. On those nights when Mary couldn't sleep, Kelly tried her best to comfort her.

"If only God would just let me know that my girls are okay. If He would show up one night in my room and sit on my bed and tell me in His own words and voice that they are happy, it would make all of this so much easier. Then I'd be able to go on in this life for however long He wants me to." Mary knew if anyone would understand it would be Kelly.

"Mary, you know in your heart that the girls are with God. That must give you some comfort. You know that they are happy. It's called having faith," she told her.

"But don't you understand, Kelly? I wouldn't need faith if I knew for sure that they were okay! Why can't He just come out of the sky on a big bolt of lightening and tell me He has them? What would be the harm? Then I wouldn't need faith because I heard the words myself from Him!"

"Mary, do you really think God wants you to go through the rest of your life without faith? What kind of a witness would you be for Him? How could you possibly help others if He took away your faith? You know He can do anything He wants, and right now He wants you to believe and trust that He knows what He's doing. Skylar and Amy are with Him, Mary, and He will never let anything harm them again."

Their talks were often, and Mary began to understand better as time passed that Kelly was right. She needed faith, and she prayed every day for hers to return.

Justin tried hard to be a part of Mary's life, too, by making weekly phone calls and leaving her messages when she didn't feel like answering. But Mary just couldn't bring herself to see him. Deep down she knew it wasn't his fault, but she had to blame someone. Since he was the only one close enough, she turned her anger on him. Her anger and his guilt proved almost fatal.

Chapter Nine

When Justin returned home after the accident, he found it harder to cope than he thought. He had no idea that two little people who were on this earth for such a short time could make such an impact on his life and heart. He wept in silence, but the guilt inside grew stronger every day. He knew his wife blamed him for leaving them alone, and deep down he knew she was right. Although the accident report said the truck lost control due to failed brakes, Justin needed to feel the guilt. He didn't want to believe that the God he was just beginning to know would do such a horrible thing. He also knew that if he had been there when the truck lost control, he could have pulled them to safety. Even if he could have only saved one, it would be one more than he had now.

Several times over the next few months, Justin had to drag himself to the office. He tried hard to concentrate on his cases although his heart wasn't really into it. His associates felt compassion and a great sense of sorrow for the young father who stayed locked in his own world of regret, but they didn't know what to do for him. They often talked him into taking the day off because they knew Justin would be of no value to them during a trial or even preparing for one.

Without his work, wife, or children, Justin was lost. He had no direction or strength left. He often wondered what it would be like if he just ended it all. Would he finally be at peace? Would it erase his guilt? But deep down he knew suicide wasn't the answer either. "If this is God's will for me to go through life without children or a wife, then so be it," he thought out loud. But he knew he could no longer do it alone.

On the seventh–month anniversary of their children's death, Justin and Mary each decided they needed to talk to Mike Greene at the church. Neither one would know of the other's decision until later. It turned out to be the best thing they had ever done. Mary called Mike first.

"I am so glad you called, Mary. I've been thinking about you for the past few weeks and prayed that you would eventually return my calls. How are you?" the pastor asked, though he imagined it wasn't good. How wrong he was.

"Mike, I think it's been long enough. I can't do this by myself any longer. I just don't have the strength. I'm ready to bring Jesus into my life again, only this time on firmer grounds. Maybe what I had before wasn't faith at all. Could you help me?" she asked.

"Of course I'll help you," Mike told her. He could barely contain his excitement. "I am so pleased that you have finally chosen the only way to feel true comfort and peace. Do you want me to come over right now?" Mike responded, more anxious than he had been in years.

"I would love it if you came over, if it isn't too much trouble or too short of notice. If it is, I can wait. Lord knows I've waited this long, another night certainly won't hurt," she said laughing. It was the first time she had laughed in months.

"Oh, no you don't. I'm getting while the getting is good. I'll be there within the half hour." He hung up the phone and turned off his computer. Then he headed over to Mary's to share the Gospel and to place her into the arms of God.

When he arrived, they went into the den and began what turned out to be a four–hour ordeal. It was bittersweet and glorious. Sometimes too sad to remember, other times too beautiful to forget.

"Do you remember that first time I came to your church?" Mary asked her pastor.

"As a matter of fact, I do. You were just going through a separation with Justin, and you stood out like a sore thumb. You looked like you needed a friend. I was so happy that you turned to God for answers, Mary, but this really isn't any different than that was," he told her.

"How can you say that? I didn't kick my children out of the house like I did Justin. My kids aren't coming back! They're dead! There is nothing I can do to undo any of it," she said.

"Oh, that's where you are wrong, Mary. First of all, none of this is your fault! Your children are with God. They are safe in heaven, and they will be forevermore. You have to stop feeling guilty. You didn't do anything wrong. Justin messed up, but he didn't do anything to hurt your children either, so stop blaming him and yourself. God has everything under control. When you go through these hard times, God waits for your call. He is so pleased when you turn to Him for comfort because He knows you finally understand that He is the only One who can give it to you." Mike knew the evening was going to be a long one, but he was quite prepared. He would stay as long as necessary, until Mary trusted God again.

"But Mike, how can God do this to us? If He really cares, how can He make it so we hurt this much and then tell us He loves us more than anything? I wouldn't do that to my children!"

"Accidents happen all the time, Mary. And whatever God's reasons are for allowing it, you may never know in this lifetime. His original intent was for us to live in a perfect world free of pain, sickness, and accidents. We were meant to live forever, without death or sin, in perfect harmony. But Adam and Eve changed all of that when they were in that beautiful garden called Eden. In the center of the garden, there was a tree. It was the Tree of Conscience, which gave knowledge of good and evil. God told them that they could eat the fruit from any tree in the garden but this tree, but they didn't listen. Satan tempted them, and they fell from God's grace. The perfect world God intended changed drastically. They were disobedient, which was sin. And the result of sin was death.

"God is in heaven, where we are all meant to be someday. Sadly, not all of us will be allowed. Only those who believe that Jesus is their Savior will be welcome there. But before we get there, we have to go through certain challenges and struggles here on earth because it is an imperfect, sinful world. We will lose our loved ones to many things because death is part of this life. But once this life is over, if we are God's chosen ones, then we will spend our eternity with Him.

"I have children, Mary, but I've never had to mourn any of their deaths. I know it would be hard to accept, and I would be devastated, too. But I know that I would never blame God for whatever took them. I would grieve terribly and miss them tremendously, but I would pray that God would comfort me through it all, as He will for you and Justin if you let Him. You need each other more than ever. You need to go through this loss together and then mend your differences and start over, if it isn't too late. Please try. I will pray for you and be here for you whenever you need me. And Kelly is here for you, too. She's come such a long way in her grief and belief. I am so blessed to have her available for people like you. She's been through so much and she is still so faithful. That faith is there for you, too, Mary, if you open the door and let God inside again. Only this time, don't shut Him out, no matter what you are going through. He will never leave you in your time of need. I promise you this!" Mike was kneeling beside her by then, as Mary cried tears of joy and sadness.

"I know what you're saying is right. I think it's time for me to come back to God and this time trust Him with everything," she said, joining Mike on the floor. They got on their knees and bowed their heads, and Mike led them in prayer.

"Father, as much as we try to do things our own way, we never get very far. We should know by now that we can't do anything without You. Please, come to us this evening and surround Mary with Your love, comfort, and strength. She needs You more than ever to get her through this painful struggle. Keep Your loving hands on her, Father, and guide her to where she needs to be in You, now and for eternity. In Jesus' precious and holy name. Amen."

Mike left Mary's around two in the morning, after he felt sure that she was finally at peace and ready to move on. On the drive home, he was overcome with a strange yet wonderful feeling as to how this would end. For no apparent reason at all, his thoughts turned to Justin and he smiled.

The next afternoon while Mike was finishing up his message for the weekend, his assistant tapped quietly on his door.

"Come in, Susan," he said.

"I don't mean to disturb you, Mike, but Justin Burgoff just came in and asked if he could speak to you. I think it could be important."

"Sure, send him in," Mike told her, cleaning up the papers from his desk. As he stood and walked toward the door, Justin made his entrance. Mike could sense there was something different about him, though his overall appearance came as a total shock. All evidence of the good–looking successful attorney Justin once was had all but vanished. The man that stood before him looked gaunt, pale, and in desperate need of a shave, yet there appeared to be a sense of peace as well. Both men shook hands and embraced.

"Mike, I hope I am not intruding, but this couldn't wait," Justin said a bit nervously.

"Not at all. I'm glad you came. It's really good to see you, Justin. You look like you've been through a train wreck, but it's good to see you! Why don't you sit down and we can talk," the pastor suggested, pointing to a large chair in front of his desk.

"I know I must look a sight. I haven't slept in months. I haven't showered or shaved in almost a week. For the last few days, I've been walking the streets not knowing where to go or what to do. I didn't think I was going to get through this, Mike. I even had contemplated suicide at one time. But I'm too chicken for that. Then just a few hours ago, it hit me. I knew that if I came here you would have the answer. It was as if I didn't have any say so in the matter at all. I just drove here without even thinking about it. I know I need help, Mike. And whatever it was that led me here is telling me that you are the solution to my pain. Please, I just can't do it alone any more," he begged. Though visibly broken, Justin looked relieved and almost renewed.

"My friend. You have just experienced firsthand how the Lord works when He wants to get your attention. He waited until you were at your weakest and could no longer resist. He wants you to know Him, Justin. And I am here to help you get there," Mike told him. "If you're ready, so am I."

"I am ready, Mike. Show me the way. Help me to understand."

For the next several hours, Mike answered all types of questions. Justin needed to hear about death, eternity, and why his babies had to die.

"Accidents and illness are a part of this world we live in, Justin. But God promises to get us through the bad times if we lean on Him for support, strength, and love. His grace and mercy are sufficient for anything and everything we have to endure. We are not meant to live on earth forever though. If you read Psalm 39, you will know that your life is no longer than your hand. You are here but for a moment more. God has a plan and purpose for all of us. Your daughters fulfilled His plan. They were not meant to get any older than what they were, or they would still be here.

"God knows what you and Mary are going through. He remembers the pain of watching His own Son die! He feels your heartache and sees your grief. The only way to get through all of this is to lean on Him and let Him give you the strength you need to get through. Skylar and Amy are in heaven right alongside of our Heavenly Father. He will never let them out of His sight, you can be sure. And if tonight you decide that where your children are you want to be also, then let's take the next step and repent, asking for His forgiveness and love, and opening your heart to Jesus. I don't know why your children had to die, Justin, but God does. Nothing is forever except eternity; the life you will live after you die on earth. The only question is will you spend that eternity with God or apart from Him? It is your choice." Mike was exhausted, but he had to get Justin to break. He knew he was close.

"I want to be with Him. What do I have to do?" he asked.

"Ask for forgiveness of your sins and let Jesus come into your heart and change it," the pastor answered.

"Okay, Mike. That's what I want. I want to see my babies again, and I want to do what God intended for me. I want my wife and my life back. Can He help me?" Justin asked in a voice that sounded desperate, even to him.

"Yes, He can and He will. Say this prayer with me. 'Father, I come to You this day on my knees. I admit to You that I am a sinner. I need You in my life, to guide me and show me where I need to be in You. Forgive me for all that I have done in the past, Lord, and let me live my life from this day forward seeking Your will and knowing that Jesus died on the cross for me so that I may someday live in heaven with You. Help me to understand Your ways, and let me lead others to know them as well. I ask this in Your Son's holy name. Amen.'" When he finished, Mike noticed that even with all the distractions from his untidy appearance, Justin Burgoff was glowing.

"Wow, I can't even explain what is going on in my heart. What an incredibly awesome feeling this is. I don't know why I didn't do this sooner!" Justin said with a smile on his face and tears rolling down his cheeks.

"We are called to come when it's time. Your time wasn't due until now. Praise the Lord that He has blessed you. This will help you get back on track with everything in your life. By the way, have you talked to Mary today?" he wondered.

"No, I haven't talked to her in a couple of days. I was going to call and check on her. But I always feel like I am pushing her or making a pest of myself. Now maybe with my news and new heart, she will want to hear what I have to say. Do you think I have a shot?" Justin still had high hopes of rebuilding the relationship with his wife.

"I would say your chances are very good. In fact, I would give her a call right now, from my office," Mike suggested. He had a feeling this would be a start of something very special for the two of them. Justin had no idea that the pastor had prayed with Mary the night before, and that she, too, had regained her faith. With the two of them now protected by the love of their Father, the chances of them working out their differences were very good.

"Really? You think I should call her now?"

"Absolutely. Here, let me dial the number, then I'll leave you two alone." Mike was anxious for them to talk. As soon as he heard Mary's voice, he handed the phone to Justin and winked. "She's all yours. God bless you both," he said and left the room.

"Mary? Hey, it's me. How are you?" Justin felt like a schoolboy again.

"I'm doing great, Justin. How are you?" she asked, feeling a little timid herself.

"As a matter of fact, I'm the best I've been in a very long time. Mary, can I come over? I need to explain some things. I also want to tell you what I just went through. I can't think of anyone that I would rather share my news with first than you. Please, may I see you?"

"I was just going to ask you if you were busy. Yes, please come over. I need you here with me, now more than ever," Mary told him honestly, smiling through her tears.

"I'm on my way. I just need to run by my house for a minute." Justin left in such a hurry he didn't even say goodbye to Mike. But he knew that the pastor would understand.

After a quick shower and shave, he headed for Mary's. Twenty minutes later he pulled up in their driveway. When the door opened, Justin stood there with the biggest grin, and Mary could not resist any longer. She ran into his arms and held him close, begging for his forgiveness.

"I am so sorry for all that I have put you through. Please, Justin, forgive me. This is all my fault! The girls should have never been at that house because you should have never left here. I was angry and hurt, and I let it consume me. What a mess I have made. Come home and be with me again. I love you. I have never stopped loving you!" she sobbed.

"Please don't blame yourself, sweetheart. It wasn't you. I am so sorry I neglected you and the girls. It wasn't fair, and it wasn't right. Let's start over. I don't want our babies to have died in vain. If something good can come out of their deaths, then I can accept it better. Let's go sit down. I have to tell you something," he said and walked with her into the den. "I was over at Mike Greene's office today, and I asked him to help me know Jesus. After several hours of explaining and many questions later, we said a prayer together. I asked Jesus to come into my heart and forgive me of my sins. I have been reborn, Mary, and I want to start all over again the right way, with God being our focus and foundation." While Justin talked, Mary's smile broadened.

"Justin, Mike came here last night and helped me to understand all that I was feeling and that it was okay to be angry and hurt. He helped me to find my heart again and give it back to Jesus. We were both on our knees right here in this room. I am so grateful that God didn't give up on me. I'm embarrassed to admit that I blamed Him for their deaths. Then, as if that wasn't bad enough, I blamed you. I am so ashamed. But last night I asked for His forgiveness for my hurtful words towards Him. God knows I didn't mean them. I am so blessed to know He will always forgive my mistakes. I just hope you can as well. Forgive me, Justin, please?" Mary begged.

"There is nothing to forgive. It is all in the past. We have a future, and we will live it like yesterday never happened," he told her.

"Oh, no, Justin. We must never forget the circumstances that brought us to know Jesus, no matter how painful they are. For without them, we wouldn't be here right now. If our babies had to die, I thank God it was now before they were tainted and tempted by the ways of the world. They were still protected by God's grace as they were when they were first given to us. God took them knowing that we would find Him in the midst of all of this pain. There is a reason for everything that happens. We should be grateful even if our babies aren't here. And I am. But I miss them so much, Justin. But I can handle the grief as long as you are here with me." Mary still hadn't let go of her husband's hand since she had opened the door. She wasn't sure if she ever would.

"I'm grateful, too, Mary. I don't know how long this pain will last, but without His love or presence, I would have never understood any of it. I thank God He rescued us both before it was too late. Now we just have to wait to see them again. I can if you will promise to wait with me."

"I promise. How about we go to your house and get your things?" she asked sweetly.

"How about we wait until tomorrow? I have a better idea," he said, picking her up and carrying her upstairs to their room.

Chapter Ten

For several months Justin and Mary were inseparable, like they were when they first met. He cut down his workload and only went in twice during the first few weeks he was back, then only three days a week after that. He knew his associates were perfectly capable of handling the business, and because he missed many days after the girl's death, a lot of them knew more about the cases than he did anyway. He took full advantage, only leaving Mary when it was absolutely necessary.

It was on one of these days when she knew Justin would be gone all afternoon that Mary went to see her doctor. She was once again feeling uneasy and tired and thought she might be getting the flu. But to her delight she was told that she and Justin would be parents once again, only this time they were having twins.

When her husband came home that evening he knew something was up. Mary was acting smitten and all aglow.

"What's going on? Are you hiding something from me?" he asked her when she came into the living room.

"That's a strange thing to ask. What could I possibly be hiding from you? And why haven't you noticed, Mr. Burgoff? Look at me. I am twice the size I normally am, and you never said a word!" she teased.

"I thought you were trying to make up for all those months you didn't eat. I think you look great with a little meat on your bones. So don't worry, I would love you if you weighed two hundred pounds!"

"Oh sure you would. They all say that! Well, by the time these babies are here, I could very well be two hundred pounds!" she answered back, not realizing she gave away her secret.

"What are you talking about…? Are you pregnant?" Justin asked.

"Yes, as if you didn't know, Mr. Smooth Talker. It sure didn't take you long to get me this way again, did it?"

"Oh, Mary! I love you! I—wait, you said babies, as in plural. Does that mean there's more than one?"

"Yes, my sweet. There are two. And next month we will know what they are, if you so desire." By the time the words were out of her mouth, Justin was at her side, holding her closer than ever before.

"Thank You, God! Thank You! Thank You! Thank You!" he whispered in her ear.

The next month Mary had an ultrasound. They both watched as the screen projected the images of their children. As it became clear, they both noticed what appeared to be a little boy.

"Yes, there is a little boy. See? Right there is his manhood. But take a look over here. See this one? That is your daughter," the nurse informed them.

"Oh, Justin. We have both! What an incredibly miracle this is! To be able to do this again and have one of each!" Mary spoke with tears streaming down her face. "I never thought it would be possible to love this way again. But I already love them so much!"

"What a gift you have given me. Thank you, Mary. Thank you for this chance to be a father again. I promise I will not let you down. I will be there with you through it all and for them, too," he told her sincerely.

The next four months went by quickly, but they took a toll on Mary's health. She was always tired and could barely keep down any food. When her blood pressure shot up into the danger zone, the doctor ordered her on complete bed rest, but Mary had a hard time staying there. She was uncomfortable, and it was hard for her to lie down for very long. Her stomach was so big she could no longer see her feet.

Mary tried to blame most of her discomfort on her pregnancy, but deep down she felt there might be something else. She had discovered a lump on her oversized breast a few weeks before, but she didn't want to alarm Justin if there wasn't any reason. It could just be a swollen gland or something related to her condition. She also had been having terrible pains in her lower abdomen, but once again decided it could wait. She would have it all checked after the babies were born.

Mary put it out of her mind and concentrated more on getting through her pregnancy. When she felt strong enough, she even tried fixing up the babies' rooms in between her naps. Her mother and Justin's mother came by every other day to assist, and Mary was extremely grateful for the extra help. They were both there when her water broke.

"Call Justin, Mom, and tell him to get to the hospital as soon as possible. Make sure you tell him I feel fine, but to hurry. I want him there when his children are born," Mary said, trying hard not to panic.

"Don't move!" Helen Griffin told her daughter. "I'll get Audrey to call her son and have him meet us there. Where is your bag?"

"It's already packed and sitting in the entry hall. Tell Audrey to hurry! And call Dr. Hendricks, too! It feels like my contractions are getting closer," Mary informed her.

By the time the three of them arrived at the hospital, Justin was already there waiting.

"Say, what took you guys so long?" he said sheepishly, bending down to kiss his wife.

"How did you get here so fast?" Mary asked curiously.

"I was just up the street doing some last–minute depositions when I got the call from my secretary. I was only five minutes away," he explained. "How do you feel, honey?"

"I feel great. I just want this to be over so I can enjoy the babies, not to mention having this huge thing in front of me gone!" she smiled, pointing to her stomach.

"I think it's sort of cute," he teased.

"Yeah, right. Like rolls on a baby. Well, it may look cute on them, but I prefer not to have any, if you don't mind!" They were laughing when the doctor came in.

"Okay, let's wheel you in and get you checked. Why don't you folks wait here while we get her prepped? Then you can visit for a while until we're ready to deliver. Justin, you can come along if you want," Dr. Hendricks told him.

"What do you mean, if I want? I wouldn't miss this for the world."

The soon–to–be parents were taken to a birthing room where they spent the next several hours waiting for their children to arrive. They were joined by both sets of grandparents. Nurse Kelly also came by to check on her friend. She was overjoyed when she heard Mary was going to have another baby, or babies in this case. Kelly was very proud of her for turning her life around in such a positive way. Mary was truly an inspiration to everyone.

Later that evening, shortly after six, the nurse on duty announced to everyone that Mary was getting close and it was time for them to leave. At the last minute, Dr. Hendricks decided it would be best to take the babies by caesarian. Twenty minutes later, both children arrived without a hitch, perfectly healthy and extremely loud!

"So, have you made up your mind on names yet?" Dr. Hendricks asked the proud parents while they both admired their babies.

"This one we're calling Kelly Marie," Justin said proudly, holding his child in his arms. "And that guy over there is Matthew Joseph!" pointing to the baby in Mary's arms.

"No, you have it backwards. I have Kelly and you have your son, Matthew," his wife told him.

"Are you sure?" he asked. Then removing the blanket he noticed she was right. "I stand corrected."

The babies remained in the hospital for five days. Mary opted to stay there, too, as was her choice after a caesarian section. Justin was there every day to help her with feedings and visit his new family. Soon, the doctor gave them all a clean bill of health and sent them on their way. Justin was anxious for them to be home. He didn't mind the days so much, but the nights were lonely and he missed his wife and babies. He and Mary were happier than they had been in years and, because of their faith, more complete than they had been in all their lives.

After the first few weeks, the parents figured out some sort of schedule, which enabled them to take turns feeding, changing, and bathing. As the babies grew, so too, did their appetites. Both children had nearly doubled their weight in just over three months.

Soon the children were cooing and smiling and watching every move Mary made as she walked back and forth across the room. It always amazed her how quickly they learned who she was. She knew some day they, too, would call her Mommy just as Skylar and Amy had done. With just the thought of her little girls, Mary's eyes filled with tears.

"I wished you could have met them," she said to the twins as they lay in their infant seats waiting for their cereal. "I wished we could have all been a family together." Mary tried to stop thinking about them, but her mind kept going back. "They would have loved being your sisters. You guys look so much alike. Oh, Skylar and Amy, I miss you both so much! Why? Why did you have to go?" she cried out.

The young mother sat at the table with tears rolling down her cheeks as her babies watched unmoved and unknowing. They laughed and giggled and kicked as babies were supposed to do. Mary smiled at them and shook off her sadness as quickly as she could. She had other things to do and didn't have time to dwell on the past. She kept reminding herself that some day she would see her daughters again because God promised and she believed.

By the time Justin got home in the evenings, the babies were bathed and ready for bed. This was when he bonded with them while Mary took a long hot bath. Afterward, they both played with them until the babies got tired. Then they tucked them in for the night. Kelly and Mattie had been sleeping all night for the past two months. Mary was delighted.

The children continued to keep her busy, and Justin helped whenever he could. He was working three days a week and sometimes a fourth whenever he had to prepare for a large case. But he was home every night and weekend to be with all of them.

One Friday evening, Justin noticed Mary looking more tired than normal and insisted that she go to bed early. But Mary declined. She wanted to be with all of them until it was the babies' bedtime. They had just turned ten months old.

"We are so blessed, Justin," she told him as she crawled into his arms after an exhausting day. "They are so perfect and such good babies. We couldn't have done better if we tried." The happy content couple cuddled on the couch to watch the news. When a commercial came on, Justin took the opportunity to talk frankly with Mary about her appearance.

"Honey, I know how much you are enjoying the babies, but are you really doing okay?" he asked with great concern. "I know you're thinking about Skylar and Amy, but you can't let it consume you. Are you taking your vitamins like the doctor told you?

"I'm fine, Justin. I do have my moments when I question Skylar and Amy's absence. They would be having so much fun with Mattie and Kelly, but evidently it was not meant to be. I actually had a bout again last month while I was feeding the kids. I started thinking about the girls and nearly went out of my mind. But the babies started fussing and kicking, which immediately brought me back to reality. Why do you ask?"

"You just don't look like you feel very well. You're pale and getting way too thin. Is motherhood a little much for you this time, with two of them? Can I do anything for you? Do you need a nanny or a maid or something?" Justin was worried, but he tried not to let it show.

"Of course I don't want a nanny! And let her have all the fun? Not a chance! A maid might be nice, though," she teased. She didn't want anyone else around to take away her joy from being with her children. "But I know what you mean about me not looking well. I noticed it, too. I am feeling a bit tired lately, sometimes even more than when I was pregnant. I think carrying these kids just took its toll on me and this worn out body of mine. Maybe I'll go see Dr. Hendricks, and he can prescribe something stronger than the vitamins I'm taking." Mary made light of their conversation, but she was a little concerned herself since she stopped nursing. The lump in her breast seemed to have gotten bigger and she needed to do something. "I'll make an appointment with him soon, I promise."

Justin made it a point to ask his wife every few days if she had made the appointment to see the doctor yet, but Mary always had an excuse. Nearly six weeks passed before she actually called. Then, making light of it to the receptionist, Mary said there was no hurry. Her appointment was made for two weeks later. By the time she actually got in, the babies were a year old.

Mary dropped the children off at her mother's that morning and drove herself to the doctor. After her examination, Dr. Hendricks told her that after she got dressed he would like to see her in his office.

Ten minutes later, he sat across from her at his desk.

"Is there something wrong?" she wondered.

"How long have you had that lump on your breast?" he asked Mary point blank.

"Well, I'm not sure. I think the first time I noticed was when I was about six months along. But I thought it was just something related to the pregnancy," she answered.

"You should have told me, Mary," he scolded.

"Should I be worried?"

"Let's not go there yet, but we need to get you in for some tests and a biopsy on the tissue from the lump. I am concerned about its size. I want to start ruling things out, so the sooner you get this done, the better. I am definitely troubled by your overall appearance. You're too thin, and you look pale. Do you get any rest at all with these kids?" Dr. Hendricks wanted to know.

"I don't get as much as I used to, but Justin gives me a break when he gets home. He is really very good to me. He enjoys these babies so much. Maybe I just need some stronger vitamins."

"I'm prescribing some for you with additional iron. You seem to be a little anemic, and this should help. I'm making an appointment for you tomorrow afternoon to do the biopsy. As soon as I get the results, we will decide what needs to be done next." He made his way to the other side of the desk and took Mary's hand. "I want you enjoying these kids as much as your husband is, Mary. But you need your health first. I will call you as soon as I hear something from the lab. They will give me the results of your Pap smear, too."

The doctor led her out of his office and over to his assistant, who already had an appointment for her.

"Thank you, Dr. Hendricks. Please don't say anything to Justin just yet. I don't want to alarm him unless it's absolutely necessary. Can we wait until after I get the results from all the tests?" she asked sweetly.

"I can do that. Now don't you worry your sweet little head about any of this stuff. We'll take it all a step at a time. It will be fine, I'm sure," he said and patted her hand. Then he walked into his office and shut the door.

Dr. Kyle Hendricks sat in his chair and put his head on his desk. He was deeply troubled and concerned. This was the part of his job that he hated the most, especially when he had to be the bearer of tragic news. Kyle didn't believe for a moment that Mary Burgoff was going to be fine. He had seen it too many times before. All the symptoms were there. It did not look good for the new young mother, who had had her share of heartache already.

Justin was already home when Mary came in with the babies.

"So, what did the doctor say?" he asked taking Mattie from her arms.

"He did some blood work on me while I was there, and he wants to do some other tests, too. He says I am anemic and I need to take some stronger vitamins with iron. I had to stop by the drugstore on my way to get the kids from Mom. After all the results come in, I will know more. Then he will prescribe whatever I need to get me better. He also said for us not to worry, so don't start. I'll be fine," Mary assured him. She intentionally left out having the biopsy done the next day.

"Well, why don't you go soak in the tub and let me tend to the babies? I can feed them their dinner and get them ready for bed. Then we can snuggle on the couch after they go to sleep. What do you say? Does that sound like a plan?" Justin asked. He was trying not to act too concerned, but it got harder every time he looked at her. She was obviously not well, and he prayed that the results would be nothing more than iron deficiency.

"I like that plan," she said. "How about we meet in an hour in the kids' room? Then we can read them their story, tuck them in bed, and be by ourselves afterward. Maybe we can even have some fun of our own," she whispered playfully in his ear.

The next afternoon as planned, Mary had the biopsy. Kelly drove her there and back without question. The following week, Mary was home alone when the phone rang. It was Dr. Hendricks and he asked if she could come in.

"I'll have to see if I can get my mom or Justin's mom to watch the kids. Can you tell me anything over the phone? Should I be prepared for the worst?" she asked somewhat jokingly. But something in the doctor's voice told her the news was not good.

"I need you to come in. Then we can discuss your results in person. Is Justin available?" he asked.

"Dr. Hendricks, I would rather you tell me first. Then you can tell Justin whatever is necessary," she requested.

"Okay. I'll be waiting for you."

Mary called her mom and told her she had an errand to do. Helen was more than happy to take the children.

"How about if I just come over there?" her mother suggested. "That way you won't have to lug all of their things over here. Besides, they'll be going down for a nap soon, and it would just be easier for everyone."

"That would be great, Mom. I need to leave in an hour," Mary informed her.

"I'll be there."

Chapter Eleven

Mary sat in the chair in Dr. Hendricks' office and waited. She drifted into her own world, thinking of all the things that she needed to do after she left. When the door opened suddenly, it took her by surprise and she jumped.

"Sorry, Mary. I didn't mean to startle you. How are you feeling?" the doctor asked, sitting on his desk in front of her.

"I think maybe you should be answering that question yourself. How am I feeling?" she shot back.

"I wished there were an easier way to say this, but I have learned that honesty and directness is best. Mary, I am so sorry to have to tell you this. But it is cancer, and it doesn't look good."

"Where is it?"

"It's breast cancer."

"Well, that doesn't sound so bad. So I have to live with breast implants. Lots of women do that, and they don't even have cancer! Breast cancer is still curable, right?"

"I'm afraid it isn't that simple. One of my very good friends is an oncologist, a cancer doctor. He looked over the results with me, just to make sure there were no mistakes. Mary, you are in a very advanced stage of breast cancer. And it has metastasized, which means it originated in your breasts, but has moved to other organs," he told her honestly.

"So, what are you saying? Am I going to die?" Her lower lip quivered as she waited for him to respond.

"Mary, Justin needs to be here. We need to go over all our choices, and it isn't fair to leave him out. He should be here supporting you and the decisions you make!"

"That tells me that you don't think I have much time. Just be honest with me, Dr. Hendricks. You've known me all my life. Will I see my children grow up? Will I be there when they start school? Will I see their next Christmas?"

"Mary, please."

"Tell me! For heaven's sake, I have a right to know!" she yelled.

"I don't think so," he said in a voice barely loud enough to hear.

"You don't think so, what? Which one is it? Growing up, starting school, or seeing their next Christmas?"

"None of them, Mary. If I had to say honestly, right now, it would be none of them."

"But, Christmas is less than five months away! How can that be?" the young mother questioned.

"Because of how advanced it is. The cancer has been growing there for quite some time, Mary. Possibly even before you got pregnant. It's in an extremely advanced stage and has spread to your uterus and colon, for sure. There may even be other places it has attached itself." Kyle had no intention of telling his patient this news without the support of a family member present, but she insisted and he had to oblige.

"Oh dear God. How can this be happening? We haven't even begun to live. Poor Justin. I don't know if he will be able to take this," she sobbed.

"Mary, I'm calling Justin. He needs to be here with you. You cannot possibly drive home alone knowing what you know."

"I know. But, please, let me be the one to call him," she said hesitating just a bit.

"Okay. You can use my phone. I will wait in the hall. Tell me when it's okay to come in." He slid the phone across his desk and left.

Mary pushed the buttons and dialed Justin at work. She didn't let on that she was ill. She just asked him if he could meet her at the doctor's office because the results were in and she wanted him to be there with her for the news. He had no idea she was already there.

"I'll be there in twenty minutes. Is that too soon? Do you need me to come by and get you first?" he asked.

"Twenty minutes is great, and no, I need to do some errands afterward, so you don't have to come get me. My mom is here watching the kids, so I'm leaving now," she lied. "See you soon. I love you, Justin."

"I love you, too, Mary. I just have to make one phone call and I'll be there."

As soon as they hung up, Mary opened the door and told Dr. Hendricks she was through.

"I need to go freshen up a bit. I'll be right back," she said and headed for the bathroom.

When Kyle returned to his office, his receptionist told him he had a phone call.

"Justin Burgoff is on line two," she said, and his heart sank.

The doctor gathered his thoughts and then picked up the phone.

"Justin, how are you?" he asked more chipper than he felt.

"I'm fine, doctor. Mary just called me and said the results are in from all her tests. She wants me to meet her at your office. Can you tell me anything before I get there, so I can prepare myself, just in case?"

"I have to go by her wishes, Justin. She wants to be here so I can tell you both together. I'm sorry, but it's policy that I do this her way," Dr. Hendricks informed him.

"Oh, I understand. I was just hoping that if it was something a little worse than was expected, that I would be able to comfort her better because I already knew."

"That makes sense, but I can't. I am more sorry than I can say," he told him. "I will see you in a few minutes."

The conversation struck Justin as a bit odd, especially with the doctor's last comment about how sorry he was. But he decided it was nothing and put it out of his mind. It had to be Mary's lack of iron and that the kids were probably just too much to handle. He vowed to get her some help at home and would make a phone call as soon as he got back to his office.

Twenty minutes later, the couple sat in the office of Dr. Kyle Hendricks and waited. When Kyle walked in with a folder in his hand and a solemn look on his face, Justin immediately became uncomfortable. It appeared to him that this was more than just an informative meeting and that his wife might need a lot more than vitamins and iron to make her well.

Mary decided she needed to be the one to break the news. She took her husband's hand and looked into his eyes.

"Justin, I've been here all morning, and I found out the results of the tests. Dr. Hendricks followed my wishes to tell me first. Then he insisted that you be here, too. Now there is something I need to tell you," she said as tears filled her eyes.

After Mary broke the tragic news, Dr. Hendricks took over the conversation, giving them options and telling them how much time he thought she might have left.

"At this point, I don't know if radiation or chemotherapy would be of any value, but that is always an alternative. It could very well give you a little more time, but it would be a painful and very tiring ordeal. If I had to make a guess, because of where the cancer has spread, I would say that you have no more than three months. I can't tell you both how sorry I am that this wasn't found earlier. But there were no signs, and obviously Mary didn't say anything either," the doctor said sadly.

"You mean to say that my wife won't be here for the holidays?" Justin asked, trying hard to comprehend it all.

"I don't have a crystal ball, Justin. I can only tell you what the tests show me as a doctor. The rest is up to God," he answered.

"But how can this be? Why would God be so gracious and give us another chance with a new family, then take it all away like this? That doesn't make sense!" he yelled.

"Justin, please. It's okay. I am really okay with this," Mary interrupted, surprising even herself. "God knows what we are dealing with, and we really don't have much choice but to leave it in His hands. He knows what He is doing! He must."

"I need to get out of here. Let's go, Mary! You can ride with me. We'll come back for your car later. We need to go see Mike," her husband stated firmly. Pastor Mike Greene seemed to be the only one they could rely on lately. "Thank you, Dr. Hendricks. Just so you know, we don't plan to just give in to any of this," Justin said with more determination than he felt.

"I'll do whatever you want, Justin. You just let me know. I will back you one hundred percent whatever you guys decide."

Justin could not get out of there fast enough. He felt smothered and claustrophobic, and he needed air desperately. When they reached his truck and climbed inside all his strength and determination vanished. He broke down and cried like a baby.

"Oh God, how can this be happening?" he sobbed, holding his wife closely. "Mary, I won't let you go. I can't. We need to fight this together. We have babies who need you. I need you. Please, don't leave me! Please, don't ever leave me!" he begged over and over.

Mary held her husband close as they sat in the truck and cried together. A short while later, they entered the church and headed toward the back to Mike Greene's office. Susan looked up from her desk and knew immediately that something was terribly wrong.

"Is the pastor available?" Mary asked.

"I'm sure he is, for you. Let me tell him you're both here." Susan was only gone for a minute. When she came back, Mike was right behind her.

"Hey, you guys. Come in," he said, holding the door open. When the couple sat down, they could longer hold back their grief.

"Oh, Mike!" Mary wailed, covering her face with her hands.

"What's going on? Is it the kids? Are they okay? Are you?" the pastor asked.

"We just came from Dr. Hendrick's office. He told us that Mary has terminal cancer and that she probably only has three months to live! How can God do this to us again, Mike? How much does He think we can take?" Justin pleaded.

"Oh, my! This is absolutely unbelievable! I am so sorry. But you can't let any of this change what you know, no matter how hopeless it seems right now. But before we get into any of that, tell me exactly what the doctor said." Mike was calm, trying not to jump to any conclusions.

For the next twenty minutes, the distraught couple explained what they had been told only an hour before. Now, they desperately needed answers.

"How does our God work, Mike?" Mary asked. "It seems the more I try to understand His ways, the more sorrow He gives us. After our loss, God was so gracious to bring us together and allow us to have children once again. Justin and I did everything He asked and expected of us as Christians. We followed His word and shared the Gospel like the Bible says. Then, only with His grace, we were finally able to enjoy our little babies without the guilt of losing our daughters. And now this! How can God be so cruel and take all this away? What have we done so wrong that He continues to let this stuff happen?" she sobbed.

"Mary, you haven't done anything wrong. God knows everything you're going through! You must not be afraid or lose hope. He is on your side, and will never leave you in your time of need just like He promised when your daughters were taken. He got you through it, and He will this time again. God hasn't singled you or Justin out! There is a reason for all of this. And maybe someday you will know what it is. Just don't lose your faith. All of this means something, I promise. That is why it is so important for us to do all we can to share the hope and love of Jesus with everyone we know. One day, at a time only God knows, He will bring an end to this world as we know it. Our job as Christians is to be prepared and to do whatever we are able to do to help others be prepared. With this new challenge you're facing, you can be sure that God will use it for His glory. No matter what happens, He will be there. When challenges, illness, or tragedies fall on any of us, could He stop it? Sure He could! But you have to know that if He doesn't, He has a darn good reason for it," Mike reminded them.

"So, if God already knew all of this, do we just ignore it? Should we just succumb to her illness and not even bother with any of the remedies that may be able to help?" Justin asked, sounding as desperate as he felt.

"If Dr. Hendricks thinks there is something she should do, then by all means do it. These doctors are gifts from God! We need to remember it is God who gives them all the skills they need to help us heal. He gave these doctors the knowledge and wisdom to make us better. Without their ability to operate and medicate, there would be a lot more sickness and deaths in this world." It always angered Mike when he heard about certain religions that were forbidden to seek the help of doctors. How could these people just sit back and do nothing and watch their loved ones suffer or die? How sad for them, he thought.

"We don't know yet if there is anything that can help," Justin explained. "But we will do whatever it takes. The doctor mentioned radiation and chemotherapy, but he didn't seem very keen on either one. He thinks Mary is too far along in her illness for anything to help, but he said he would do whatever we decided."

"Then we have to pray, and then wait and see what the choices are. The most important thing now is that you don't give up. Don't let the fear of the unknown drive you to making the wrong decision. Give this to God and let

Him handle it! He's the only One who will do it right!" Mike assured them.

As it turned out, Mary didn't go through radiation or chemo. Her cancer had spread too much for either one to make a difference. Mary and Justin knew that any treatment at this stage would be difficult to recover from, which would leave Mary too tired to enjoy what time she had left with her family. They opted for putting her on medication and praying every day for another day. In the end, having more days together was all that really mattered anyway. Mary felt incredibly blessed that she made it through Christmas and was able to spend it with her family.

Justin remained strong, at least in front of Mary. He still went to work, but only once or twice a week when it was absolutely necessary, and even then he only went at Mary's insistence. Helen came over to help with the kids when he was gone, but Justin couldn't stay away for long. He knew he was on borrowed time, and he wanted to spend as much time with his wife as he could.

Occasionally, Justin broke down, but she never saw him. He always did it alone in the basement or at his office. But in all the months since they found out Mary was sick, he never gave up hope. When her pain became unbearable, Justin prayed daily, sometimes hourly, to take away her burden and let her be at peace.

"Father God, I know there is a reason for all of this, and I will accept and respect Your will, whatever that may be. I know that Your plan will be revealed in Your time, not mine. Until then, Father, please keep me strong for Mary. My only request now is that You make her last days on earth as comfortable as possible. Lift this pain from her, Lord. Give her peace and hold her in Your arms until I can be with her again."

Chapter Twelve

As Mary grew weaker, her spirit and faith grew stronger than ever. She was able to reflect on all that life had been to her and her family as she spent her days resting in the den. Her life was so perfect in the beginning, or so she thought. But thinking back now, it was never really complete until she found God.

When she first separated from Justin, God was there to make sure she got through it. Then when she lost her daughters, He was there once again, with all His strength and love, showing her the way, helping her to cope, and giving her hope. She knew that what she was going through now was His plan all along. It was for His purpose that she had lived in His grace and mercy in the first place. She felt her life had been blessed beyond all expectations.

Early Friday afternoon just after Christmas, Mary was once again resting in the over–stuffed chair in her husband's den. Evidence of her love was everywhere in the room, which had been decorated with her special creative touch and décor, splashed with brightly colored pillows, knick–knacks, and rugs. It was the most used room in the house. Justin sat at her feet. Kelly Oliver Rubin; Kelly's husband, Dr. Keith Rubin; and Mike Green were present, as well as both sets of parents. Her precious children played quietly on the floor.

Mary asked for their attention as she rustled with the note in her hand.

"I need to talk to all of you," she murmured softly. Her health had rapidly declined since Thanksgiving, and she was grateful to have made it this far. "I have written a little something that I need to share with you. So if you can bear with me for just a few minutes, I'd like to read it. I have come to terms with my illness, and I am finally able to understand why all of this had to happen. But I admit it took me awhile to put it all together. When Justin and I had separated that time, I was so lost. But I realized I needed to be in order to hear God calling me. He took me in with open arms, and He got me through it. Then, just as our relationship was on the mend and as I grew closer in my walk with Jesus, we lost our daughters. I can't even begin to tell you what that did to my faith." Mary looked over at her friend, Kelly, and smiled.

"I'm ashamed to say I didn't handle it very well. To date, that was the hardest thing I ever had to go through. I was so angry and bitter, first blaming God, then Justin, and then both of them. But, even as much as I struggled with the anger, I felt this urgency inside that I needed to understand it better. I begged and cried out, and somewhere in the midst of it all, God heard me again. I learned that He had a plan, as He does for all of us, and all that we were going through was part of that plan. I may not understand His ways, but recently I have been more willing to accept them. And through our incredibly tragic loss, Justin and I became firm believers in our Father and in Jesus Christ as our Savior.

"For the past few years, the two of us have been reaching out and ministering to anyone and everyone who we come into contact with. We tell them how to open their hearts to know Jesus better and let them know how much He loves them. We share our testimony, and let them know that we could never have made it through our loss without His strength. He gave us the courage, comfort, and peace we needed to go on. Then, by the grace of God, these precious little babies were born and life was good again!" she beamed proudly.

"Then lo and behold, I got sick. What a difference it is when you're the one dying. I was very confused, to say the least. I kept wondering what happened to the original plan God had for me? Was I done? Wasn't I supposed to be telling the world how great our Father is and that Jesus died for them? Shouldn't I keep teaching others how they should be living, no matter what their circumstances? When God gave us this latest challenge, I didn't know what to think or what to do. Then one night, Justin and I got on our knees and prayed like we never prayed before. We prayed over and over again, and begged God to give us the answers. And miraculously He did just that! But it wasn't what we expected at all, which is pretty normal when we're dealing with God's plan and will for us. He always has a way of making a bad situation better and more suitable for His needs.

"For the past two years I have been incredibly blessed by helping others get through their struggles and showing them how to live their lives for Jesus. But, now all that has changed. Instead of me showing them how they're supposed to live, God has decided He wants me to show them how to die. He wants me to do it with complete faith and trust in Him. And that is what

I will do." A sob escaped the young mother's lips as she looked down at her children. Justin took her hand and held it tight. The scene was a somber one as everyone watched with tears flooding their vision and sorrow tugging at their hearts.

"I'd be so scared right now if it weren't for my faith. I know where I am going when this is all over, and it is very comforting to me. It should be for all of you, too. Please, don't cry. You'll make me start crying, and I don't want to any more. I am really okay with all of this, I promise. I know my babies will be just fine. With all of you taking care of them, how can they not be? I know you will never let them forget me, even though they are too young right now. They will grow up knowing that I loved them more than anything in the world! I thank God for all He has done, sending me all of you, especially you, Justin. I could not have done any of this without your unconditional love and support, nor would I have wanted to. Thank you, sweetheart. And Mom and Dad, and Audrey and Phil, you've been the best grandparents to all our children and so good and supportive to us. And you, Kelly, there are no words that can describe what you have been to me. You were my rock when I needed one the most. And Pastor Mike, what a wonderful friend you have been. You've helped us to stay focused on what is really important. Thank you for everything, all of you.

"I know my time is running out, and I needed to tell you all of this while I still could. I want to go with dignity and be as courageous as God allows me to be. I will see you again someday, when we're all in heaven. And when you get there, it shouldn't take you too long to find me. I'll be the one playing in the sandbox… with Skylar and Amy!"

Mary let her tears fall freely down her cheeks. She no longer tried to stop them. She hoped that her friends and family would always remember her. But not in a sad way, in the way that God intended—that she was here on earth for His purpose. When that was carried out, she knew His plan was complete.

Two days later, Justin woke to the sound of gurgling. It was coming from the other side of the bed.

"Mary, are you okay, honey?" he asked his wife. But she didn't answer.

She didn't have the strength. Her eyes were open, but he could barely detect any breathing. Justin knew what was coming next, and he prepared himself. He crawled over beside his still beautiful wife and held her closely to him, vowing to never let go until her last breath filled her lungs and escaped her lips.

"I'm here, Mary. I'm with you. It's okay, my love. Soon everything will be okay and you won't have to worry or hurt anymore. Don't ever forget how very much I love you. I will always love you. Hug my little girls for me!" he whispered softly.

As she lay in her bed watching the curtains blow in the breeze, Mary felt the life slowly drain from her frail body. She knew it was time and she was ready to go. In the distance there was a light. It was the brightest, yet most comforting light she had ever seen. But it didn't hurt her eyes like she first thought. Mary reached out and waited until she felt the warmth and peace rush through her. Then she was quickly enveloped in a love she never knew existed.

She moved forward ever so humbly toward the glowing mass ahead. Just as she crossed over into the divine realm of eternity, Mary became aware of all the thousands of colors, magnified to perfection, crystal clear, and brighter than anything she had ever seen before. It was much too beautiful to describe with only the earthly words she had once known.

As she searched in awesome wonder of the heavenly grounds, Mary looked over and noticed two young children at play. When they saw her, they stopped what they were doing and ran toward her calling out her name, the only name they ever knew her to be…"Mommy!"

Andy Lynch

Thirty–three–year–old Andy Lynch had finally made it big. He was the king of the screen and the most sought–after actor in Hollywood. He was also one of the kindest, most caring men in the movie industry. Andy gave thousands of dollars every year to hundreds of different charity organizations all over the world.

When he first came to Hollywood in his early twenties, Andy began his new career by playing in several sitcoms. Then his agent got him bit parts on made–for–television movies and the small screen. But his public wanted more! The megastar soon reached the top of the popularity charts, starring in more than twenty major motion pictures and having three Oscars to his credit.

Andy had been a confirmed bachelor up until he was thirty two. But all that changed when he met twenty–six–year–old Meagan Marini, star of stage and screen, and designer of her own clothing line. Meagan was gorgeous, tall, and very good to Andy. A short eight months later they were married. They made the perfect couple.

Shortly after taking their vows, the twosome joined the Church of Scientology, which was the choice of many celebrities in Hollywood. Its claim to offer a clear, bright insight to help individuals blaze towards their mind's full potential attracted the two. Believing whole–heartedly that all of life's difficulties and contradictions were due to occurrences from past lives was very appealing. Andy and Meagan desperately craved direction, answers, and purpose, and this particular "church" filled that need for them. It also contradicted everything that Andy had been taught as a child. But for him, this new way of studying religion made much more sense and also fit into his lifestyle better. "What could be the harm?" he thought.

A few years later, Andy realized how wrong his choice had been. That early Sunday morning after Christmas, on the set of what turned out to be his last movie, the young star suffered a massive heart attack. Andy was rushed to the nearest hospital and immediately put on life support. His diagnosis was not good, but the verdict for afterlife was worse than he ever imagined…

Chapter One

The downtown area was lit up with more than a dozen high–wattage spotlights placed from one end of the street to the other, blazing their way upward into the darkened skies overhead. It was quite apparent that something big was going on. The roped–off area was packed with fans from all over the world.

Cameras were flashing, people were screaming, and hearts were pounding. It was the biggest movie premiere of the year, and America's hero of the film industry was its star. Thousands of loyal fans pushed and fought their way towards the red carpet, trying to get a closer look at their idol. Security was tight in front of the theatre as Andy Lynch exited the stretch limousine with his wife, Meagan Marini, on his arm. The crowd went wild as they screamed out his name.

"Andy, Andy, over here!"

"You're my hero, Andy!"

"I love you, Andy! Will you marry me?"

"Can I have your autograph, Andy?"

This scene was a familiar one to the superstar. But even after more than ten years in the business, it never got old. Andy was always very cordial and appreciative to all the people who continually showed up for these premieres and other special events. It was the fans who paid the money to watch his movies, and it was the fans who kept him at the top of his profession. So even when some of them tried to get too close, he didn't get upset. In fact, Andy really didn't mind it at all.

Andrew Michael Lynch grew up in the small town of Carthage, Texas, near the Louisiana border. His father, George, was the senior pastor at His Word Christian Church, one of the largest churches within a fifty–mile radius. His mother, Ellen, was a second grade teacher. She also taught Sunday school in her husband's church every week for twenty years.

As a young boy, Andy read the Bible every day and memorized many Scriptures. He believed there was a God and was told all about His Son, Jesus. But the thought of Satan scared him straight. When Andy was twelve years old, he heard one his father's sermons, a sermon which had the most impact on him growing up. It was what kept the young man in line.

That week the message was titled "*Spiritual Warfare: The Prince of Darkness...Hollywood or Foe?*" as part of Pastor George Lynch's continuing series on The Power to Persevere.

Andy sat in the front row as he always had since he was just a toddler. He preferred to attend the church service rather than to go to Sunday school with the other kids his age. He became a symbol, of sort, to many of the faithful churchgoers.

When the music ended, Pastor George Lynch stepped to the podium.

"Good morning, everyone. C.S. Lewis once said, 'there are two equal and opposite errors into which our race can fall about the devils. One is to disbelieve in their existence. The other is to believe and to feel an excessive and unhealthy interest in them. They themselves are equally pleased by both errors, and hail a materialist or a magician with the same delight.'

"There is an increasing fascination with the dark side in our world today! Let me show you what people are watching on the big screen and even TV. *The Sixth Sense*: 'I see people. I see dead people.' *The Blair Witch Project*: 'I'm sorry to everyone. I was very naïve!' *The Cell*: 'You can control how you see yourself, but the rest is up to him!' *The X Files*: 'The truth is out there!'

"I want to start by simply asking you a series of questions," Pastor Lynch said to his congregation that Sunday. "If there is enough food in the world to feed every man, woman, and child three meals a day, why doesn't that happen? Don't answer... just listen. In an educated society, why are our prison systems busting out at the seams? Why are so many people involved in self-destructive patterns? And why is there so much evil in the world?

"The answer from Scripture is that Satan and his kingdom have been waging war against God, against God's purposes, and against God's people ever since his unsuccessful coup attempt ages ago!

"Now, let me ask you another question. What is spiritual warfare? This is an important question because 'spiritual warfare' means different things to different people. The term itself is not found in the Scriptures, but the concept is taught. The Apostle Paul wrote two of the most commonly associated passages. You'll find them in II Corinthians 10:3–5, 'For though we live in the world, we do not wage war as the world does. The weapons we fight with are not the weapons of the world. On the contrary, they have divine power to demolish strongholds. We demolish arguments and every pretense that sets itself up against the knowledge of God, and we take captive every thought to make it obedient to Christ.' And also in Ephesians 6:10–12, 'Finally, be strong in the Lord and in His mighty power. Put on the full armor of God so that you can take your stand against the devil's schemes. For our struggle is not against the flesh and blood, but against the rulers, against the authorities, against the powers of this dark world and against the spiritual forces of evil in heavenly realms.'

"Satan is our adversary. He is a created being and a fallen creature. He seeks to be like God and even tries to impersonate Him. He is known by many names: Satan, Lucifer, Beelzebub, the devil, ancient serpent, dragon, the evil one, and many more. He is evil in his character! He is a murderer and a liar. He is known as the father of lies in John 8:44. In John 10:10 he is a thief, who tries to steal, kill, and destroy. But he is limited in his powers. Romans 8:38–39 tells us that Satan can never separate the true believer from the love of God. Nor can he keep God's grace from being extended to the believer. God's people are able to overcome the activity of Satan even as he tempts, tricks, and torments us. Satan's business is not so much in scaring us to death as it is persuading us that the danger of a spiritual fall is minimal! He promises the best but pays with the worst; he promises honor and pays with disgrace; he promises pleasure and pays with pain; he promises profit and pays with loss; and he promises life and pays with death!

"Look in I Peter 5:8. It reads: 'Be careful! Watch out for attacks from the devil, your great enemy. He prowls around like a roaring lion, looking for some victim to devour.' His most powerful tool is discouragement though he has many others like shame, pride, confusion, deception, conflict, and fear!

"There are two big lies that Satan has been perpetuating ever since the Garden of Eden. The first is that God is mean, vindictive, a spoilsport whose main role in life is to keep us from being fulfilled and happy. When we step out of bounds, He takes delight in making us pay.

"The second lie is that God really doesn't care what we do and probably doesn't know either. And if He does, His business is to forgive us. He'll always forgive no matter what, so it really doesn't make much difference how we live and what we believe.

"But Satan's pitfall is the believer's trust in God! It's prayer! The devil hates it when we pray. James 4:6–8 says, '…as the Scriptures say, "God sets Himself against the proud, but He shows favor to the humble." So humble yourselves before God. Resist the devil, and he will flee from you. Draw close to God, and God will draw close to you. Wash your hands, you sinners; purify your hearts, you hypocrites.'

"When I was in high school, I never got in one fight. The reason was simple. My best friend was 6' 5" —and a shot putter! My friends, you are no match for Satan. When he wants to fight you, just run to your elder Brother who is more than a match for all the demons in hell! Our spiritual warfare is prayer, identity, and truth. It's how we fight the fight! If we use prayer, identity, and truth, we can and will win every time! Let's pray.

"Father, we are sometimes so weak. We know that it doesn't take too much for Satan to work his deception and evil into our lives. Whenever things don't go the way we expect or when someone says something to hurt or offend us, we are all targets for Satan and his corrupt, deceiving ways. Please, Father, protect us all. Cover us in Your coat of armor. We can't do anything without Your love and mercy over us. Put Your hand on all of us and guide us through each day safely and in Your grace. We ask these things in Your Son's mighty name. Amen.

"Thanks for coming today, everyone. We'll see you next week." And with that George exited the stage and joined his wife and son at the entrance of the church to say his good-byes.

From that day forward, young Andy Lynch was more terrified of Satan and what he could do to destroy and devour mankind than anything God could ever do. After all, God was good, and Satan was evil.

Chapter Two

Throughout his adolescence and teens, Andy never missed a Sunday service that his father preached. He was his parents' pride and joy. He never gave them any trouble even after he entered high school. After graduation, Andy attended a Bible college in nearby Marshall, Texas, with every intention of becoming a pastor like his father and grandfather before him. But during a summer break in his second year, twenty–year–old Andy Lynch took a trip to Southern California to visit his aunt for a month. It was a trip that changed his life forever.

One afternoon several of his cousins and their friends were hanging out at the beach playing an intense game of volleyball. With his baby–face good looks, wavy black hair, and dark complexion, Andy stood out among his peers. Everyone noticed the tall, handsomely proportioned athlete, especially one man in particular. His name was Rudy Begossi, the most famous agent in Hollywood.

Rudy was amazed as he watched Andy interact with everyone around him. Andy had a certain charm and magnetism and spoke in a slight Southern drawl, leaving behind a touch of refreshing innocence that was rarely seen in that part of the country. He left the girls speechless and the boys in awe.

Later that same day, Rudy approached the young stranger in hopes that he could persuade him into possibly doing a screen test. But in less than twenty minutes of conversation, the trained eye of the agent realized that Andy wouldn't need one. The young man had exactly what it took to be a star. After nearly two hours of interviewing, Rudy handed Andy his card.

"You're just what America has been looking for, son. If you move to L.A., I can make you a household name in less than a year. And I will make you the biggest star in Hollywood since Clark Gable before you turn thirty," the agent promised.

"Clark who?" Andy asked innocently.

"It doesn't matter. I keep forgetting this generation has never heard about so many of the great ones. Just mark my words, Andy. If you come back and follow my lead, you will have everything you have ever dreamed of and then some." Rudy tried not to show his excitement, but he knew he was standing in front of a gold mine.

"But I don't know if I want to be a big star. I never thought about it before," Andy told him honestly. "Besides, my dad would be so disappointed. He wants me to follow in his footsteps and take over the church where he is the pastor. I just always thought that was my calling."

"Andy, think about it. You'd be making millions of dollars a year! If your calling is to help the less fortunate, you could give money away to thousands of needy people all over the world and still have plenty for yourself. As a pastor, you could never make that kind of money. You'd be much more powerful having the ability to help all those people as opposed to only a few of them somewhere in a desolate corner of Texas," Rudy tried to explain.

Andy's cousins, who were standing close enough to hear the conversation, suddenly felt compelled to give their opinion.

"Come on, Andy. Take the offer," one of them said.

"Yeah, Andy. Stay here with us and become a star. You could help everyone with the money you'd be making, especially me!" said another.

"Your folks would understand. They'd want what you want, Andy. Go for it!"

It didn't take a great deal of encouraging for the soon–to–be actor to take the bait. He was reeled in hook, line… and paycheck. Just before boarding the flight home, Andy signed a three–year contract with Rudy's company, Nightingale Productions, for $100,000 a year. He was bound by the contract to return within three weeks, and even though he was uncertain of his future, Andy Lynch suddenly felt a burst of excitement he had never known before. This exuberant feeling of power and security stayed with him until the wheels of the jet touched down on the tarmac in Shreveport, Louisiana. That was when Andy realized that he still had to face his dad and try to convince him that the choice he made was the right one.

George and Ellen Lynch were waiting curbside in the car when Andy walked out. They sensed something different immediately. Yet even with the phone call warning them of their son's surprising decision, Andy's parents were caught completely off guard.

"How was your trip, son?" his father asked trying hard not to notice the boy's cocky new demeanor.

"It was great, Dad. Probably the best time I have ever had," he told him honestly. But as hard as he tried, he couldn't look either one of them in the eyes.

"Andy, it's okay. We already know," his mother said, trying to ease some of his guilt. "Let's talk about this when we get home."

The rest of the drive was mostly small talk. Few words and little laughter filled the space between the front and back seat of the car. One hour later, they arrived home and gathered in the living room where they normally had their family talks. Ellen picked up the conversation where she left off.

"Aunt Judy called last night and told us what happened. Andy, before we get into any of this, please know that we want what you want. But we also want the best for you. Only God can do this. He has a plan for you and it is very special. I don't know if taking this movie offer is what His plan and purpose is for you, but it has to be your decision, not ours." Ellen was normally quite strong and rarely emotional. But this took its toll on her heart and the tears poured heavily down her cheeks.

"Mom, Dad, I really do believe this is God's will for me. Why else would the timing be so perfect? It was my first trip anywhere! I never knew I wanted to act. I never even thought about it before. And then all of this happens. It's like it was planned all along. My agent, Rudy, really opened my eyes and showed me what I could be if I wanted. He also said that with the money I'd be making someday, that I could help thousands of causes all over the world, instead of just here in Carthage. I couldn't do that being a pastor."

"No, you're right. A pastor doesn't make as much as a movie star. But he has riches more powerful and satisfying than all the money in the world.

All that green stuff can be as evil as it is good, Andy. You have to know how to handle it. I just pray that what your mother and I have instilled in you over the years about the Bible will stay with you through all of this and that you never forget where you came from and where you belong. But no matter what you do, I don't think I will ever understand how you could change your dream so quickly," George said sadly.

"I don't think it was as much my dream as it was your dream for me, Dad. I wanted to please you so much. I thought by being a pastor like you that it would. But I don't remember it ever really being a dream of mine." As much as Andy's words stung, his parents appreciated his honesty.

"I can accept what you're saying. But I just have to know that this is totally your decision and not your agent's and what he can make off of you. We all make mistakes and bad choices in our life, son. But there is a lesson learned in every one of them if we seek God's will for us. Every time we fall, He is always there to pick us up if we ask. But regrets can be a whole other ball game. I just don't want this decision of yours to be a regret, that's all. Make sure it's what you want and no one else and that you're doing it for the right reasons." George still couldn't believe what was happening.

"If we were having this conversation last month, I might have had a different response. But today I can honestly say that this is my decision and my choice. Let the chips fall where they may. If this ends up being the worst mistake of my life, I can live with that. I don't want any regrets either, Dad. But I feel if I don't at least give this a shot, someday I might really regret it. I couldn't live with knowing that God practically put this opportunity on a silver platter for me and I blew it off."

"How can you be so sure it's from God, Andy?" his mother asked curiously.

"Mom, how could it not be? The whole thing fell into place too perfectly. I'd be foolish not to think it was His doing."

"Andy, don't be so naïve," his dad interrupted. "You know that Satan has powers, too. He could be trying to lure you away from what God wants, which would stop you from being a pastor and spreading the good word of

Jesus Christ. It's what he does best. This could very well be his doings and not God's," George said, trying hard to reason with his star–struck son.

"I don't think so, Dad. I really want this, and I truly believe it is a godsend. Besides, if you look at how many people I can help this way, how can that be from Satan? He certainly doesn't want me helping anyone! That would be a good thing, and he doesn't do good things."

"Very well. I won't argue with you anymore. If this is what you want, then so be it. We love you, and we will stand by your decision. But please don't go out there and act like all those high society snobs who get caught up in the power, glamour, and lust of Hollywood. You're better than that, Andy. Always remember that you are a child of God and you're welcome back here any time. There will always be a place at the pulpit for you if you ever change your mind." George walked over to his son and held him hard against his chest. His doubts were strong that this was God's will for him, but he knew that Andy's mind was made up. All he could do now was pray that God would watch over him in Hollywood, as He would have in Carthage, Texas.

Before Andy left for California, he said good–bye to all his friends and family with the promise to return as soon as he could, but he never made it back. This was the last time Andy was in his hometown, and the first of many promises he neglected to keep.

When Andy first arrived in California, he felt out of place. He missed his friends and family and called home every day. He wasn't sure if he made the right decision by coming, but he didn't want to give up just yet. Andy decided to stay and give this new life a try. After all, how bad could it be? He had everything he needed at his fingertips and the promise of fortune and fame in his future. But he still needed to be reassured that he had made the right choice. Andy turned to the only person he trusted… his father.

"I miss you and Mom," he said over the phone one night a few months after he arrived.

"We miss you, too, Andy," George replied, fighting back his tears. "How is it going so far?"

"It's okay. I made the rounds at the studio today and met a lot of pretty important and very influential people. But it sure isn't Carthage," he laughed.

"No, I wouldn't think it was even close!"

"Dad, be honest with me. Do you think I've done the right thing by coming out here? I know it was my decision, but I really want your approval. I trust you more than anyone I have ever known, but you're not saying too much about any of this," Andy stated somewhat confused.

"I can't say if your decision was the right thing or not. I already told you. If you truly feel this was the Lord's calling, how can I tell you it isn't? We all hear His voice in different ways. If you heard Him leading you there, then He must have a plan for you. Just make sure you keep your eyes and ears open to His words. Sometimes we get led down a path that we think is God, and it turns out to be our own fleshly desires. All I ask is that you be careful, and make sure you pray with every move you make. God will reveal His divine plan for you and let you know if it is His will. And don't do anything if you're not sure!" George advised. He knew he had to let his son make his own mistakes.

"Right now I don't feel too sure about anything, but I want to see where this goes. If I still feel uncertain about my choice in a year from now, I am coming home. I think that should be enough time for Mr. Begossi to make something out of me."

"Andy, my boy, you are already something very important. Don't ever forget that. But if fame is what you're seeking, all I ask is that you keep your eyes on Jesus, no matter what happens in the next twelve months." George knew that his son was confused, and he wanted so much to just tell him to come home. But he knew it had to be Andy's decision.

That first year went by quickly, and Andy made his mark on the streets of Sunset Boulevard. His stardom rose rapidly with each appearance, whether starring in his own television show or playing a small part in a big movie. As his popularity grew, so did his bank account. Soon Carthage, Texas, was just a faded memory in the young actor's mind.

Rudy Begossi knew what the fans wanted and he gave it to them as quickly as he could, which put money in his pocket and gave massive power to his young client's ego. It was only a matter of time before Andy gave up all that he had been taught, burying all his Christian beliefs somewhere in the desert sand near his Hollywood Hills estate.

Chapter Three

Andy soon adapted well to his new life. He had all the dates he wanted and more money than he ever dreamed of. But even with all that he had acquired—his mansion, furnishings, and bank account—Andy was still not totally satisfied. He never remembered being this way before he came to California. But, as hard as he tried, he could not put his finger on the problem. He continued to call home for advice.

"I don't understand any of this, Dad. I have everything I have ever dreamed of and so much more, but it doesn't seem to fill the gap. I don't know why I still feel so incomplete. I crave something, yet I can't put my finger on what the problem is. What should I do?" he asked his father one night after his appearance on a local talk show.

"I can only surmise that your incompleteness is directly related to your lack of fellowship and knowing who to turn to in a time like this. It isn't me that you should be asking. It's God. He is the only One who can give you comfort and peace and fill that emptiness you're feeling. You have distanced yourself lately, ever since you left here. I know it's different out there, but Jesus hasn't changed or left. He is right there if you call on Him," George explained, trying hard to help his son keep his faith.

"I don't know if that's the reason, but it's sure confusing. One thing is for sure. It's hard to stay focused on God out here, because of all the other distractions—all the parties that you have to attend, not to mention all the premieres and fund–raisers. It gets pretty overwhelming at times. These people don't put a great deal of importance on God or His Kingdom. It's scary, but true. I've tried not to get sucked into any of this secular stuff, but, Dad, to be honest, it's really hard not to fall out of balance. There are so many other religions out here that it gets confusing, to put it mildly. I find myself being drawn to some of them just because they make so much sense. No wonder Hollywood is so lost. But I know I can make a difference if I can just get my foot in the door as a respected actor. Right now they still consider me too young and very wet behind the ears. So it may take me a while, but I feel real strongly about this." Andy was determined to shake the Hollywood scene and continue his work for the God he grew up to believe in.

"It sounds like you know what you're doing, Andy. I'm very proud of you. If you can just stick it out and not get caught up in all the sin, you will make it. Just keep praying for your heart to be filled with His love and peace, and you should be fine. If you need anything, I am always here for you," his dad told him, and he meant every word.

"Thanks, Dad. I love you. Tell Mom I love and miss her, too. I will talk to you soon," Andy said. Unfortunately, these were the last words he shared with his dad about God and sadly the last words he spoke that remotely related to Christianity.

The next time Andy called his parents was after he made his first big movie. He didn't even sound like the boy who left home a short time before.

"Whasup, Dad? How be everything out there in your world?" he asked in a slang he had never used before.

"It's going really well, son. It's been almost nine months since we've talked to you. You sound different. How are you holding up?" George asked, but he could tell in the tone of Andy's voice that he had changed.

"Totally awesome! I am having a ball and making a bundle of greens. I'll send you some for the church and maybe even a little extra so you can take Mom somewhere really cool," Andy said proudly.

"I'd rather have you home. We haven't seen you since you left over a year ago. Do you plan to come back anytime soon?" his father asked.

"I doubt it! I'm going crazy with all the appearances I have to attend on late night television to promote my movie. Well, it's my first big movie anyway, but I still need to be around. I'll be heading to New York next week, but I don't see me getting away to come to Carthage. It's just not feasible right now." Andy never gave any indication that he missed his parents.

"Well, we think about you all the time. We see your picture everywhere. Are you still trying to spread God's Word out there to all those Hollywood heathens, or have you given up?" his dad asked curiously.

"Oh, they don't want to hear any of that stuff. I figured that out a long time ago. There's too much to think about with all the contracts and movie deals, so I don't have a lot of opportunity to do much of anything else. But don't worry, Dad. I'm still the same," Andy assured him. But George knew better.

Andy stayed in Hollywood, but over the next several years he wasn't strong enough to make his mark the way George had hoped. It was obvious to him that his son had finally turned into one of the elite Hollywood icons of his generation who turned his back on God. Andy stopped trying to find the peace and tranquility he so desperately sought when he first arrived. And with the passing of time, it seemed quite clear that Andy forgot he even needed it. More and more Andy began to seek material things for instant gratification and selfish satisfaction, which made him feel less desperate for peace and whatever else he thought he was missing.

Chapter Four

After many years of bachelorhood and dating, the megastar thought it might be a good time to start looking for steady companionship. He was tired of going home alone and hoped that this venture would fill a lingering void and make him happy.

Meagan Marini came from Connecticut, where she grew up an only child. She left home at eighteen with her dreams and $200 in her pocket, and she never looked back. She struggled for several years, ate lots of Spaghetti O's, but never gave up. In the end, it paid off.

Her first job was waiting tables at a small soda shop on the outskirts of Culver City. One afternoon Rudy Begossi walked in, hungry, tired, and very irritable. But when his eyes found the young beauty, his mood changed quickly. With flaming red hair hanging down to her shoulders and a face that turned every head in the room, she was hard not to notice.

"What can I get for you today?" Meagan asked. Her innocence was refreshing, to say the least.

"I… I… let me see your menu," Rudy babbled, unable to speak. He felt himself flush with embarrassment. He was rarely caught off guard by a pretty face, but clearly this one was different.

"The menu is on the wall, sir. Our special today is a club sandwich with avocado and a cup of cream of mushroom soup," she told him. Then leaning over, she whispered, "It's actually really good. I had some myself before I started my shift." Meagan had no idea who the stranger was, but she always tried to be friendly and helpful.

"You talked me into it. Put it on whole wheat and give me a cup of strong black coffee," he said, trying to regain his dignity. As she walked away, he turned his thoughts to what her talent might be and how he could get her to sign a contract, even if she couldn't act. He knew with her looks that she could very well become someone famous and extraordinary. It was his job to know this about people, and he was never wrong.

Though she liked her job as a waitress, Meagan was desperate for fame. It had been her passion and dream since childhood. As a little girl, she was always the "star" of the show, the hit of the neighborhood, whenever she and her friends put on their own "movie premiere." She even designed and made her own wardrobe for their backyard blockbusters. Meagan took that dream and passion with her when she came to Southern California. She had the drive and willpower to make it a reality, no matter what the cost.

Over the next few months, Rudy frequently visited the café. He was determined to see that his little prodigy was discovered and told her what he had in mind.

"I have several people who can help you get into theater. If you do a good job, that will only be the beginning of what could be a very successful career for both of us! Do you think you're ready for a live audience?" Rudy asked.

"Ready? I've been ready all my life! Let's do it!"

Meagan was thrilled at the prospect of being on stage. A short time later, she auditioned for and got the part in a small theatrical production, which lasted nearly a year. Meagan eventually was financially stable enough to leave her waitress job and devote all her time to acting. She spent several years doing theater where she eventually made her mark. The audience fell in love with her no matter what part she played.

As her popularity grew, Meagan decided it was time to bring out her other talent. She soon opened her own elegant and very unusual clothing line called M & M Designs, which she eventually sold exclusively to several shops on Rodeo Drive. The designer clothes became very popular among the rich and famous, and Meagan made quite a name for herself. But the young woman was not satisfied. She desperately wanted stardom on the big screen.

Her agent began pulling in all his resources and got Meagan small bit parts in several major motion pictures. A few years later, the young starlet got a major break when she was given the lead in the smash hit movie *Almost There* starring alongside Andy Lynch.

When Meagan first set eyes on the Hollywood hunk, she fell in love. She spent the next few months making sure he knew it. Soon they became an "item," promoting the buzz around Tinsel Town that wedding bells could be ringing at last for the confirmed bachelor. Eight months later the couple married.

Chapter Five

George Lynch couldn't get away from all the publicity surrounding his son. Everything Andy did was plastered in every magazine and newspaper across the country. George was barely able to make it to church in the morning without seeing his son's face on the cover of something. It broke his heart when he saw what Andy had become and what Hollywood had done to him. Though Andy was totally accountable for his actions, George thought he had taught Andy better than that. Through all the years his son had been gone, George hoped and prayed that he had given Andy a strong foundation, one that would prevent him from falling into the ways of the world and Satan's web of deceit. But it was not to be. Andy chose another direction, which was totally unacceptable to George and Ellen.

When they first heard that Andy and his new wife were members of the Church of Scientology, their hearts were crushed and their spirits were broken. They knew they could no longer support their son's ambitions and told him so the next time he called. It was against everything they believed. George talked while Ellen listened on the extension.

"I can't believe what you're doing to yourself! How can you even think that Scientology is the answer to prayer or salvation? It isn't the answer to anything, Andy. It's a cult! Your whole life here in Carthage was centered on your faith in Jesus Christ and what the Bible says. The Bible is the ultimate authority and the only book written by God. It's where you go for truth, not to that Dianetic's book! That book by Ron Hubbard is a farce, a lie! Someone who knows nothing about the One True God of the universe drives its whole concept. In fact, any religion that refers to any other book besides the Bible in their teachings is propagating a lie! And they're all going to hell on a bobsled!"

"Dad, wait… listen to me a…" Andy tried to interrupt, but George wouldn't let him.

"Did you know that Ron Hubbard thinks we were all gods in another life and that we can become gods again through some hocus–pocus ritual? How can you consciously believe any of that? Just because you have a bank account that most people would kill for, you think you have to go along with all those pagans out there in Hollywood and join this ridiculous mockery of a church because it's fashionable and popular. Well, I won't stand for it! It is not the way you were raised!" his father yelled.

"Dad, please, let me explain. I haven't forgotten anything that you've taught me. I just think we should open our eyes to other ways of doing God's work. There are hundreds of other religions all over the world, and we'd be crazy not to check some of them out. If the ways of Scientology work better for me, then why should it upset you? I'm still the same person I was when I left there twelve years ago," Andy said, trying hard to get his father to understand.

"You're not the same person, Andy. How can you even say that? Listen to yourself. I know how that cult operates. It's like all the other cults. I've read about them years ago. Scientologists prey on the young, the emotionally distraught, or those who are hurting or lost and looking for hope, especially the ones hooked on drugs. Then there are people like you who just want to throw their money away on unrealistic ideas and ridiculous theories because it's the 'in' thing to do. Whatever your reason is, it isn't acceptable. You know the truth. What's the matter with you? Have you lost your mind?"

"No, I haven't lost my mind, nor anything else. I just took another direction. It works for us, me and Meagan. It gives us answers that we never knew before."

"You never knew them because they aren't the truth, Andy!" George screamed into the phone.

"How do you know that for sure? How can you say that any of this isn't something God wants me to learn and then tell others about, too? Aren't we allowed to make our own choices?"

"Yes, Andy, God does allow us to make our own decisions, but He wants those decisions informed by Him. He wants you to follow what the Bible teaches, that the only way to salvation is through Jesus Christ. Don't you understand? You are making a decision that has grave consequences, maybe even eternal consequences. If you are a true believer, your heavenly Father will be forced to discipline you to put you back on the right path. And believe me, you don't want that! If you're not a true believer, then you are throwing away eternal life. Scientology members don't believe in creation or in heaven and hell. How do you explain that one? Where do you suppose all of them go when they die?"

"That's the beauty of it all, Dad. They don't die! They believe they are reincarnated and that they have many lives," his son told him. "And it's exactly what I need to believe. You know how I've always been deathly afraid of hell and of Satan, ever since I was really young? But Scientology people don't believe in hell, so this is perfect for me. Now I have no reason to be afraid anymore!"

"Andy, just because they don't believe in something, doesn't mean that it doesn't exist! What is wrong with you? Why are you so afraid of Satan, anyway? Don't you know that the wrath of God is far worse than anything Satan can do to you?"

"That's what you say, but how do you know that for sure? Besides, I need to believe that this is how it works—that there is no devil or hell or anything like that. It makes it a lot better for me and far less frightening!"

"But it isn't the truth, Andy! Use your head!" his father shouted. "Besides, if reincarnation were possible, then why did Jesus have to die on the cross? If you can just live your life over because you didn't do it right the first time, why did God send His Son to earth to save the world?" George could not believe he was having this conversation.

"Well, I don't know if I can answer that, Dad. I guess the way you put it, it would be senseless for Jesus to have come, if that is what He did."

"What do you mean, 'if'? The Bible tells us that is what He did! But your new religion doesn't believe that, do they? For some idiotic reason, they think that Jesus Christ was one of their thetans, a god of sort, in a past life. They believe He was 'cleared' so that He could regain His powers like all the rest of you, but you guys now have to use some sort of lie detector machine to accomplish this! What do you suppose they used two thousand years ago on Jesus to 'clear' Him? And a theory like this would totally erase what the Bible teaches. It would also put the Son of Man in the same category as you and me! How can you even begin to think that this is truth?"

"Because the way they explained it to us makes sense. It's called auditing, Dad. And the machine they use is an e–meter. It works like a lie detector and helps to remove all the engrams, which are, in a sense, mental blocks due to traumatic experiences we suffered in another life. It's sort of like going to confession. Once this is done, the psychic hindrances of our engrams are 'cleared.' I don't know what they used on Jesus, but I'll ask. I'm sure there is a perfectly good explanation. And yes, Scientology members do believe that we were gods in another life. But is that really so bad to believe that the world is full of many gods as opposed to just One? Wouldn't their way of thinking make this a better place to live?" he asked, trying hard to sound convincing. "Please don't be upset. It isn't that I don't believe anymore. It's just that out here it's an entirely different world than it is in Carthage, Texas. You've been here a few times, so you know what I am talking about. No one would listen or understand if I started talking about Jesus being our Savior. Besides, Scientology works better for me here than all that stuff I was taught before. But I haven't forgotten anything, I promise!"

"Oh dear God, how foolish you are! What are you doing to yourself? How can you possibly think that what you're doing is what God wants? How can you believe any of this? It's a farce. It's brainwashing. Don't you get it? There is only one God of the world, and He is the One in the Bible! If you continue with this outrageous practice acting as if you're some kind of non–believer, then you'll be treated like one. And you'll send yourself straight to hell, Andy! And contrary to your new beliefs, there is a hell. I just don't understand what happened. I thought your faith was strong enough to carry you through the rest of your life, no matter where you resided or who you became. But I guess I was wrong." George was beside himself with anger, frustration, and a sorrow he had never known before.

"Dad, please. I am a grown man, and I will make the choices that are right for me. Meagan and I discussed at length if this church would work for us. We did a great deal of research and soul–searching, and talked to a lot of other well–known people. Scientology came highly recommended. So, please don't preach to me any more. This is what we are, and this is how it is!" Andy stated firmly.

"I'm sorry you feel that way, son. You know there's a big difference between confessing Christ and possessing Christ? Someone who professes

Christ and falls away is not a genuine believer. Satan himself believes in God, has faith that He exists, but that is not saving faith. True believers persevere to the end. You obviously are not, nor have you ever been, one of these believers, as I had hoped. Your mother and I will once again accept your decision, but this time we cannot be a part of it. I wish you all the happiness in the world, and I will pray for you every day of my life. But we won't be coming out there to see you any more. We just can't take seeing you fall. And you won't be welcome here, either, until you come to your senses. It will break our hearts, but there's nothing more we can do for you. You have obviously made your choice. I hope you know what you're doing. May God forgive you, Andy. Good–bye," George said and hung up the phone. Ellen stood at his side as she had done for 35 years. Her heart ached with the loss of their son, but she hurt even more watching her husband crumble.

"How can he do this, Ellen? Where did we go wrong?" He sat in the chair with his hands over his face and cried like a child.

"George, it wasn't us that went wrong. It was Andy. It was his choice, not ours. We showed him the way a long time ago, but his spirit weakened. Then by falling heavily into the secular world with all his fame and fortune, he himself has chosen another route. It's what we're allowed to do, remember? Free will, our own choice, being in charge of our own spiritual destiny," Ellen said, trying hard not to break down herself.

"This wasn't part of the plan. Andy was supposed to go to heaven. Through God's mercy and grace our foundation was laid from the very beginning. I did my job as a father, but Andy threw it all away. I just can't take knowing he won't be there in heaven with us, Ellen. To picture my blood, my son, my heart, crawling in the black slimy pit of hell, where he will rot in unimaginable pain and grief, with no signs of God anywhere, until the end of days. How can I live the rest of my life knowing that?" he sobbed.

"Faith, George. We need to have incredible faith right now. God will get us through this like He has all the other times when we called out to Him. He promises to never leave us, especially in the bad times. Trust Him. It's all we have. Maybe Andy will turn out to be our prodigal son, like the one in the Bible. He came home after all his philandering and rebellion, remember? And his father welcomed him with open arms and a huge celebration!"

"I can only hope and pray that is what happens for us, too, but I am fearful that Andy is too lost. I think it's time for us to admit that the spiritual seeds planted in Andy as a boy weren't deep enough to take root if something like moving to Hollywood can change his entire beliefs. Soon Andy won't know how to come back. And worse, he will forget why he should."

Ellen and George had been through difficult, heartbreaking times before. The most heart wrenching was losing their young daughter, Sarah, to cancer when she was barely five years old. Andy was only eight at the time. The only thing that got them through was their faith, knowing they would see her again someday when their duties on earth were complete. But even as painful as that time was, it was nothing compared to what they were both feeling now with Andy's sudden change of heart. They didn't feel as confident about where he would be in the afterlife, and it scared them to death.

Andy sat in the spacious living room of his Tudor–style mansion staring out the window toward the foothills of Southern California, the phone still cradled in his hand.

"Do you think my dad is right about all this stuff, Meagan? Maybe we aren't choosing wisely or correctly. Maybe I have lost my mind," Andy said a bit confused.

"I can't tell you if your dad is right or not because I don't know what his beliefs are. But we chose what works for us, Andy. Based on that, how can any god deny us our human right to choose? Your dad said we are allowed to make choices. But then we do, and if they're wrong according to some higher power, we get punished. Is that the kind of god you want to answer to and serve?" she asked somewhat confused herself.

"I guess not. But how can my dad do this to me?" he asked Meagan. "How can he just walk out of my life and never want to see me again? It makes no sense at all!"

"Is that what he said, that he doesn't want to see you any more?"

"Yes, he said he couldn't be a part of any of this Scientology nonsense and that he wouldn't support my decision to join. Why can't he just be my father and not try to control me all the time?"

"Andy, you know your dad loves you. He just doesn't understand right now that we live in a different world than he does. Give him some time and he will come around. You are all he and your mother have, and they won't be able to go without seeing you again. You know that. Let's wait a few months for them to adjust to this new choice of yours… ours, then you can call them. I'm sure they will have come to their senses by then!" Meagan tried to make light of a very sad situation. She knew how close Andy was to his parents and how much he adored them.

"Maybe you're right," he agreed. "I'll wait until the holidays and call them. That's only six months away. Besides, they love that time of the year and might be more forgiving and more apt to accept our decision by then. Speaking of which, we have to go. There's a meeting tonight at the church."

Chapter Six

The couple continued to grow closer in the Scientology faith. Their fame and fortune were impressive and rising. Andy continued to believe that everything he was blessed with was God's will, but it wasn't the same God that he grew up with. As the days and weeks passed, he and Meagan became inseparable, especially with his parents out of the picture. For Andy, there was no one else.

A few months later, Andy's agent, Rudy Beggosi, called him one afternoon and told him about a picture he thought would be perfect for him.

"It's all action and very physical. It will definitely be a challenge, but it's a great script. With the right cast, this could be Oscar material for sure! I'll have my assistant drop it by in the next hour or so. Look it over and tell me if you think you'd like to take a crack at it! I think it has your name all over it!" the agent said.

"Maybe that's just what I need to get out of this mood that I've been in for the last several months. Send it over, Rudy! I'll read it. But I can tell you right now, if you think it's right for me, then I'll do it. You've never been wrong yet," Andy bragged. He felt very lucky to have Rudy as his agent. He was always looking out for him and making sure he did the right movies for the critics as well as for his numerous fans.

Two months later, Andy was on the set of his latest movie, *Thunder Canyon*. Rudy had been right. It was a very physical and very exhausting role, but exhilarating as well. It gave Andy a new satisfaction to be able to keep up with the younger actors on the set. And he did most of the time. But no one ever thought it would kill him.

Christmas came and went, and Andy still hadn't heard from his father. He attempted several times to call, but no one answered and no one returned his messages. Andy tried hard to ignore the hurt inside, throwing himself into the character of his new movie. But it didn't help him at night when he was lying in bed, trying hard to understand what went wrong. Early Sunday morning right after Christmas, he called his wife and talked to her about it, but she didn't have any answers either.

"They'll come around someday, Andy. I know they will. They love you too much," Meagan assured him.

"I am so confused. I never thought they would just blow me off like this. I must have really upset him when I went another direction with my faith. I just don't understand. My dad was always so open and so supportive in whatever I did before. I never realized that it was based on where I went to church. I thought he and my mom loved me more than that." Andy was so hurt he could hardly sleep at night.

"Honey, don't worry. You have too much to concentrate on with this movie and all the lines and physical conditioning. I am sure once they know they are going to be grandparents, they'll be calling very soon!" she told him. They had just found out the week before that they were going to have a baby, which left them both ecstatic. Andy just knew that this child would be the cure to his overall dissatisfaction and emptiness, because nothing else he did seemed to work. At least it didn't for very long. He never mentioned to Meagan this grief or the void he sometimes felt. Because he wasn't sure how to explain it, he felt it was better left unsaid.

"Maybe you're right. I sure hope it does something to their attitude and their hearts. Well, my love, I'd better go. I need to get some sleep before the alarm goes off in three hours. I will call you tomorrow night. Are you feeling okay?" he asked.

"I feel like a million dollars. This baby is so easy. I don't even have the morning sickness that everyone told me about. I sort of feel like I'm missing out on something. But at least I can act normal for a while anyway. No one knows yet, so don't tell anyone around the set. I think you need to tell your parents first before they see it on the news," she said, and Andy agreed.

"I will call them next weekend again. I've left two messages, but they don't return my calls. I think if they know they are going to be grandparents this summer, they will jump on the first plane to get here! At least that is what I am hoping. I love you, Meagan. I'll talk to you soon. Sweet dreams," he said and hung up the phone.

At five–thirty in the morning, the crew was preparing for an intense action scene, where a full–scale helicopter was actually supposed to crash in a fiery blaze at the bottom of a deep canyon. Just before the director called out for "action!" a scuffle was heard in the back of the set. Before anyone could find out what was going on, someone screamed.

"Oh my God, get the paramedics! Andy Lynch is on the floor, and I don't think he's breathing!"

An ambulance was already on the premises just in case there was an emergency. The paramedics put the actor on a gurney and transported him to the nearest hospital, performing CPR all the way. They managed to revive Andy several times, but in the end, it wasn't enough.

Chapter Seven

As Andy drifted in and out of unconsciousness, he watched his life pass before him. Suddenly, the emptiness and void he had felt for months was gone. In its place was the most incredible feeling of love. It was more intense and powerful than he had ever experienced before, a calming peace that covered his entire presence. It was only a glimpse of what should have and could have been, but it didn't last. As quickly as the feeling overcame him, it was gone.

In what seemed like a millisecond, but could have been years, his spirit began to plummet on its final journey into a darkened world full of pitiful cries, unbelievable chaos, and massive, painful confusion. Andy discovered, far too late, that his earthly father had been right. His eternal days were very real, very permanent, and beyond anything he ever imagined. The pain his body suffered, from the time he left the realm of one world to join the next, was too hideous to conceive. No earthly words could ever describe the heartache, remorse, or misery that he was doomed to endure, and the worst was still ahead.

During his final days on earth, Andy had let the secular world of Hollywood sway him into thinking that what he was doing was acceptable and had let his fleshly cravings get the best of him. John 6:37 makes it very clear that salvation cannot be lost or traded. Jesus said, "All that the Father gives Me and the one who comes to Me I will by no means cast out," which means that Andy had never been a true believer, or God would not have let him go. And, more importantly, Andy would have never wanted to. In the end, the young star from Carthage, Texas, turned his back on the only One who should have mattered.

Like a fool, Andrew Michael Lynch gave into his own selfishness, replacing all he had been taught with the likes of Scientology, stardom, fortune, and lust, like so many others had done. Those non–believing, high society tycoons had no idea that they, too, would be joining this superstar someday in a treacherous pit of no return. And the monarch of hell was gloating through it all!

In the midst of this terrifying holocaust stood a disgusting being. His cold, soulless eyes oozed with vindictive evil as he roared in satisfying laughter, penetrating deep inside Andy's doomed and ill-fated soul.

"Oh God, what have I done? What have I done?" Andy screamed, as he fell further into the oblivion of suffering and remorse that would be his world for all eternity.

Charlie McGee

Charlie McGee was nearly at the end of his rope. His construction business had been struggling off and on for several years, but he managed, by the grace of God, to keep it running. He continually prayed for a miracle, and every month he was blessed with one… he made payroll again. But without a big contract of some kind, Charlie knew his failing business couldn't last much longer. But he was faithful in his belief that God was in charge and knew exactly what he needed. Charlie knew there had to be a reason for this newest test and challenge. He knew, too, that someday it would eventually work itself out. What he didn't know was what God's plan was for him.

Charlie was ready to go in whatever direction God was leading. Whether his business would be a part of God's plan or not was another story entirely. But Charlie remained confident that God's purpose for the continual setbacks would soon be revealed. Until then, he was suffering the effects of his loss daily. He knew it was just a matter of time before it would all come tumbling down around him.

Charlie and his wife, Lisa, knew that times could be rough and that their faith would often be tested, but lately it was almost more than they could bear. Besides having to deal with the rapid decline of the company, the beautiful home that they worked so hard to get was about to be sold because they could no longer keep up the payments. Then the month before, Charlie discovered a leak in the roof after an unmerciful rainstorm had hit the region, and there was no money to fix it. Their worst news came two weeks later when Lisa's father was diagnosed with lung cancer and had to undergo emergency surgery. It seemed that every time the couple thought it couldn't get any worse, it always did. Their faith was dangling by a thread.

Charlie hadn't always been a God–fearing man. In fact, at one time he was quite the opposite. He used to drink too much and party too hard, even after marrying Lisa. But one day shortly before the birth of his second son, Bryan, Charlie stumbled onto a Christian radio station, where the subject of having hope was being discussed. That broadcast eventually turned his life around.

Afterward, Charlie started going to church and reading the Bible, which eventually brought him into a relationship with Jesus Christ that lasted more than seven years. He was very thankful that he made the decision to become one of God's children, especially on that weekend after Christmas, when Charlie hit a truck head-on and was immediately, upon impact, catapulted into eternity.

Within an instant, Charlie felt himself falling into a totally different kind of peace and tranquility. By the grace of God, the only One true God whom he had grown to know and worship, Charlie was completely and mercifully surrounded in a love he had never known before, where his heart danced and his hope was everlasting.

Chapter One

"Honey, come quick!" Charlie yelled from the backyard. "Look at this sunset! It's the most beautiful one I've ever seen!"

"Oh, Charlie, that is beautiful," Lisa told him as she hurried outside. "But you said that about the one last night!" After ten years together, she was used to his sensitive and very sentimental observations.

"Yeah, I know I did. But they seemed to be getting prettier lately, don't you think? Sit with me for a few minutes. Let's watch it disappear."

The couple climbed into the wooden swing, and Charlie put his arm around Lisa's shoulders. They both looked around in amazed wonder at their incredibly beautiful home spread out on five gorgeous acres in the middle of dense pine trees, and began to reflect back on all they had been through.

"We are so blessed, honey. I know times are tough right now, and it doesn't feel like they are going to get better anytime soon, but I promise they will," he told her.

"I know, Charlie. But I am very confident that all of this is leading somewhere. God does strange things when He needs to get our attention, even if we think we're doing it all the right way. He lets us know when it's time to go in another direction," Lisa replied.

"I don't understand any of it yet, either. But I feel that all of this interruption of life as we knew it and these continual challenges are leading us to other blessings He has waiting. I just wish I knew what they were and when all of this other stuff will end. But I would venture to say that Job felt the same way at some point in his life."

"Job had it a lot worse than we do, Charlie McGee! He not only lost his fortune, but he lost his entire family, too, remember? We've had a wonderful life, sweetheart. And we're a long way from being like Job. But I just want you to know that I am ready to do whatever we have to do, even sell the house and move. I can adjust to anything, and the kids are willing to let all of this go, too.

It isn't that important when you think about the overall picture. This life goes by way too quickly, and before we know it, it's gone. There isn't anything here that is worth holding onto, except our beliefs. You know, Charlie, if we were still living the way we used to, we'd sure be running scared right now!"

"Boy, isn't that the truth! Can you even imagine us going through all of this without God's strength? We would have given up a long time ago! Thank you, Lisa, for hanging in there. I know it hasn't been easy and it doesn't look like it will be for a while, but it's only material stuff we're talking about right now. We all have our health, thank God. And your father will be fine, too. At least he knows Jesus, and we can give thanks for that. Someday we know that we'll all be together, and nothing can ever change that!"

"I am very thankful that my dad knows Jesus! It could be so much worse if I had to worry about his salvation as well as his health. But I still pray that God will see His way to let Daddy live just a while longer. He just has to. At least he seems to be doing better since his operation." Lisa knew that the surgery had gone well, but her father was still not out of danger. The doctors were hopeful that they had removed all the cancer, but they didn't know if it had spread to any other organs. The results would be known soon.

Charlie took his wife's hand and held it tightly, reassuring her that all things were possible through Christ. Words weren't always a necessary form of communication, not after ten years together. They knew with a touch or a glance what the other was thinking.

Of course, it hadn't always been this way. When Charlie and Lisa were first married, neither of them knew what God was able to accomplish in their lives and in the lives of anyone who put their trust in Him.

The husband and father of three remembered the day when he first heard the powerful words from a pastor on the radio. Trevor was two, and Lisa was pregnant with Bryan. They were going through extremely difficult times, not only in their finances but also in their relationship. Each day their problems seemed to get worse, and Charlie would stay out later, drinking and trying to forget. Soon, he was reaching out to another source of satisfaction and was about to make the worst mistake of his life. He felt a sudden urge to wander and to seek pleasure from someone he had met only a few hours before, hoping it would distract him from the mounting pressures of his job and his seemingly hopeless relationship with his wife. His distraction came in a slender, five–foot–six frame, with copper brown eyes and long blonde hair. Her name was Mindy.

Chapter Two

Mindy was lovely, luscious, and very available, and she didn't waste any time letting Charlie know she was interested. They spent the evening talking and flirting. Then one thing led to another as their conversation took them to the next level. When Mindy came back from using the restroom, she made her move.

"Hey, handsome! Want to buy a lady a drink? I could sure use another one!" she told him seductively, rubbing purposefully against his arm. Charlie smiled knowingly and ordered her another Vodka martini.

"I'll buy you whatever you want, gorgeous!" he said as his eyes tried to focus on her face.

As soon as the bartender set her drink in front of her, Mindy downed it quickly. Then she leaned over and whispered in Charlie's ear.

"What do you say we get out of here? I just live down the street, and I have plenty of stuff to drink. And plenty of other things to do, too, if you know what I mean," Mindy said with a playful wink. She reached over for her coat and keys. Then headed quickly toward the door. And, like a fool, Charlie followed.

It took all of ten minutes for Charlie to come to his senses. He walked Mindy to the front steps of her apartment and then proceeded to explain to her why he couldn't go inside.

"I'm really sorry. But I can't do this. I'm married, and I have to go home before I do something I will live to regret," he said in a voice barely loud enough to be heard. And with that, he turned and left. As he drove the twenty miles back home, Charlie was lost in his own thoughts. The radio was playing, and he leaned over to adjust the station. He was looking for a familiar tune, but what he got was God.

At first he thought he came across the broadcast somewhat by accident, but soon he realized it had been God's plan all along. As the pastor on the radio spoke, Charlie listened intently. His heart began to stir with feelings both old and new and one that he thought he had lost forever. It was the feeling of hope.

"Our message today is 'Living With Hope.' Let us begin with the significance of hope. Psychologist William Marston asked three thousand people, 'What have you to live for?' He was shocked to discover that ninety-four percent were simply enduring the present while they waited for the future: waited for something to happen, waited for next year, waited for a better time, waited for someone to die, waited for tomorrow to happen. All human beings are hopers. Hope is why people get married. Hope is why people have children. Hope is why they pay to send their children to college. Hope is why people buy those 'Ab' machines. It's why people pay for makeovers and read self-help books and go to counselors and play the stock market. It's why we go on blind dates!

"Just how important is hope? The word 'hope' is found 141 times in the Bible, so it is a major theme! In my opinion, it is the defining characteristic of the believer. There is nothing worse than losing hope.

"Proverbs 13:12 says, 'Hope deferred makes the heart sick.' The human spirit can survive just about anything, but it cannot survive the loss of hope.

"Last week I read about one of the experiments that the Nazis did with victims in the concentration camps. They would assign people meaningless work. They would have them shift mounds of dirt to one place and then shift them to another and then shift them to another until it was quite apparent that there was no purpose behind it. One of the things they found was that people died at a faster rate when assigned a meaningless job!

"Now with that in mind, I want to talk about the source of hope. Romans 5:1–2 reads, 'Therefore, since we have been made right in God's sight by faith, we have peace with God because of what Jesus Christ our Lord has done for us. Because of our faith, Christ has brought us into this place of highest privilege where we now stand, and we confidently and joyfully look forward to sharing God's glory.'

"The believer's joy, confidence, and hope are all wrapped up in one very significant truth. It is the security of salvation! If we truly understand our destiny, then we can endure the journey. When we stand in God's grace, we walk in hope… I repeat, when we stand in God's grace, we walk in hope. But wait, there is more.

"The strategy of hope is found in Romans 5:3–5. 'And not only that, but we also glory in tribulations, knowing that tribulation produces perseverance; and perseverance, character; and character, hope. Now hope does not disappoint, because the love of God has been poured out in our hearts by the Holy Spirit who was given to us.'

"In this Scripture, Paul describes this basic process underlying the Christian life. He talks about how suffering can produce endurance, which can produce character, and character produces hope. Paul explains this process at the beginning of Romans 5:3 when he says, 'we boast in tribulation.'

"In Greek, it is 'the tribulation.' In other words, the general experience of pressure we all come under as Christians. The word 'tribulation' actually means 'pressure, hardship, suffering.'

"Now, think of your own life for a moment. What are your main pressures? List them out in your mind or on paper. This is 'the tribulation' for you at this time. Now, look at that list. Is Paul serious? How can we boast in this? How can this be an 'X' marking the spot where we find confidence?

Charlie did a quick mental note and thought about all he was going through and what his main pressures were. His list seemed to be a mile long. He continued to listen to the voice on the radio.

"We can all agree with Mark Twain who wrote, 'By trying we can easily learn to endure adversity. Another man's, I mean.'

"But what about agreeing with Paul? I weary myself when I hear my self–pitying questions repeated yet again, 'When will I get a break?' 'When will things ease up a bit?'

"The point is simple: things won't ease up! Christ will be sufficient, and I will be conformed to the diamond He is. Our God has great confidence in His Son within us to carry us through everything we face. Thus, we can boast confidently in this pressure because our God who brings the heat lives within us to withstand the heat. And we need to remember the heat always has a purpose!

"It is not a capricious and malicious pressure. God's purpose is to produce His character in us so that our hope in the glory of God will be realized as the life and character of Jesus Christ shines through us.

"This is the defining process of the Christian life: pressure mounts up, and God works within us to patiently endure the pressure. This is the perseverance that comes from pressure when we walk right through it with Christ.

As Charlie listened, he felt a calming surge of hope flair up inside. He had no idea what was happening, but he knew he was right where he was supposed to be. The pastor went on.

"Then from this perseverance comes proven character. This is literally 'approved character,' which in this case means the approved character of Jesus Christ shining through us. Then, as His character shines through us, we find our hope fully realized, our sure expectation that He lives in us and through us comes to full fruition.

"This hope will not disappoint us or leave us ashamed because we can see through all this process the love of God at work in us, standing with us in the pressure, whispering His love to us while the heat goes up. And that His perfect love will cast out our fears!

"Thus, the pressures we experience come into our lives for the purpose of forging the character of Christ in us. His character is indeed forged within us, and our hope in Him living through us is certainly realized in the midst of our pressures. This is the defining process of the Christian life the world over.

"Hope is a confident expectation as you continue to do what God wants you to do! Hope always expresses itself in perseverance. So the question is, are you clinging to hope? Are you growing as a hopeful person?

"Followers of Christ are hopeful people. How can you cling to hope? There are two issues here. First, you must believe it is possible to grow in hopefulness. And second, you must learn a new way of thinking.

"You must believe you can become a hopeful person. It really is possible. Listen to what Paul says in his letters to the Church of Thessalonica. 1 Thessalonians 5:8 says, 'But since we belong to the day, let us be self–controlled, putting on faith and love as a breastplate, and the hope of salvation as a helmet.

"Let's break this down. 'But since we belong to the day,' we've been transferred into the Kingdom of the day; we're out of darkness now. 'Since we belong to the day…'

"Now go to the next line. 'Let us be sober and put on the breastplate of faith and love, and for a helmet, the hope of salvation.' The helmet represents a way of thinking. The key is how you understand and explain your failures, setbacks, criticisms, or bad events.

"There's a character in *Winnie the Pooh* that is a very hopeless character. I don't know if any of you watch or know *Winnie the Pooh* and its characters, but the character I'm referring to is Eeyore. Now, this is what might be called a kind of 'Eeyore syndrome.' It is a way of thinking that produces this sense of 'Why bother?' It has to do with how you understand or think about setbacks, failures, criticisms, bad events, and so on.

"There are three words that describe this wrong thinking. Permanent is the first one. It's going to last forever. In other words, 'this stuff that is causing problems for me is going to be permanent and will never go away!'

"Let's say you try to lead a small group and the small group doesn't go well. A hopeless person will tend to say something like, 'I just can't lead a small group. I can't contribute to the ministry, and I'll never be able to.' Then, they'll just quit! They will neglect alternative possibilities like maybe it was just an off night. Or maybe it was just a cranky group. That's what happens in small groups sometimes, just cranky people that may not be attracted to each other. Or maybe the chemistry was off!

"Aaron Beck, one of the leading researchers in marriages, says, 'The number one defeating belief in marriages, the belief that will kill a marriage faster than any other, is the belief that says, "My spouse will never change. Because once I think that my spouse will never change, I am not motivated to do anything. I am not motivated to persevere, so I will give up. I won't be a faithful and loving person.'" Permanence is the first deal.

"The second is pervasive. In other words, 'it's going to undermine everything in my life' ". If I experience a setback, a failure, if there is a problem that I see in my character and so on, then it's pervasive. In other words, not just that it's permanent and it's going to go on, but also that it's going to affect everything in my life!

"Have you ever been turned down for a job? Okay, you get turned down, and you have a series of thoughts. For some people that lean towards hopelessness, it will feel like this is a pervasive situation. 'I guess I am just not worth much. Nobody is interested in me.' Therefore, this person may just quit looking for work thinking he isn't good enough for anything.

"The third is personal. 'It's all my fault and there's nothing I can do about it.' Some people hang on this and believe that everything is their fault.

"Now, I need to tell you the right way to think! First of all, Christ is eternal; therefore, problems are temporary! Secondly, Christ is everywhere; therefore, problems are limited! And lastly, Christ is in me; therefore, I am not alone. Therefore, I can and will persevere!

"When I think in ways that lead to perseverance, tenacity, faithfulness in life, I am practicing Christian hope. When I think in ways that lead to discouragement, defeat, despair, giving in, then I need grace to change the way that I think.

"A Good Friday service in Bangladesh was packed. Little children sat on the floor in the aisles and across the front of the church. Rows of people stood in the back, craning their necks to see the crucifixion scene depicted in the 'Jesus Film.' Weeping and gasps of unbelief could be heard in the shocked hush as Jesus was crucified. As the Bengalis watched, they were feeling the agony of Jesus' pain and the disappointment in the disciples.

"In that emotional moment, one young boy in the crowded church suddenly cried out, 'Do not be afraid. He gets up again! I saw it before.'

"'He is risen!' is the cry that gives new hope to all! And if there is anyone listening to this program that would like more information on how to receive God's free gift of salvation, please call the prayer line. We're ready to help you turn your life around."

By this time, Charlie was in his driveway. He quickly wrote down the number and called immediately from his cell phone. After all, it was free! How could he not at least inquire? As he listened to the voice on the other end, Charlie realized how lost he had been. He quietly unlocked his front door and tiptoed into the den. Then, without a moment's hesitation, the one–time nonbeliever was soon on his knees in a prayer that would change his life forever. Charlie repeated the words with the man on the other end of the line. Tears fell from his cheeks as his heart filled with love.

"Forgive me, Father, for all that I have done against You. I have spent my life ignoring You and all Your gifts and blessings. I am ready to change, Lord, and do what You have intended for me, no matter what the cost. Take away my sinful ways and thoughts, and replace them with what Jesus would do. Where there was greed, lust, and selfishness, let me feel Your loving kindness for all mankind. Help me to forgive as You have forgiven me. With Your grace, help me be a better person to all that I am in contact with. Help me to know that I can do nothing without You and everything with You. Guide me, Father, to a better life in You. In Jesus' name. Amen."

When Charlie finished, he was instantly filled with a hope he had never known before. He immediately woke Lisa and shared his news. She could sense the change and heard the excitement in his voice as he told her what he had done. Lisa soon realized that God was something she needed and wanted as well. The next night the young mother was on her knees in prayer next to her husband, humbly begging for forgiveness and asking the Lord to come into her heart. Over the next few weeks and months, the couple grew closer to God. He soon became their foundation in marriage as well as in their life.

The family attended church each Sunday morning and held a small Bible class every Friday night. As they came to know God more intimately, they also came to know His Son, Jesus, who mercifully died on the cross for all of them. Jesus was their Lord and Savior. And the entire McGee family became extremely devoted followers of Christ, dedicated to serving Him and spreading His word. Their fruit was plentiful and very obvious to everyone.

Chapter Three

Their daughter, Jenna, was born two years later. Soon, their lives flourished and stabilized, with income and blessings beyond anything they ever thought possible. Eventually, Charlie started his own business, and it blossomed into a huge success. In less than a year, he had twenty–five employees and several large, future contracts that would surely guarantee them security for many years to come.

But five years later, everything changed drastically when a great deal of money came up missing. Soon the finger pointed to one of Charlie's most trusted employees who had been with him since the beginning. Hundreds of thousands of dollars were unaccounted for, and the rock–strong business Charlie had started was beginning to disintegrate.

With only his deep conviction for God to keep him from running away and hiding, Charlie tried to stay focused and endure the ongoing phone calls and pressure he continued to get from the contractors and businesses who wanted their money. But in reality, there was none left to distribute. He could barely stay above water as he struggled to make payroll each week. Several times he had to take the money from his own personal account to pay the very few loyal employees he had left. Charlie knew that God would never leave him and that He would see him safely through this struggle. But not knowing how long it had to go on was grinding away at the young man's faith as it clung to his heart by a prayer.

The couple eventually put up their beautiful home for sale and downsized all their belongings. The fancy cars were gone. The motor home, ski boat, jet skis, snowmobiles, and four–wheelers were sold along with thousands of shares of stock. Charlie completely forgot about being a stockholder in a software company called Hightech Incorporated, or these shares would have been sold as well. Two years before, on the advice of his stockbroker, Charlie had invested ten thousand dollars for just over three thousand shares of Hightech stock, with hopes of the small company becoming highly successful. Three months later, the stock was selling for less than half of what he had originally paid.

Charlie talked to Lisa often. She always turned out to be his saving grace sent by God to help him endure.

"Listen to me, honey. You know that God has a plan for all of this mess we're in. Maybe we just got too big for our britches with all our 'stuff.' Maybe He needed us to come back down to earth and focus more on what is really important. Or maybe He has an incredible plan for you, and He needs you to show others how they can get through their trials and struggles by successfully withstanding your own. He isn't going to let this trial destroy your faith, Charlie! It will get stronger. You wait and see," she told him confidently.

"I sure hope you're right. I am so glad tomorrow is Sunday. I need a heavy dose of God in a very big way. I hope Pastor Ray gives me some encouraging words to hold on to and to get me through the next few months. I need them more than ever." He smiled and drew her closely into his arms. Lisa wanted desperately to believe the words she just told her husband, but inside she was falling apart.

The next morning, Pastor Ray O'Neil gave the perfect message for both of them. It was entitled *Knocked Down but Not Knocked Out.*

"Many people see the Bible as a collection of fairy tales and bedtime stories. It's like the little girl who felt a little jealous that her older sister could read. One day she picked up her Bible and pretended to read, 'and Jesus said, "Little pig, little pig, let me come in."' But the Book of Daniel is not a bedtime story. It is a story of the power of God… and the faithfulness of a man who got knocked down by life! It is a story of a man who was just trying to serve his God and he got shafted. Daniel was not thrown in the lion's den for what he had done wrong, but for what he had done right!

"Have you ever said, 'Why do things like this always happen to me?' Then the Book of Daniel is for you. Our story begins in Daniel 6 with Daniel in captivity.

"At this point the Babylonians had fallen. The Medes and the Persians had conquered Babylon just as Daniel predicted. A man by the name of Darius was king. At this point, Daniel was about eighty years old. He has worked his way into a very powerful position. And Darius was the third king that he has served.

"Out of our text today, I want to point out four pillars of truth that you will require in your life if you are going to get up when life knocks you down. First, you need the right spirit!

"Turn to Daniel 6:3. 'Then this Daniel distinguished himself above the governors and princes, because an excellent spirit was in him; and the king gave thought to setting him over the whole realm.' Daniel had an excellent spirit! If we are not going to get knocked down by life, we need the spirit of Daniel.

"What was the spirit of Daniel? For this we go to verse four. 'So they sought to find some charge against Daniel concerning the kingdom; but they could find no charge or fault, because he was faithful; nor was there any error or fault found in him.'

"Three things describe this excellent spirit that Daniel had: faithfulness, integrity, and purity. Daniel was faithful to his God. How does a person develop faithfulness to God? The answer is that you start with the small things. Do you know where the Bible tells us to start? It's with the discipline of giving. In Luke 16:11 it says, 'So if you have not been trustworthy in handling worldly wealth, who will trust you with true riches?'

"Daniel was faithful! The second pillar is the right expectation. First, let me tell you what you can't expect. Don't expect that life will be fair! This world is filled with cruelties and harsh realities. The reason for this is that we live in a world where sin abounds!

"Daniel 6:6–7 reads, 'So the supervisors and governors went as a group to the king and said: "King Darius, live forever! The people who advise you have all agreed that you should make a new law for everyone to obey: For the next thirty days no one should pray to any god or human except to you, O king. Anyone who doesn't obey will be thrown into the lion's den."'

"They were jealous, and Daniel was the curve buster! He was making people look bad, so they had to get rid of him. They elect Darius god of the month, and anyone, meaning Daniel, who prayed to anyone but Darius, would get munched by lions. They knew he would be faithful to God!

"Don't expect life to be fair! The famous game of 'Monopoly' has one card that is discovered occasionally when someone lands on 'chance.' On it the card reads, 'return to 'go' and collect $200.' In life, don't expect to get this card!

"Here is what you can expect. The first thing is that you can always expect God to be with you. And always expect God to bring good! Daniel had the right spirit and the right expectation.

"The third thing he had was the right motivation. There are two things that motivated Daniel. They are great trust and gratitude. Daniel 6:10 says this, 'But when Daniel learned that the law had been signed, he went home and knelt down as usual in his upstairs room, with its windows open toward Jerusalem. He prayed three times a day, just as he had always done, giving thanks to his God.'

"Have you seen that commercial that begins with a young girl standing alone in a picturesque meadow? The camera then pans to another part of the field where it shows a gigantic African rhinoceros.

"The ominous beast begins a lethal charge towards the girl, whose serene and happy face remains unmoved. As the rhinoceros gets closer, the words appear on the screen, 'Trust is not being afraid.' A split second before the rhino tramples the helpless child, it stops, and the girl, her smile never wavering, reaches up and pets the animal on its massive horn. The final words then appear, 'Even when you are vulnerable.'

"The commercial was designed to tout the abilities of an insurance company to protect its clients from the uncertainties of life. How much more does it describe the believer, who can confidently say with the psalmist, 'I will say of the Lord, "He is my refuge and my fortress, my God, in whom I trust."'

"Daniel was also motivated by gratitude. Notice something: Daniel is not acting out of desperation. He simply did what he had been doing for probably seventy years! He didn't whine, whimper, or complain. His alarm clock did not make him arise and whine! Daniel had a walk with God that was rooted and grounded in God's character. The lifestyle that he had established with God was one of continual thanksgiving.

"Then lastly Daniel had the right perspective, which is imperative! One morning after a terrible snowstorm, Susan was outside shoveling her driveway. She stopped to wave to her neighbor, and he asked her why her husband wasn't out there, helping her with the chore. She explained that one of them had to stay inside to take care of the children, so they drew straws to see who would go out and shovel. 'Sorry about your bad luck,' he said. To which Susan replied, 'Don't be sorry. I won!' The roar of laughter filled the church.

"Never underestimate the power of your witness," the pastor continued. "Daniel 6:13–14 reads, 'That man Daniel, one of the captives from Judah, is paying no attention to you or your law. He still prays to his God three times a day.' Hearing this, the king was very angry with himself for signing the law, and he tried to find a way to save Daniel. He spent the rest of the day looking for a way to get Daniel out of this predicament.' Daniel had a significant impact on this unbelieving king.

"During those times when you are discouraged and ready to quit, just remember that you never know who is watching your life! Our greatest problems are God's greatest opportunities. Go to Daniel 6:17–20. 'A stone was brought and placed over the mouth of the den. The king sealed the stone with his own royal seal and the seals of his nobles, so that no one could rescue Daniel from the lions. Then the king returned to his palace and spent the night fasting. He refused his usual entertainment and couldn't sleep at all that night. Very early the next morning, the king hurried out to the lion's den. When he got there, he called out in anguish, "Daniel, servant of the living God! Was your God, whom you worship continually, able to rescue you from the lions?"' What is important here is that Daniel was not delivered from the lion's den but in it! It is important to note that these aren't just toothless, vegetarian lions retired from the circus!

"We tend to believe that God is working in our lives when everything is rosy and to believe He is absent when we have problems. The truth is that God always has the final word! Daniel's accusers think that they have him. That curve–buster is gone! But the king rushes to the den the next morning and cries out to Daniel.

"Go to the next few verses from 21 to 24. 'Daniel answered, "Long live the king! My God sent His angel to shut the lion's mouths so that they could not hurt me." The king was overjoyed and ordered that Daniel be lifted from the den. Not a scratch was found on him because he had trusted his God. Then the king gave orders to arrest the men who had maliciously accused Daniel. He had them thrown into the lion's den, along with their wives and children. The lions leaped on them and tore them apart before they even hit the floor of the den.' And so I repeat, God will always have the last word. You can bank on it!

"Always look for the main character in the midst of your hardships. The main character was not Daniel. It was the king. Daniel 6:25–26 says, 'Then King Darius sent this message to the people of every race and nation and language throughout the world: "I decree that everyone throughout my kingdom should tremble with fear before the God of Daniel. For He is the Living God and He will endure forever. His kingdom will never be destroyed, and His rule will never end."'

"Back in the year 1873, Horatio Spafford, a Christian lawyer from Chicago, placed his wife and four children on a luxury liner sailing from New York to France. Spafford expected to join them in about three or four weeks after finishing up some business, but with the exception of his wife, he never saw them again. On the evening of November 21, 1873, the ship was suddenly struck by another vessel. It sank a mere thirty minutes later, with the loss of nearly all on board.

"On being told that the ship was sinking, Mrs. Spafford knelt with her children and prayed. A few minutes later, in the confusion, three of the children were swept away by the waves, while she stood clutching the youngest. Suddenly, the youngest child was swept away from her arms, too. Mrs. Spafford became unconscious and awoke later to find that she had been rescued by sailors from the other vessel.

"But the four children were gone! Back in the United States, Horatio Spafford was waiting for the news of his family, and at last, ten days later it came. 'Saved...alone' was his wife's message. That night Spafford walked the floor of his room in anguish as he shared his loss with his Lord. Through that loss, which could not be reversed in this life, he found, as many have, a peace which indeed passes all understanding.

"As he reflected on this disaster at sea, he wrote this hymn:

When peace, like a river, attendeth my way,
When sorrows like sea–billows roll;
Whatever my lot, thou hast taught me to say,
It is well; it is well with my soul.

Though Satan should buffet, though trials should come,
Let this blest assurance control:
That Christ has regarded my helpless estate,
And hath shed His own blood for my soul.

My sin – oh, the bliss of this glorious thought!
My sin – not in part, but the whole
Is nailed to the cross and I bear it no more,
Praise the Lord; Praise the Lord, O my soul!

And, Lord, haste the day when the faith shall be sight,
The clouds be rolled back as a scroll;
The trump shall resound and the Lord shall descend,
Even so – it is well with my soul.

"Evidence of Horatio's pain is written throughout this hymn, but so is his incredible faith. He knew his children were safe with his Savior, Jesus Christ, and for this father of four, it was all that counted. His sufferings and sorrows on earth would soon be in the distant past. All that really mattered was their eternal future. The Spaffords knew that someday they would be together again when they crossed the realm of eternity into the glorious wonder of their Father's home of heaven. And I am confident that they are there right now: a family reunited!

"Ladies and gentlemen, I spend a great deal of my time trying to explain to Christians, as well as many non–Christians, that life was never supposed to be the way it is today. To put all of this into the right perspective, you have to understand that when God made man, He intended him to be perfect. He was never supposed to get sick, feel pain, or go through trials.

In fact, man was never supposed to die. Death became the result of his disobedience in the Garden of Eden. Because of this action, sin was born. And because of this sin, pain, tears, heartache, and confusion are all a part of this life. Deadly diseases like cancer are ravaging our bodies and all too often lead to death. And as Christians, because we know what is waiting for us after we die here on earth, we need to be more understanding and accepting of what God's will is for us.

"It won't ever be easy. In fact, the more you lean on God, the harder Satan will make it for you which sometimes steers the lost even farther away! But for those of you who truly believe and don't give up hope, I promise it will all be worth it someday. Everything you ever go through in this life will someday be erased and made perfect. Let us give thanks to an awesome God, who will never leave us no matter what challenges we face in this life, as we make our way to Him.

"Father, we are so grateful for the challenges You enable us to get through each day, and that they bring us closer to You. You are so faithful, Lord, as You continue to give us hope in everything that life brings our way. In the midst of all our struggles, Father, let us hear Your voice. Let us seek Your will before we take steps forward, and if those steps produce pain and suffering, let us know that You are there to guide us through. Give us the strength to get through all that You have for us. I thank You, Father, for this day, and every day we are allowed to praise Your name. We ask all these blessings in Your Son's precious name. Amen.

"Thanks for coming today, everyone. We'll see you again next week."

Charlie and Lisa sat in awe of what they had just heard. They knew God worked in wonderfully mysterious ways, but they were amazed how the entire message fit everything they were going through. It was truly sent from heaven. From beginning to end, their pastor's word gave them both a hope they had almost forgotten they had. They felt somewhat embarrassed to think that God would ever let them go through their struggles alone. As they left their seats, the twosome reflected once again.

"Can you believe what we've been doing? Shame on both of us! We were nearly allowing Satan to destroy our faith, Lisa. That makes me sick to my stomach to think he could crawl inside of me so easily," Charlie told her with deep regret.

"I am ashamed to admit that he almost had me going, too," she replied. "I was nearly convinced that we should throw in the towel and give it up. I just knew no one in the world was going through what we are going through and that they would never understand. And to think all we have to worry about is the financial junk and maybe a challenge of health for my father. But I realize now that God has it in His control, too, because even if He takes my dad from this life, my dad will never die. He will live with God forever. So we win! I am just so grateful that Daddy was able to put his trust in Jesus when he got sick. If he hadn't, I don't know what I would be feeling right now. I would no doubt have a lot of grief and fear of where my dad would be spending eternity. So go ahead and do your stuff, you devil, and don't bother me with this other garbage. You don't scare me anymore!" Lisa proudly announced.

"You tell him, honey! That's my girl. Now let's go get the kids and get them something to eat. My treat!" he smiled.

"Say, Mr. McGee, where did you get the money to take us to lunch? Have you been holding out on me? Did you rob a bank or something?" she asked, as she gave his arm a playful punch.

"Well, not exactly. It was just a little stash I'd been saving for a rainy day. But it isn't big enough now to make a dent with the major storms we've had lately, so we may as well enjoy a little treat. Don't get used to it though. It might be the last one you have for a while. I have enough to do a little better than McDonald's, but nowhere near enough for the Palace Steakhouse. So what's your pleasure, my queen?"

"Oh, I don't mind McDonald's, really. The kids love it and I can have a salad. So let's not go crazy and blow the whole wad. Save a little for later. Maybe we could even splurge again and go to a movie or something later on." Lisa felt closer to her husband than she had in a long time. The strain and stress were all but gone, though the challenges ahead were still very real. But they knew they could get through anything now because their faith had been restored.

Chapter Four

Five days later their faith and endurance was tested once again. Lisa got a phone call from her mother very early in the morning. The news was devastating.

"Oh, Lisa, your father's gone!" Martha Brown sobbed. "He passed away about an hour ago. I didn't even have time to warn you."

"But Mom, how? I thought he was getting better," her daughter said somewhat confused.

"I thought so, too, honey. He was doing so well after his surgery, but late last night he had a major setback and took a turn for the worse. I only just got here myself. Can you come? I need you."

"We'll be there in less than half an hour. Remember, Mom, Daddy's with Jesus, now. Nothing can ever hurt him again," Lisa told her, desperately trying not to cry. But her control only lasted until she hung up the phone. Her husband was already by her side.

"I am so sorry, Lisa," he said sympathetically, trying hard to hold back tears of his own. He loved her father as if he were his own.

"Oh, Charlie. Daddy's gone. How can this be happening? Why would God take him now? Haven't we had enough? I just don't know if I can do this. It hurts so bad!" she cried out painfully, smothering her tear-stained face into Charlie's robe.

"Lisa, look at me. Remember what you just said to your mother? Your dad is in heaven. He's okay, and nothing can ever hurt him again. His pain is finally gone. We just have to stay strong for your mom. She's never been without him."

Martha and her husband, Jerry, had been together for over forty-five years. But they had known each other all their lives. Her loss would be unimaginable.

Lisa quickly changed her clothes and woke the children. As they dressed, she broke the painful news.

"Kids, I have something to tell you. I just got off the phone with Nana. She's over at the hospital because Papa got really sick last night and they called her. Sit down here with me for a minute, you guys, and listen carefully. You know Papa's been really sick for a while, right? And he gets better, but then he gets sick again. But this time, he didn't get better. This time God took him home to heaven and Papa isn't going to hurt anymore," she said, pulling her children close to her. Her heart ached but she didn't break down. The thought of her father being gone forever hadn't totally sunk in yet.

"You mean that Papa is dead?" Trevor asked, as his little mouth quivered.

"Yes, honey. He is. He died just a little while ago. We have to go help Nana because she isn't doing very well. She misses Papa so much, just like we all will," Lisa told them, as the tears spilled down her cheeks.

"But if Papa is okay and he's safe in heaven, why are you crying, Mommy?" Trevor started to cry himself when he saw his mother's tears.

"I'm just sad because he isn't with us here anymore. But he's with God, and that should make us all very happy!" she said.

"But, I didn't get to show him my new truck! I promised him that I would bring it over. Papa wanted to see it, Mommy. Can I still bring it?" Bryan asked innocently.

"No, sweetheart. Why don't you leave it here? I'm sure Papa saw it when he got to heaven. I'll bet he's looking down at your new truck right now and smiling."

"But that isn't fair. I wasn't through loving him yet. He was my best, Mommy, my very best!" Bryan sobbed in her arms.

"I know, baby. He was all of ours. But it will be okay, I promise. Now let's go help Nana so she won't be alone. She needs all of us right now, so we have to be really strong for her, okay?" she asked them.

"Okay, Mommy!" they all answered simultaneously.

When they reached the hospital entrance, Martha was waiting at the door. She was instantly drawn into her daughter's arms. They held each other close.

"Oh, Mom, I don't know if I can do this! I know I should be happy that Daddy is out of all that horrible pain, but it hurts so badly. I just wasn't prepared at all!" she whimpered.

"Me neither, Lisa. What am I going to do? I have never been without your father. I don't even know where to start."

"Mom," Charlie interrupted, "what you're going to do right now is not worry about anything. Lisa and I will take care of all the funeral arrangements. Then we'll talk about the future. You don't have to concern yourself with any of the legal stuff. What I want the two of you to do is go sit down over there and let me handle this here. Then we'll go to your house and pick up some of your things. We still have that spare room, and we want you to stay with us. The kids need you around them right now, and I'm sure you need to be around them, too. So, go sit down, and I will be right back!" he told them gently but firmly.

"Thank you, Charlie. Thank you for being here and coming to my rescue. I don't know what I would do if I didn't have you and Lisa and my grandchildren. I just can't believe he's gone. My sweet, wonderful husband—what am I going to do without him?" she said, as her daughter led her into the waiting room. The kids followed closely behind and sat on the floor near their grieving grandmother, while Lisa held her hand. They waited for over a half hour for Charlie to return.

"Okay, I got all the legal stuff here out of the way. They know what they have to do, and I will call the funeral home later this morning and get that taken care of, too. Now, let's get out of here. We need to go home and do some heavy duty praying. It's going to be a very long day and even a longer week. But, I have faith that we can all get through this if we stick together and give it to God. He knows what we need right now, and He needs to be in charge," Charlie announced, while making his entrance into the room.

After a brief stop at Martha's house to pack a few of her belongings, the family went home. The new widow spent the rest of the day talking, laughing, and crying as she remembered her beloved husband, lifelong companion, and very dearest friend. As they all sat in the den, Martha reminisced.

"Lisa, do you remember that time when your father fell in the river?" her mother asked, with a smile that lit up her face. "He was trying to teach you how to fish. You were probably all of five at the time, but he was bound and determined to have you throw that line out and catch your first fish. He ended up getting tangled in the line, and then the line got caught on a log, which was caught in a heavy current. It was so funny! It looked like he was hanging on for dear life! Your father struggled for a good five minutes because he thought for sure that on the other end of the line was going to be the biggest fish ever! Then lo and behold, he lost his balance and fell face first into the water! It took him downstream at least a half a mile! By the time he recovered, he pulled the line in and all there was on it was a bunch of weeds and that log! We laughed so hard. You thought that was the funniest thing you ever saw. And to tell you the truth, I did too!" Martha confessed.

"I don't think I really remember the incident, Mom, but you've told me the story often enough that it feels like I remember," Lisa said honestly. "It's one of my favorites."

"Tell us more, Nana. We want to hear more funny stories about Papa and how he made you and Mommy laugh!" the children shrieked with delight.

"Oh, I could probably go on all night with stories about your grandpa. He was so funny. Let me think, oh yes, there was this other time when we were out camping when your mother was around eight, and Papa got stuck in a tree! Your mom and I had just gone into the tent to get ready for bed. Your grandpa stayed outside to make sure the campfire was out. Your mom fell asleep immediately, and I waited for a good hour for Papa to come in. But he never did. Of course, I didn't realize that until the next morning because I fell asleep, too. When I woke up, I noticed he wasn't in the sleeping bag next to us. Your mother was already awake, and she asked me where her dad was. I had no idea. So we got dressed and went out to find him. We started calling out his name, but there wasn't any answer. After about five minutes, I decided to walk around and see if I could find him." Martha started laughing before she could even finish the story.

"What happened then, Nana?" Trevor asked, eager for her to continue.

"Sorry, but I still laugh when I think about it. Anyway, I was beginning to get a little worried. Then I saw him. He was about twenty yards from the campsite and not in a usual place where we would have looked."

"Where was he, Nana? Tell us!" Bryan asked excitedly.

"Well, it seems your grandpa heard noises that night while he waited for the fire to cool. He walked around the back and saw a big shadow. He just knew it was a bear! The only thing he could think to do was climb the closest tree. And that is exactly where we found him the next morning. His pants had gotten caught on a branch. So instead of him taking his pants off and climbing down, which he never thought of doing, he spent the entire night up there in the tree. When we found him the next morning, I suggested that he pull off his pants. He did, and that was when he was able to get down. It took him about ten minutes though because by that time he was really tangled."

"What about the bear, Nana? Was it still there?" Bryan asked.

"Oh, there never was any bear. That shadow your grandpa saw was just a silly old sheep dog that had wandered into our camp from a few miles down the road. It hung around the tent for a long time. Papa felt pretty silly by the time he got down. I wasn't allowed to talk about it for the longest time, at least not with his knowledge. But I shared it with many of my friends, and we laughed about it for years!" she giggled.

"Tell us another one!" they all screamed anxiously.

"Okay, I promise I will later. But I need to go lie down for a little while. I'm really tired right now. How about we do this again tomorrow? I have lots of crazy stories, and you will laugh so hard! Now you guys give me a big kiss.

It has to last me until I wake up, so it better be good!" she told them, and they fell into her lap and smothered her with their kisses.

Later that night, when they were all in their rooms, whimpers and sobs could be heard from outside each door. Martha lay alone for the first time in decades in the spare room and cried herself to sleep. Lisa crawled into her husband's arms and wept as well, unable to withstand the heartache. And even the children, as young as they were, understood that their Papa was never coming home again. They mourned his loss, each in their own way, remembering the kind and gentle man he was and the funny things he did. Jerry Brown would be sorely missed by all.

The funeral was scheduled for that Friday. Martha, Lisa, Charlie, and the children made it through with tears of joy and some of sorrow. Friends and other family members attended, bringing their condolences and prayers and filling the church with love and laughter. Many of them stood at the podium to share a brief experience or event that they would always treasure, made special by a man they knew to be good and kind, honest and sincere, and extremely entertaining. But most importantly, they shared how Jerry, in his final days, had become a strong and willing follower of Christ.

After the service, dozens of friends gathered at the home of Charlie and Lisa McGee for a celebration of life. There were tables full of delicious casseroles, assorted meats, salads, breads, and several desserts. Everyone ate until they were full. Many of Jerry's closest friends came and stayed late into the night, sharing more of their favorite stories. Then one by one they slowly began to leave. Eventually, the noise died down, as did the laughter. The tables of food had all but disappeared. But the tears and sadness remained in their hearts for many years to come.

Weeks went by and Lisa constantly begged her mother to sell her home and stay with them. Eventually, Martha did just that. She moved in permanently two months later. Though a very big part of Martha had been taken away, it didn't seem quite so lonely when she was with Lisa and her family.

And then early that fall, their beautiful house was sold to a wealthy couple with four young children. Charlie moved his family into a smaller, but adequate home not quite so far outside of town. They all knew it was only temporary until they got on their feet once again, which made the move easier for all of them.

Chapter Five

Days turned into weeks and the weeks into months. Charlie managed somehow to stay afloat. But as winter settled in, most construction businesses in the area slowed way down. Charlie grew more concerned by the day. He knew if his business slowed down any more, it wouldn't make it past Christmas, which was only a month away.

The bitterness Charlie felt inside for his friend and trusted employee who had put his business in financial despair seemed to surface more often. He tried hard to keep his feelings under control, but sometimes the feelings were just too much to bear. How much more was he expected to do under the circumstances? There were many times that Charlie wanted to scream out and, on occasion, even to hit something or someone. He prayed often, in hopes that God would soften his heart and give him clear direction.

"Father, Thank You for this time together. Even with all the challenges I have to deal with, I am still so grateful for all of Your blessings. I know if I wasn't struggling right now, that our time might be less important to me, and probably less often. If this is what I am to learn from this experience, then please help me to be better at it! Give me a heart like Jesus, Father. Loving, caring, and forgiving no matter what goes on in this world. Help me to truly forgive the man responsible for the hardships I am going through. I know that You would never have allowed it to happen if it wasn't Your will for me. Please, Lord, open my eyes and heart to hear Your words and to be willing to do whatever You need to fulfill Your plan and purpose for me. It's not clear yet, Lord, what I am supposed to be doing. Please help me to see it more clearly. Please help me hear Your voice."

Praying always made Charlie feel better. Though his heart was still somewhat hardened by the events that brought his business into its current state, he was beginning to feel stronger and more confident about being able to forgive everything someday. He knew God would show him the way.

Soon the holidays were upon them. Christmas wasn't quite the celebration that it had been in the past. Charlie and Lisa had to cut back considerably on their spending. But their children didn't seem to mind.

The McGees had a whole new perspective on Christmas this year. It was completely centered on Jesus, as it should have always been. But because of what the world had turned the season into—having to spend too much money on too many unnecessary gifts—somehow Jesus always got pushed aside, even in the most Christian of homes. And it had happened in theirs.

Jesus Christ's birth was most important, and Charlie and Lisa wanted their children to know what Christmas was really all about. If going though this trial was what they needed in order to bring them back to reality, then it was all worth it!

A freshly cut pine tree was put up in the corner in the den, beautifully trimmed and decorated with hundreds of lights and ornaments. And though gifts were scarce beneath it, love was abundant.

Martha got into the spirit as well, cutting back on many of her gifts to everyone. She noticed how unaffected they all were by the lack of presents under the tree, especially the children. In fact, the whole family seemed to be happier and more content than ever before. Martha thanked God for all that she had been blessed with, and for giving her such a wonderful family to support her and care for her in her time of need.

Christmas morning arrived and the family celebrated. They all gathered around the tree together. Once they were situated, Charlie said a quick prayer and then passed out the gifts. Each child got four presents apiece and a few small things in their stocking. They were more than satisfied and very grateful, too. When the events of the day were over, everyone went back to his or her normal routine.

Chapter Six

Charlie continued to pray for a miracle. With all the pressures, stress, and uncertainties in his future, he hadn't been sleeping very well lately. He was usually the first one awake as he was that early Sunday morning after Christmas. The sun had not yet crested the mountaintops, and the stars had not quite disappeared from the sky. Charlie got dressed and drove to the office. He planned to be back home before the family had to leave for the 10 o'clock service at church. His wife and children were still sleeping. Martha was reading the paper in her room.

Charlie arrived at the office a half an hour later. He was alone in the building. It was a little eerie and very quiet except for the heater blowing through the vents. Charlie liked being there by himself. It gave him a chance to reflect and to plan what his next move would be, if there were any left. As he looked around, he made a decision that should have happened months ago. He couldn't fight this any longer. He needed to file bankruptcy. The stress was just not worth the outcome anymore.

Charlie sat at his desk in his office and thumbed through his mail. All the unopened bills stared back at him, reminding him of his failure. But he knew he had to look at them eventually. And so he began the task of opening them all one by one. The first few envelopes were advertisements. Most of the others were the unpaid bills that got bigger each month because of interest and service charges. He stared at them, willing them to disappear. But they never did. The last envelope he fingered for several minutes before he opened it. It took him a few seconds before he recognized the return name in the corner. It was from Hightech Inc. When he tore at the corner, the check fell out and Charlie almost fell out of his chair. He picked it up and inspected it closely. His heart began to race, nearly pounding out of his chest. He covered his mouth and tried to muffle the scream that was slowly building up inside. But it could not be stopped.

"Oh my God! Praise the Lord!" Charlie screamed out over and over, as he jumped high into the air. "Praise the Lord and thank You, Jesus! I knew You were listening. I just knew it!" He immediately grabbed for the phone.

Charlie tapped his fingers on the top of the desk and waited patiently as he counted the rings. Martha picked it up on the third one.

"Hello," she said.

"Hey, Mom. Is Lisa up yet?"

"Yes, but she's getting ready for church. She may still be in the shower. Let me check."

"Tell her it's very urgent and to come to the phone now!" he told her firmly.

"Okay, Charlie. I'll get her. Hang on." Martha set the phone down and went to find her daughter. She could tell that something was up by the sound of Charlie's voice.

Another minute passed before Lisa picked up the extension.

"Hello, Charlie? What's wrong? Tell me you're all right and that nothing else is wrong. Please? I don't think I can take any more bad news right now!" she said.

"Oh, Lisa. This news isn't bad at all! In fact, everything is going to be perfect. I'm coming home. I need to show you something. And when we get to church, we are going to get on our knees and thank God in front of everyone. Oh what a testimony we have! Then tonight we're going to celebrate! You are going to get yourself all dressed up, and we're going to the Palace Steakhouse. The kids and your mom are coming, too!"

"But, Charlie. We can't afford to go to…" but he interrupted her before she could finish.

"We can afford anything we want! We have been so blessed! I'm on my way. I'll be there in a half an hour." Then without waiting for her response, Charlie hung up quickly and dashed to his truck. But he never made it home.

As he drove on the freeway, Charlie didn't notice the congestion ahead, nor did he see the truck full of steel pipe that had slowed down in front of him. Charlie was still so engrossed in the check that protruded from his wallet on the dash that he didn't look up until it was too late. He didn't even have time to hit his brakes.

The last thing he remembered was the massive load of steel that quickly engulfed his windshield. He never knew what hit him. He was gone in an instant.

Suddenly, Charlie was blanketed in a calming peace he never knew existed. Within what seemed like seconds, dozens of angelic beings encircled him and carried him off into another realm that would be his world forevermore. Once his spirit reached the outer part of this wondrous New World, Charlie discovered a breathtaking beauty that was beyond anything he had ever imagined, displaying multitudes of brilliant colors everywhere he looked. No earthly words could ever describe the radiant images that were before him. It was a place where time stood still and dreams came true. Also present was the most incredible feeling of complete and utter love, one he had only dreamt about in another lifetime.

For Charlie there were no more tears, sorrow, pain, or shame, nothing sad and nothing bad. Never again would this faithful child of God be expected to feel the hopelessness of earthly life that had him imprisoned and down to his last prayer. Never again would he know despair, remorse, temptation, or fear. Charlie was finally home where he belonged, where he would praise and worship his Lord and Savior for all eternity.

Chapter Seven

Lisa didn't start to worry right away. She knew her husband was easily distracted and rarely on time. But as the clock rounded the second hour since their phone conversation, her heart filled with fear. Charlie would never miss church no matter what! She made several calls to his office and cell phone, but there was no answer on either one.

"Mom, I'm getting worried. Charlie should have been home by now. What could be keeping him? It's Sunday, and he has never been away this long, especially when he knows we're going to church," Lisa said in a voice full of uncertainty.

"Oh, you know Charlie! He's probably on the phone and that's why you can't get through. You know how much he loves to talk. Or maybe he wanted to stop somewhere and get you something special. He'll be here soon, don't worry," her mother told her, trying hard not to be concerned herself.

But another hour passed and still there was no Charlie. When Lisa finally heard someone driving up the gravel driveway, she jumped up and ran to the door. She wanted to meet Charlie before he came inside. But it wasn't Charlie. It was the Highway Patrol. When she opened the door, three State Troopers stood outside with solemn faces and a wallet in their hand.

"Are you Mrs. McGee?" one of them asked.

"Yes, I am. What's wrong, officer? Is it Charlie? Is he okay? Please tell me he's okay!" she begged. But the look on their faces said otherwise. She knew immediately that something terrible had happened to her husband.

"I'm so sorry, Mrs. McGee. This must be your husband's. We found it at the scene," the trooper said, handing her the wallet. The check was folded neatly inside, though she wouldn't notice it for several weeks.

Martha came around the corner just as her daughter's knees gave way, and she collapsed to the floor in a fetal position. Her mother dropped to her side as Lisa screamed out in anguish and despair.

"No! No! Please, not Charlie! Oh, Lord, this can't be happening! How can God do this to us?" she wailed, hugging her knees tightly to her chest.

"Lisa, what is it? What's going on? Is it Charlie?" she asked, looking up at the men standing at the doorway.

"I'm afraid it is, Ma'am. He was in a terrible accident on the freeway about three hours ago. If it helps at all, we know he didn't suffer," he said, hoping to dull the pain a little.

"You mean he's really dead? But how?" Martha wondered.

"He slammed head–on into the back of a truck. Because there were no skid marks, I would venture to say that he never saw it coming. There were long steel pipes hanging over the back of the truck, and they went straight through the your husband's windshield. He was killed instantly. We are so very sorry."

"Oh, dear God," Martha cried. She bent down, gathered her daughter into her arms, and gently rocked her. No one noticed Trevor standing nearby until the troopers left. When Lisa looked up, her son was staring at her with fear and confusion as tears flooded his young eyes.

"Oh, Trev," she cried, reaching out to him.

"Mommy," he whimpered softly, "is Daddy… is he dead, too?"

"Please, Trevor. Come over here, son. Let me hold you, please?"

"Tell me, Mommy! I want to know," her oldest son demanded, suddenly seeming much older than his nine years.

"Yes, Trevor, I'm so sorry, but he is. Daddy is dead," she told him, holding onto him desperately, barely able to comprehend her own words. "He was in an accident, and God took him to heaven to be with Papa," Lisa blurted out. How was she ever going to explain it all to her young children when she didn't understand it herself? "When will it be enough, God?" she wondered silently. "When?"

Early that afternoon, the young mother told her children to meet her in the den next to the Christmas tree. She needed to tell them that their father was never coming home. But, before she said the words that would change their lives forever, she knelt beside her bed and silently prayed for strength to get them all through this tragedy and any others that they were destined to suffer in this lifetime.

"Father, I need You. Please let me hear Your voice. Show me You're with me right now as I try to tell my children why You had to take their daddy away. Help me explain to them that life here on earth is in Your hands and that there really are no accidents. You are in control of everything that happens to us. Help me to explain that even with this horrible news, that You still love all of us! Let me say the right words, Lord, so that they will continue to trust You and in Your will and purpose for them. And, Father God, help me get through all of this as well, feeling Your love and grace, and guide me to where You need me to be. Let me use this unbelievable heartache You have bestowed on us, and let it be turned into something good some day. Help me to understand that it was Charlie's time to be with You and that one day I will be with him again, when it's my time. I miss him, Lord. Oh, God, I miss him so very much! Let my time here go by quickly so I can see him again, soon. Help us all to get through these next few months and years without him. Protect us from all the evils of the world. Let the accidents be minor and our faithfulness in You be plentiful! In Jesus' name. Amen."

When she finished, she walked into the den to face her children. Lisa sat on the couch and looked into their young, innocent eyes. They watched her closely and hung on her every word.

"I need you to listen very carefully to what I am going to say. I never thought for a moment that I would be sitting here with you about to tell you the worst thing that will probably ever happen to you in your whole life. But I promise that something good will come out of this someday. God has His hands on all of us, and He will never let us go! You must never forget this, even when you are older and bad things happen!" She took a deep breath and let it out slowly. "Kids, Daddy had to go to heaven today. God needed him there more than He needed him here with us. Daddy's work here was all through. But he is watching us right now, and he's smiling because he knows that we can get through this. He wants us all to stay together and keep the other ones from hurting. That means, Trev, when you see your sister or brother crying because they don't understand why their daddy had to leave or they just miss him so much that they can't stop crying, you need to help them get through it. The same goes for me and for Nana, too. If any of us gets too sad, we need to support and comfort each other. It's going to take a long time, maybe years, before we don't hurt anymore, but we can do it if we remember all the good stuff about Daddy and that some day we will all be with him in heaven. Do you think you can do this?"

"Sure we can, Mom," Trevor said bravely, trying hard to hold back his tears. "I will hug anyone who starts to cry and not let go until they smile!"

"I can help, too, Mommy. I will hug someone, too, and be their friend," five-year-old Jenna announced.

"I don't want Daddy in heaven. I miss him and I want him here with us! I don't want to play like everything is okay. It isn't okay! Nothing is okay! And it never will be again!" Bryan wailed out in heart-wrenching anger.

"Oh, Bryan, we all miss him, honey. It's okay to be mad and cry. It's okay to be confused and hurt. But we won't always have to be sad. Some day the hurt will go away, I promise. But we can get through all of this if we just stick together and help each other. I can't do it all by myself. I need you to help me. Do you think you can?" Lisa asked her middle child.

"I guess so, Mom. But I don't care what you say, I'm going to be sad for a long, long time," he told her with tears streaming down his young face.

"I know, sweetheart. I will, too. Come over here and let me hold you. All of you!" Lisa held out her arms and they all gathered together. They held on in desperation and cried for their loss and for the uncertainty of a future they never dreamed they would ever go through alone.

Chapter Eight

Charlie was cremated the next afternoon, and his memorial service was three days later. Lisa stood up in front of the church and bravely gave the eulogy as she praised her husband's character and integrity.

"I don't know how long I'll be able to stay up here without breaking down completely. I can't even imagine what my life will be like without Charlie. He was my soul mate, my best friend, and my whole world. But I know that somehow all of this fits into God's plan. He is in control of everything. Charlie was an upright and honorable man, as you all know, and he loved his God more than anything in the world. I know, too, without a doubt, that he is in heaven right where he belongs. I only wished that I could be there with him.

"For those of us who are left behind, death can be so hard to deal with, especially when we aren't sure where our loved ones will be in his or her afterlife. But if they know Jesus like Charlie did, we can be comforted knowing for sure that our precious loved one is with the Father and will be forevermore. The hard part now will be waiting until it's my turn. Which brings me to something else we sometimes have trouble with, even as Christians, and that is forgiveness. I'm not sure how many of you are aware of this, but I was informed this afternoon that Charlie's death was completely preventable. The man who was driving the truck that Charlie hit didn't have any brake lights. By the time Charlie noticed the truck had slowed down, it was too late. Charlie didn't stand a chance. The man also didn't have the red safety flag that is required when their loads hang over too far." There were gasps of surprise throughout the sanctuary.

"But I hold no blame on anyone. And because our Lord is such a forgiving God, I, too, need to forgive this man for causing my husband's death. When I think of the pain this man will suffer for the rest of his life, I hurt for him. I know Charlie is safe in heaven, but this man will never be released from his guilt until I let him know that I forgive him, totally and completely. If God didn't want Charlie on that freeway, on that day, at that particular time, He would have never sent him! And I do forgive this man with all of my heart. I hope some day I can tell him.

"Now, before I go today, I want to read something to you. I think this pretty much sums up everything I am feeling. It's from the father of a young cadet who was being initiated into the Cadet Corps at Texas A&M University. One night this young man was forced to run until he dropped, but he never got up. Bruce Goodrich died before he even entered college. A short time after the tragedy, Bruce's father wrote this letter to the administration, faculty, student body, and the Corps of the Cadets. 'I would like to take this opportunity to express the appreciation of my family for the great outpouring of concern and sympathy from the Texas A&M University and the college community over the loss of our son, Bruce. We were deeply touched by the tribute paid to him in the battalion. We were particularly pleased to note that his Christian witness did not go unnoticed during his brief time on campus.' Lisa paused to turn the page and then went on. 'I hope it will be some comfort to know that we harbor no ill will in the matter. We know our God makes no mistakes. Bruce had an appointment with his Lord and is now secure in his celestial home. When the question is asked, "Why did this happen?" perhaps one answer will be, "'So that many will consider where they will spend their eternity!'"

"Now change the name in this letter from Bruce to Charlie and make it from me to all of you who don't know Jesus. I pray that my husband's untimely passing will bring you more awareness of what eternity really is and make you wonder where you will be spending yours. We will all have to go somewhere when our time here is done. I hope that Charlie's life will never be forgotten. But more importantly, I want his tragic death to be a reminder for everyone that life is so very short. It can be taken away in a split second, leaving behind tears and sorrow for the rest of us to endure. But our pain doesn't have to last forever! One day, it will all be worth it if we make the choice now to follow Jesus and believe with all our hearts that He loves us and He died for us on the cross so that we can live eternally in heaven with Him, just like my Charlie is now.

"I know Charlie would love to see all of you again someday. And so would I. If you don't know Jesus, I beg you to find Him! Put your life in His precious hands and trust Him. I promise you will never be the same again. Thank you all so much for being here and supporting my family and me. And thank You, Father, for keeping me strong enough to say what You needed me to say. God bless all of you!"

Pastor Ray O'Neil carefully led Lisa to the stairs. Then she stepped down and walked over to her children and mother, who were seated in the front row. A few of Charlie's former employees and several friends took the opportunity to say a few words about him. When the service ended, once again there was a celebration of life held at the home of Charlie and Lisa McGee, minus the presence of Charlie. But through it all Lisa stood tall, courageous, and incredibly strong. Her determined and willing spirit was like a magnet, and everyone was drawn to her.

Before the evening ended, several family members and friends approached Lisa and asked her about salvation and what they had to do to receive it. The brokenhearted widow knew once the shock wore off and reality set in that she and her children would go through extremely mournful times, as they dealt with their enormous loss. But Lisa was so humble and grateful when she was temporarily distracted from her grieving in order to bring ten people to know Jesus Christ as their Lord and Savior right there in her den.

And the heavens rejoiced… as Charlie watched in awesome wonder at the miracle of it all!

A Plan of Salvation

Although the characters in this book are fictitious, the places where they ended up are not. Fire Captain Dave Sanders was a nice enough guy who was always willing to lend a hand to anyone in need, but in the end, being nice wasn't enough to get him into heaven. Where Dave will be spending his eternity is so unbelievably painful that mere words cannot describe what awaits him. Worst of all, this world full of agonizing darkness and regret that he chose for himself will be with him forevermore.

Poor, young Taylor Morgan threw her life away before it even began. Unable to recover from the heartache of losing her caretaker and best friend, Taylor committed suicide. How sad it is when a teenager can't decipher between the realities of life and death because of the pain, turmoil, and confusion he or she is going through? The alcohol Taylor turned to didn't help her make the best decision either. The young woman found out too late that death was not the answer to her painful existence.

Raised as a Christian by a father who was a pastor, megastar Andy Lynch knew what he needed to do to get into the streets of heaven better than all the other characters in this novel. Yet, it was clear that Andy never truly believed or he could have never been so easily swayed into the lust and sins of the secular world of tinsel town or joined the Church of Scientology. In the end, the choice was Andy's, and he knew the instant his heart stopped beating that it was the worst choice he could have made.

There were only two people who truly understood what they needed to do and in whom they needed to trust: Charlie McGee and Mary Burgoff. No matter what life did to them or how bad it became, they remained faithful and left all their struggles, losses, and heartache in the hands of God. In the end, when they took their last earthly breath, they were immediately covered with the Holy Spirit and taken to a place about which we on earth can only dream.

If this book made you realize that you need to change the way you are living your life, then it has done its job. Don't wait until it's too late. Don't live your afterlife in regrets that can never be undone! If you want to spend eternity with Someone who loves you more than you have ever been loved before, surrounded in a peace that surpasses all understanding, then ask God to come into your life and change your hardened heart. He hears, sees, and knows everything about you already. Offer your life to Him, too.

If you want the free gift of eternal salvation that our Heavenly Father promises to all of us, say the following prayer out loud. Say it with passion and mean it and believe it with all of your heart!

Dear Father God,

I am here for the taking, with my heart in hand and my trust in You. I am a sinner, and I want to stop, Lord. Please forgive me and all that I have done against You. Come into my life and make it whole. Lead me down a righteous path and help me to know You better. I know that Your Son, Jesus Christ, died for me on the cross and rose again so that I may one day live with You forever. I am so very humble and grateful for Your sacrifice. Help me to know You better, Lord, and open my heart so that I may help others to know You as well. Let me spend the rest of my days here on earth spreading Your Word and telling others what an awesome, forgiving, and loving God You are. Guide me to do the right things now so that one day I can be comforted knowing that I will have eternal life with You. In Your Son's precious and holy name I pray. Amen.

If you need more help learning about salvation, go to my website at www.justfaith.com and click on the word Jesus in blue or go to Bill Keller's website at www.liveprayer.com/bdy_salvatn.html, where you will find many of your answers. If you need additional encouragement you can email me anytime at tjmartini@justfaith.com or Bill Keller at bkeller@liveprayer.com.

This will surely be the most important decision you have ever made. Don't put it off. Time on earth is very short; like vapor in the wind, it is here today and gone tomorrow. So much more awaits you in a world too wonderful to fathom, but it's your choice. Choose life! You will never regret it! God bless you all!

OTHER BOOKS BY T.J. MARTINI

Wings of Pride:

The Story of Reno Air and Its People (2001)

Joe's Bible:

A Teen's Journey to Salvation (2003)

Blue Side Up:

An Angel Among Us (2005)

Destruction of Innocence:

A Mother's Guilt – A Daughter's Shame (Summer 2005)

To help you through your struggles or to learn more about Jesus Christ, visit our Web Site at www.justfaith.com. If you have any comments or stories you want to share you can contact TJ at tjmartini@justfaith.com